SUSPICIOUS BY DESIGN

A

GENEIVEVE BENOIT

NOVEL

Dedication

This book is dedicated to all the women in the world who put on a uniform and stand bravely in the face of danger regardless of their own safety, insuring that all citizens are protected from the perils of daily life.

Table of Contents

Prologue

Stepping through the airport in the North African city of Algiers was a common occurrence for most international travelers privileged to visit the former French colony. For Nazim Aziz however, traveling under his alias of 'Louis Remesy', it was always with a sense of trepidation and uncertainty. Dressed like most European executives, he was traveling to discuss a business transaction with very lucrative benefits, if successful.

The warm breeze, its origins deep in the Sahara, blew through the doors of the terminal, as Nazim walked out towards the line of taxis waiting for a fare. Coming to the first one, he announced his destination to the driver, "To the Hotel Sofitel Algiers Hamma Garden please," sliding into the back seat.

Tugging the meter flag upward the driver replied, "Yes sir," before slipping the car into gear and heading towards the city. Nazim sat in the back, contemplating what today's' meeting would produce for his fledgling drug empire.

Resting in the hotel café' in the center of town, Sean Gilmore sipped his mineral water, working hard to keep his nerves calm. This was the first time his employer, 'Mr. Higgins', had asked him to undertake a negotiation away from Belfast. Sporting a wig of jet-black hair and horn-rimmed glasses obtained from a local theatre troupe, he fought his emotions and tried his best to appear at ease. The thought of making a mistake was wearing on Sean, visible by the perspiration moistening the armpits of his dress shirt.

Heavy gilded doors to the hotel swung open as Ismail Ghazi, the mediator for today's meeting, strolled into the hotel lobby before making his way to the café. The Algerian criminal was dressed in a traditional gandoura robe and linen slacks, complete with a burgundy-colored fez and a tarnished golden tassel. Crossing the threshold of the café doorway, he saw the person he'd arranged to meet with, noticeable not only by his attire but likewise his pasty complexion.

"Monsieur Higgins?" he asked with a slight bow. "I am, Ismail Ghazi," he said extending his hand to the Irishman.

Pushing up to his feet, Sean shook hands with the Algerian. "Hello, thank you for arranging today's meeting" Sean said returning the greeting, still uneasy answering to his boss' alias. "It's a trifle warm for so early in the morning," wiping the beads of sweat from his brow.

"Yes, it is, and it will get warmer in the coming months," Ismail said taking a seat at the table. "My associate is on his way, so if you don't mind, I'd like to wait for his arrival before we begin our discussions."

"By all means, I understand," Sean said returning to his seat.

The waiter soon arrived, and Ismail ordered a pitcher of spring water and two glasses expecting Nazim's arrival. "You had a pleasant flight?" he asked the Irishman.

"It wasn't without its bumps," Sean said. "Seems the only flight I could secure was through Paris."

"I see. I've never had the pleasure of traveling to France myself, I've only been to…," Ismail said stopping in mid-sentence glimpsing Nazim entering the lobby.

"You were going to say?" Sean asked turning to look what caught the Algerian's attention.

"It turns out my associate has arrived," waving the French-Algerian traveler to their table. "Louis, it's good to see you again," Ismail spoke greeting Nazim with the feigned kiss on each cheek.

"As always, it's a pleasure to return to Algiers and see you Ismail," the drug dealer said.

"May I introduce Monsieur Higgins," Ismail said motioning to Sean Gilmore who was now standing.

Shaking hands with the Irishman, Nazim replied, "Monsieur Louis Remesy. A pleasure to meet you Monsieur Higgins," shaking hands with the Irishman.

"Thank you for agreeing to this meeting," Sean said taking his seat opposite Nazim.

As they took their seats at the table, Ismail poured a glass of spring water for Nazim before pouring his own glass. Moving the glass in front of Nazim, he wiped away the pool of condensation that had grown under the pitcher.

Nazim raised his glass, "To a successful discussion."

"Yes, to a successful discussion as you say," Sean replied bringing his bottle of Perrier to his lips. He sipped the drink, luxuriating in the coolness and the light fizz on his tongue. Setting the bottle down, he slid the costume glasses upward before speaking.

"Getting down to business," Sean said opening his leather portfolio. "Monsieur Remesy, it's been brought to my attention you have the means of moving, shall we say, a 'marketable product', via freighters into France. Over the last six months, I've seen more South American groups pushing north, with an inferior product. And I wish to stop it by providing a more robust item of my own choosing," he said. "I'd like to know if you'd accept an offer to expand your horizons to the United Kingdom."

Relaxing back in the chair, Nazim contemplated the offer and the risks. Getting the hashish and cannabis resin into France is already in motion, he thought to himself. But to have a chance to move it to the Northern European users would increase his finances tenfold.

"Monsieur Higgins, it's rather apparent you are well informed," the drug trafficker said. "With the help of my associate, I'm sure we can offer you with the robust product you want. In this case, the finest Moroccan hashish, and cannabis resin cocktail," Nazim said citing the blend of drugs. "And with the help of my partner in France, we should be able to move it onshore, with assurances of course," he added.

"I understand completely Monsieur Remesy," the Irish counselor said. "I would propose we undertake a trial run, so to speak," Sean replied keeping to the script he and his employer prepared. "That is, if you're prepared to do so?"

"And what do you recommend as this 'trial run' you mention?" Nazim asked.

"I'd like to have, say five-thousand kilos made available," Sean said. "Once the product is ready for shipment, I'd like the exchange to take place off-shore. It would be between your vessel and one of ours," the Irishman alluded. "And I'm prepared to give dossiers on the captain and his crew, for you and your associate to vet before undertaking the action," finishing his proposal.

Ismail sat back and took in the exchange between the two gentlemen seated at the table. He had no knowledge of how the drugs they were discussing were created or shipped. His only role was to have the two men meet and promote the dialogue for the transaction. His boss, Omar Khalid, had instructed him to insure no harm came to Nazim Aziz, and he was prepared to do just that if the need arose.

Sean saw the hesitation in Nazim's eyes. He saw the same look in court when a witness was contemplating a lie to one of his questions. "I'm willing to pay a quarter-million euro for this first transaction," he said planting the seed of greed — which was always money — into the game for Nazim to contemplate.

Discovering the sum of money that the Irishman was willing to pay seemed too good to be true to for the French-Algerian drug dealer. Nearly four times what can be made selling the drugs in France, and for half the quantity? His head hurt thinking about the amount of money being offered.

"And if I consent to this transaction, when do you expect delivery?" he asked knowing he'd need his mentor, Omar, to help gather the quantity from their chemists.

"Given the current weather in the Channel, the delivery should take place no later than mid-April or so, at the earliest."

Wrapping his hand around the glass of spring water, Nazim felt the cool collection of condensation under his hand. Five months to deliver, he thought. Can I convince Omar and Gregory to both help make this happen? he wondered while he emptied the last of the spring water from his glass.

"I'll agree to this transaction, but with one condition," Nazim said. "The money needs to be in place first, to this account," sliding the business card in front of Sean. "And then I'll present you with the details for making the transfer with a date," he said finalizing his demands.

Picking up the card off the table, Sean stood abruptly, causing Ismail to reach behind his back for his scabbard, before noticing that the Irishman extended his hand. "I accept your conditions," he said.

"As do I," Nazim said.

Chapter One

Bundled against the wind from a spring storm enveloping the harbor, a solitary figure strolled the brick and stone promenade along the waterfront normally full of tourists and vendors. For the second week in a row, Detective Geneviève Benoit was working with her fellow officers on an anonymous tip. This one involved a group of young men and a woman soliciting drugs to the passengers of cruise ships.

Roaming along the cobblestone path, the female detective shivered under her fleece jacket. Whispering into the hidden microphone, she said, "I'm not getting anything out here but a severe case of pneumonia."

"Maybe you should wear some long underwear under those slacks," her fellow officer said stopping to light a cigarette as he walked along the street across from her.

"I refuse to because the warmest ones are scratchy and make me itch," she said. "But maybe you should get your ass in a better position for once Guy," teasing the police officer who was never more than fifty meters from her during their surveillance.

Detective Guy Masson chuckled at the response from the newest member to the drug enforcement team. Detective Benoit had already proven her worth by subduing two assailants single handedly during one altercation.

Just beginning her fourth week since being transferred from La Havre, Benoit had started to apply her newly learned skills as a detective amongst her fellow officers. During this time, she'd single-handedly subdued a would-be thief attempting to rob an elderly couple from Austria near the cathedral. It was later learned by the officer's the suspect's action were taken to feed his addiction to heroin.

And last week, while running another 'bait and switch' operation with Detective Masson, she broke up a fight between several English soccer fans who attempted to incite their French counterparts.

Remaining in the back of the service van which doubled as a command post, the officer's senior member reminded them of their work. "Keep your discussion professional," Senior Detective Claude

Lemieux said watching the young woman and the other officer walking the wide, wind-swept pavement along the waterfront.

Going past a shuttered information kiosk, Geneviève saw their suspects. "I've got an eye on three men at the corner, and what appears to be a woman just beyond the postal bin that fit our descriptions," ambling towards the group.

As she grew closer, one of the young men wearing a weathered motorcycle jacket and heavy work boots walked up to her, "Hello there, where you from?" he asked.

"Originally you mean? I'm from La Havre. I was hoping to come down here for warmer weather, but…," she said shrugging her shoulders against the chill. "I guess I'm a little early for the summer crowds," nodding towards the empty sand.

"If you're cold, I've something that might warm you up, maybe take the chill off," the young man said.

"And what might that be? I don't see a cup of coffee in your hand," she said with a forced chuckle, straining to play the part of the tourist.

"Everyone stand-by," Lemieux said wanting to make sure the team kept their focus.

"If you're interested," the youth said glancing over his shoulder. "I've a limited sample of this," holding up a small plastic baggie containing hashish.

"It doesn't appear to be enough for both of us though," Geneviève cooed trying to coax him into incriminating himself further.

"Be careful Benoit, you're beginning to draw a crowd," Detective Masson said noticing the others moving closer to Genevieve and the drug dealer.

"That's not a problem, I've got several," pulling more from his faded canvas knapsack, festooned with various military patches.

While conversing with the young drug dealer, Geneviève saw that the young woman from the kiosk joining the group of men. "Michael, did you tell her how much?"

"No," he said turning to the group and then back to Geneviève. "It's worth fifty-euros a hit, if you want the sample."

"Fifty euros for one? How much if I want more to take on my trip?" she asked stating the code phrase alerting the other officers of a pending arrest.

"Each one is fifty," the woman declared now standing next to the one she called Michael, showing her dominance over the men of the group.

"In that case, I'll take five hits," Geneviève said reaching into her purse feigning to pull her money out but instead, flashing her police credentials. "Stand where you are, you're under arrest," shouting to insure everyone nearby heard her.

Realizing that their mark was a police officer, the group bolted, scattering in separate directions. Missing her chance to grab the suspect identified as Michael, Benoit sprinted after the woman, who'd stumbled running towards the street. In a matter of minutes though, all four of the group were in custody, having been rounded up by the other members of the surveillance team.

"Nice work Benoit," Masson said to Geneviève who'd subdued the woman before she could run over five meters. Placing handcuffs on her suspect Benoit lead the woman to the police car pulling up to the curb.

"It's a start," she said. "What do you think Detective Lemieux?"

Claude looked at the three detectives place the felons in the cars for the trip to central booking before replying. "Like you say Benoit, it's a start. But I'm afraid all we've done is kick the can further down the street," alluding to the four youths failing to turn in their supplier. It was the supplier the police needed to apprehend who was still free to peddle the deadly drugs. "Wait till the weather warms up and tourists begin crowding the city, then we'll know how we've done," watching his officers.

"You know Claude, it's like the mythological tale of cutting off one head," Detective Berger said. "And two more will grow from the wound," showing off his knowledge of all things mystical.

As the suspects were transported to the central jail, the detectives returned to the police station to file their reports. Walking down to the basement, Detective's Benoit and Masson had the unenviable task of booking each suspect, insuring the proper charges was identified.

"So, Geneviève why did you request the transfer to Marseille?" Masson asked.

"Well, mainly because I didn't want to patrol the streets in uniform anymore," she replied as she escorted the suspect named Michael in front of the fingerprint station. "Plus, I wanted a better chance at getting promoted, and Detective Lemieux's group had an opening."

"I've been with the department for over two years and haven't had my record looked at for promotion yet," the burly officer said. "And the only way we can move up is with Detective Lemieux getting promoted or we go to another department.

"If that's the case, we'll have to insure Lemieux is seen by Captain Duval as a superior candidate for his own promotion," Benoit said. "I can't imagine he enjoys running down drug dealers or addicts chasing down their next score," alluding to the burgeoning drug epidemic.

"Lemieux has a special passion for this," Masson said two of the suspects toward the vacant holding cells.

"I guess I'll have to ask him about his passion then," Benoit replied escorting the female suspect forward.

"As they say, be careful what you ask for," Masson replied.

With the suspects booked, Benoit and Masson rejoined their fellow detectives who were busy completing their reports on the day's activities. With the three detectives sitting at their desks, Detective Lemieux rose and grabbed his coat. "Once you're done filing those, you're free to head home," alluding to the paperwork. "Captain Duval is going to let the night crew do the preliminary interviews of our guests."

***

In her darkened apartment lit only by a single candle, the silhouette of Detective Benoit had just transitioned from the seal position to downward facing dog. The soft sounds of instrumental music helped with her concentration as the beads of sweat rolled down her brow and into her eyes.

Each evening she undertook a thirty-minute routine of yoga to maintain her flexibility and focus. But, Geneviève further used it to release the daily tension that comes from being the only woman on the drug task force.

Slowly coming to her feet, she stretched toward the ceiling, taking in a deep cleansing breath before exhaling it as she assumed the 'bridge' position.

Resting on her mat, Geneviève slowly stretched her pelvis upward, keeping her feet and shoulder blades firmly on the surface, her breath coming in slow controlled efforts. Someone is responsible for the drugs coming in, but whom, she asked herself.

***

Relaxing on the balcony of his apartment, Claude raised the wine glass and took in the aroma of the varietal before taking a sip of his newest acquisition. Ah, a sweet yet robust nose, with a hint of jasmine, taking in the fragrance. Swirling the deep red liquid of the cabernet in his mouth, he could sense the tingling of the wine on the inside of his palette.

Is it safe to say Geneviève and I only need to focus on the freighters and the cruise ships? If that's the case, the drugs are being prepared off shore and coming from another country. Bracing his elbow on the railing, he balanced the glass in the palm of his hand, looking through the liquid at the lights dotting the harbor in the distance.

In the distance, the mast lights from a departing ship were barely visible. Recalling the conversation with his partner he thought, if it's a freighter, is it the entire crew or just a handful and whose flag does it fly? And if it's a cruise ship, which nationality of patron do we focus on as potential traffickers? Sipping the last of the wine in his glass, he carefully emptied the remains from the bottle into the glass.

Chapter Two

The hiss of escaping air announced another tour bus making a stop along the waterfront. Observing the crowd of tourists shuffling past them, picking out the first-time visitors from Northern Europe was easy. "Will you look at the sunburn on that woman," Detective Benoit said pointing out the blonde walking past her and her partner, Senior Detective Claude Lemieux. The exposed shoulders showed the woman's complexion, once a pale white, was now aglow with a bright tinge of pink.

Angling his head to follow the woman Claude said, "She'll have a rough time sleeping tonight," observing the reddened skin that lacked sunscreen through his mirrored sunglasses.

Relaxing at a sidewalk table outside the coffee shop, the two officers seemed out of place as a couple. Senior Detective Lemieux was the typical middle-aged Frenchman, beginning signs of weight gain, his thinning brunette hair highlighted with hints of grey. He was twelve years older than his companion who sat across the table from him.

Meanwhile, Detective Benoit was just the opposite in her appearance. Sporting a slim, well-toned figure, her auburn hair pulled back in a ponytail secured with a colorful scarf that billowed with each passing breeze. Wearing a summer blouse, her tanned and toned arms showed signs of a diligent workout routine. Glancing at her, she could be mistaken for Claude's niece or worse, a younger lover to a recently divorced executive.

This was the third week the two police officers had undertaken their surveillance of the waterfront as part of a major effort to reduce the drug trade. Remaining in the fading afternoon light, they each took turns looking in opposite directions, constantly searching for the telltale sign of a drug transaction taking place.

"How did we come across making the last arrest?" Claude asked, sipping his Perrier from a straw, savoring the cool liquid as it slid down his throat.

"You mean last week? I was approached by a young soccer player near the velodrome," Geneviève said. "He said he had a quarter kilo of marijuana he wanted to share."

"Well then, it suggests you can be the 'bait' on these fishing expeditions."

"Only, if Captain Duval allows me to dress for the occasion."

"You mean slinking around in cut-offs showing off your cheeks, with tops barely covering your breasts? I'd say the chances are next to nothing," Claude said glancing at his partner. Ah, to be fifteen years younger and 20 kilos lighter, recalling a fond memory of his wife Nadine.

"True, but if the captain ever did let me go undercover, where would I conceal my weapon?" the female detective asked with a laugh.

"Mon Cheri, your weapons are always in plain sight, and you know it."

Geneviève smirked at the compliment. She was the reigning hand-to-hand combat champion in the police department, known for subduing her victims within minutes of being engaged. She learned this skill early in her youth, taking up karate as a young girl. Growing up near the docks in Cherbourg, she used the defensive moves to survive the advances of several young seamen.

Amongst the passing crowds, a local drug dealer stood near a group of bicycles his head moving left to right while watching the people walking passed him. He stopped scanning the pedestrians' as he fixated his gaze on an African making his way directly towards him.

As the African came closer, he thrust his hand into his pocket, pulling out a two small balloons. In a poor attempt to replicate the actions of Cold-War spies, the two men made an exchange, one passing the drugs to the other for a folded bundle of euros.

Pointing out a possible suspect, Geneviève said, "There, the young man in the blue shirt and cargo pants."

"You saw him pass something?"

"Yes, he handed something to the short African walking towards the car park."

"You take the first man, I'll follow the African," Claude said. Getting up from the table, they both walked away in separate directions.

Claude came up from behind the African man as they both negotiated their way thru the crowd of pedestrians. God, I hope this person doesn't run into the crowd, he thought reaching behind his back to withdraw his pistol.

Watching the first suspect, Geneviève had already closed the gap between her and the man. Having him stop at a souvenir kiosk on the sidewalk, she stepped up from behind, bumping into him while drawing her pistol from its holster.

"Oh, excuse me," she said.

Peering over the tanned figure of the police detective, the suspect said, "No problem Miss, please feel free to do it again."

Holding her credentials in his face she said, "I just might; while you're locked up in a cell."

"What's this all about?"

"I've got a few questions I'd like to ask you."

"You've no right," he said before bolting away from her racing up the boulevard.

Striking out to grab the young man, Geneviève missed her opportunity, allowing him a 10-meter head start. Dammit, I'm wearing the wrong shoes for this today, she thought cursing her choice of low-heeled footwear.

Just a block away at the nearby car park, Claude was questioning the African man under the watchful eye of a foot patrol officer. "What did you get from the other gentleman?"

"Nothing," the African said looking away from the detective.

"So, if you've nothing to worry about, empty everything from your pockets." Claude demanded.

Gradually the young African suspect placed everything on the hood of a parked car which included the small rubber balloon.

"Oh, so you've nothing. Can you explain this?" Claude asked pointing to the balloons with his pen. "Cuff the suspect if you please officer," looking at the patrol officer.

"I'll help you if you'll let me go," the African said pleading with his eyes, as the police officer pulled his arms back, handcuffing him.

"Is that so; how can you help me?"

"I've a regular contact, he knows someone who's supplying the hashish to the dealers on the street."

Putting the drug-filled balloon in the evidence bag, Claude spoke. "I'll certainly let the judge know you wish to be cooperative, after we've booked you for possession."

"Let's go," the police officer, said pulling the suspect off the parked car and through the crowd that had formed around them.

Still running as fast as he could, the other suspect being chased by Detective Benoit turned the corner at the end of the street. Here, he ran headlong into a group of elderly German women, who were stopping in the middle of the sidewalk to take in the exterior view of the cathedral.

Stumbling while skirting past them, he didn't notice Geneviève had closed the gap and was upon him, her weapon pointed at him. One woman in the group saw the gun and screamed while the others stood frozen in place.

"Don't try anything foolish or I'll shoot," she said between gasps trying to regain her breath. "Now get on your feet; slowly," keeping her weapon leveled on his head.

Struggling from his hands and knees, but doing as he was told, the young Frenchman stood. Facing Benoit, his own breathing was coming in gasps while traces of blood oozed from his skinned-up hands that shook from the adrenaline.

Genevieve grabbed the drug dealer by the arm and pushed him against the storefront. "Put your hands on your head and lean your forehead against the wall," she demanded.

Just as she was taking control of her suspect, two uniformed officers pushed their way thru the crowd to help. With one officer providing back up, she holstered her weapon while reaching for the suspect's hands, using her feet to push the suspects' legs apart. Now to see if you had what I thought you were handling, she told herself

Taking her free hand, Geneviève began the slow methodical search of the suspect, working her way from the top of his head toward his waistline. Grabbing his wallet from his pocket, she tossed it to one of the police officers standing beside her. "Check his identification," she said. Moving her way around the front of his waist, she came across something else. Feeling a slight bulge just below his belt, she said, "What do we have here?"

"Any other time I'd show you," the suspect snorted defiantly.

Carefully sliding her hand under the waistband, she pulled out a string of four drug balloons, similar to the one her partner Claude retrieved from the African. "It seems you had some selling in mind," laying the balloons carefully at her feet. As she stooped down, she finished searching the suspect by running her hands over his legs. Reaching behind her back, Genevieve retrieved her handcuffs from the waistband of her slacks.

Moving each hand down behind his back, Geneviève slid the handcuffs over each wrist, locking them in place before pulling the suspect from the wall and turning him around.

"Who's your dealer, um..., Marco is it?" she asked looking at his identification.

"Kiss my ass bitch," the young man spat back at her.

"You'll go down for possession and trafficking," she said picking up the narcotics and balancing them in her hands. "These are a kilo or more."

"I'd soon rot in your cell than turn on my supplier."

"We'll see if that's true. Officer, take him to the car," Geneviève said following the suspect down the same street they had just run up twenty minutes before. Dammit, look at my good shoes; I've broken one of the heels because of this asshole, realizing she was standing awkwardly on her feet.

After jostling the suspects through booking at police headquarters, Detective Benoit and Senior Detective Lemieux now faced the unenviable task of filling out the arrest forms on the drug dealers.

Resting in the air-conditioned office, each officer labored over the computer terminals, busy completing their respective arrest reports from the afternoon's action. "So, we've had marijuana last week and what turns out to be hashish this week," Claude said. "What's next heroin?"

"Be careful what you wish for," Geneviève said selecting the 'print' function on her computer screen for her report. "There, all done."

Shaking his head, the senior officer let out a loud sigh. "Damn you women and your inherent typing skills," Claude said, struggling with his two- fingered typing as he continued to fill in the blanks of his report.

"My fingers and thoughts are just nimbler than yours," flexing her fingers while retrieving the papers from the printer.

"Back to our current dilemma. Where are these damn drugs coming from detective?"

"Don't tell me your suspect can't furnish any information either?" she said. "Because mine hasn't said a word since we booked him."

"I doubt either of them would offer anything of substance," the older officer said. "They're more scared of what the supplier is capable of doing to them than what would happen to them in prison."

"Well, we've narrowed the activities down to the docks so far," Geneviève said sliding the papers into a folder. "Doesn't the Gang Enforcement group have any information on who controls that area?"

"I'm sure they do," Claude said. "But which one of the gangs or criminal syndicates would be difficult to concentrate on without more information. In addition, yes, the waterfront is seeing a greater number of drug deals taking place. But who's bringing the drugs onshore?" Claude asked. "There, finally done," saving his version of the arrest report on the African suspect.

"It has to be coming in on the freighters, right?" she asked.

"But we can't base our investigation on only the one occurrence," Claude replied. "And since then, they've seemed to vanish. And it's not necessarily just freighters, look at the number of times a cruise ship docks at the harbor, and where are they originating."

"But the security of the docks is so fantastic," she said sarcastically. "Just ask any DCJP agent assigned to the Central Directorate of Border Police," Geneviève said poking fun at the national police agency actions as part of border security.

"Don't be so harsh on our fellow officer's; they just might recruit you some day."

"And that'll happen when pigs fly," she declared before being interrupted by the office door swinging open.

Entering their small office, fellow detectives, Guy Masson, and Nicolas Berger saw Geneviève and Claude finishing their reports on the afternoon activities.

Berger bowed his head in mock praise as he stood at his desk. "Well if it's not the 'dynamic duo'," he said teasing his fellow detectives.

"We heard you caught two more peddlers," Masson added sitting heavily in his chair, folder in hand trying to cool down from the summer heat.

"That's right, two fewer delinquents for you gentlemen to worry about," Geneviève said with a sense of pride. "Our problem is neither of them wants to roll over on their supplier."

"We likewise heard you're trying to convince Captain Duval to allow a trip to Paris to buy some new shoes too," Berger chuckled as word spread through the station about the footwear failure.

"These were the most comfortable shoes I owned," she exclaimed holding up her broken pair of Swilden pumps.

"I recommend you find a pair of track shoes if you plan on running down anymore suspects through the streets," Masson said with a chuckle.

Having shared the events of the day amongst themselves, the four detectives of the Central Directorate of the Judicial Police (DCPJ) returned to the task at hand. Finding the responsible party or parties trafficking and selling drugs along their countries Mediterranean coast.

Chapter Three

The hustle and bustle of tourists mingling with the citizens out for a Friday late afternoon stroll clogged the sidewalks along the waterfront of the French seaside city. As groups of families and friends stopped to talk, they created an international symphony of dialects conversing in unison.

Strolling through the front entrance of a local café' near the marina's entrance, Guillermo Ochoa glanced over patrons with a casual but knowing eye. *Who amongst all these tourist looks like a possible candidate for a score? He asked himself.* It was here he planned to make his last 'street' sale before boarding the *M/V Joan of Arc*, beginning his life as a drug-dealing merchantman.

Lars and his girlfriend, Zoe were spending their last evening in France, enjoying the local ambience, sitting in the corner of the crowded café.

"I thought we'd make a score by now?" Zoe asked, her eyes darting from one table to the next, hoping no one noticed their conversation.

"I know so did I, but it's not as easy as it would be if we were back home in Holland."

"Didn't your friend Petr say you could find a seller on the waterfront?"

"He did; but we've been up and down the docks for three days and I've not sure the French are as open to making a sell," Lars said.

Shuffling past patrons sitting at small café' tables, working towards the side entrance, Guillermo caught a snippet of the couple's conversation, a wry smile forming on his face. "I'm sorry, but I couldn't help but overhear your conversation, maybe I can help you."

"I'm not sure I understand," Lars said. *Could this guy be police? he sounds too eager to help,* wondering about the olive-skinned stranger coming out of nowhere to stand next to him and his girlfriend.

"I've traveled a while myself," looking about the restaurant. "And I know it's hard to get 'recreational' drugs in a foreign country," Guillermo said shifting his satchel form behind his shoulder to his lap. *I hope I haven't judged wrong with this guy? If I did, and these two are*

French police undercover, I'll never make Germany as planned, he thought nibbling on the peanuts left on the table.

"Yes, in Holland, it's easier to enjoy oneself when you have particular pleasures," Lars said.

Zoe pulled the loose strands of hair back into her ponytail before she asked, "Can help us?"

"Yes, I've a friend who has provided me with something I can offer you, for a price that is," Guillermo said. "I recommend we discuss this away from here though," sensing the crowd moving closer to them.

Nodding in agreement, the young couple made their way out of the café'. Lars and Zoe strolled to the public square just a block from the café' like the many young people who were out in the afternoon sun, followed by Guillermo. Stopping under the shade of a small birch tree, they sat and waited for the Spaniard to join them. Glancing at the passersby's as they walked through the park, "What is it you wish to offer us?" Lars asked.

Removing the small satchel off his shoulder, Guillermo reached in and pulled out the last two 'balloons' he was selling. "I've got a hundred and twenty-five-gram balloon or a two hundred fifty-gram balloon," he said. "Which one of these do you want to buy?"

Lars looked at Zoe, then back at the drugs, "How much for the small one?"

"It'll cost you two hundred and fifty euros."

"And how much will it cost for the larger one?" Zoe asked, knowing it could be shared by both of them.

"It'll cost you four hundred euros," Guillermo said. I don't want to be too greedy; I just need to be clean for when I board the freighter, recalling the need to pass cleanly through the customs inspection point.

Glancing at each other, Lars and Zoe contemplated the buy, each knowing this would use up much of their spare cash.

Lars pulled his wallet out, "We'll take the larger of the two."

Settling the transaction, Guillermo watched the young couple leave. Now, holding the cash in his hand, he thought to get myself to the freighter before it leaves, a devilish smile crossing his face.

Sitting at the small desk in their hotel room, Lars was carefully dividing up the hashish they bought earlier in the day.

"How long before you can have it ready?" Zoe asked.

"Just a few minutes, we've spent a bunch of our cash on this so I want to make it last until we get to Athens."

Getting out her make-up kit, Zoe extracted a small glass figurine of Buddha, and handed it to Lars.

Depositing a small amount of the drugs in the recessed part of the statues stomach, he passed it back to Zoe, "here you get the first try."

With a flick of her lighter, Zoe placed the flame against the drug, lighting it and took in a long drag from the smoldering content.

"Um..., smooth," closing her eyes as the drug attacked her senses.

Taking the figurine back, Lars prepared his own piece, lighting it before taking a hit of the drug.

"This is almost better than the smoke from Columbia."

Getting up from the bed, Zoe walked out onto the balcony.

"Look at the water, it's so wonderful Lars, I want to go swimming."

Sprawling back on the bed, Lars didn't hear his girlfriend; he was experiencing his own high, envisioning a field of tulips swaying in the breeze, the colors hypnotizing him.

Resting against the rail, Zoe slipped out of her shorts and top, preparing in her mind, to plunge into the cool waters of the Mediterranean Sea.

***

Drawing the cloth away from the nude body, Captain Julien Duval noted the latest victim. A red-haired woman, appears to be in her twenties, and from a northern European country based on her features, perhaps on holiday, he thought. The grotesque contorted way the body was found led his officers to surmise the young woman fell from the top floor of the hotel.

"Make sure we question the hotel staff," he said pulling the cover back over the woman's body. Rising, he looked skyward to the rooftop trying to imagine how the woman came to fall.

"Yes Captain," the investigating officer said, the taste of bile still fresh in his mouth.

"Hopefully we can find someone who is still alive that knows her," Duval said. Another apparent drug death for us to worry about the officer thought, looking around at the gathering throng of tourists. "Please move along ladies and gentlemen," the captain said waving his arms to the crowd.

The pounding on the hotel room door by the police brought Lars out of his own high. Rolling over in the bed, he found himself alone, Zoe said she was going swimming, she must be at the pool; I guess she forgot her keys, sitting up in bed.

Teetering across the darkened room, he opened the door to find himself staring at two uniformed police officers and the hotel manager.

"What the hell do you want?"

"Are you Lars Jansen?" the senior officer asked.

"Yeah, what's the problem?" shaking the fog from his thoughts.

"Do you know this woman?" the officer asked holding a headshot of Zoe.

The unflattering black and white printout of his girlfriend shook him. Her hair had been pulled to each side of her face, but her eyes were closed, he noticed. And there were dark smudges, residual blood, under her nose and around the corners of her mouth. With situations like this, the medical staff tried to reduce the grotesque nature of death on the young woman's face.

"What's happened to her?" he asked as he trembled where he stood.

"I'm sorry, but she's dead," the officer said coldly, "we need you to come down to the station for questioning."

Learning his girlfriend was dead; Lars doubled over and vomited on the shoes of the hotel manager.

Grabbing the young man, the senior police officer said, "Let's get a medical crew up here and then we'll continue after he's stable."

Steadying Lars by the arms, the officer turned on the lights and helped him back into the hotel room and sat him at the desk.

Glancing at the desk surface, the officer saw the open balloon of hashish and the drug paraphernalia. It's sad this young man wasted his youth and the elegance of a poor girl. And for what, a cheap thrill, the officer told himself, thinking of his niece in Paris, hoping she'd not succumb to this.

As the emergency workers arrived to aid Lars, the detective reached into his coat pocket and pulled out a spare evidence bag, placing the narcotics into it. Holding the hashish up, "I'll get this to the lab; I'm sure Captain Duval will want to know what we're up against," the senior officer said. "You escort the suspect to the infirmary and book him."

***

Making a notation on his evidence sheet, the lab technician removed the drugs collected at the hotel room of Lars Jansen. Grabbing a scalpel from the tray, he sliced open one of the balloons before using a spatula to smear the gooey tar-like material on the Petri dish. Sliding his chair to the side, he grabbed three separate bottles before rolling back to his workstation.

Taking the first bottle, a mixture of vanillin and acetaldehyde in ethanol, the technician poured it into the dish, he mixed the drug until it became soluble. Next, he added hydrochloric acid before adding the last chemical, which was chloroform. In moments of starting the Duquenios-Levine test, the contents turned a brilliant shade of purple, a clear indication that some form of cannabinoids were present.

Removing some of the liquid, the technician placed a few drops on the specimen glass and placed a second piece on top of the first. Taking the specimen, he slid it into place on the microscope's turntable, while preparing another sample for placement in the labs' mass spectrometer to be analyzed.

Standing over the eyepiece of the electron-microscope, he squinted through the microscope the technician saw the microbes floating in the solution, *this is a nasty combination of cannabis*; the lab technician wrote in his notes filling out the toxicology report.

There looks to be some artificial markers in the make-up, noting the mixture of purified cannabis resin and of the refined hashish. I've not come across the likes of this before, counting the various indicators visible under the microscope. Someone with a great deal of skill has been playing with nature on this one, wiping his brow with the back of his sleeve.

I don't envy the police on this one, signing the report and closing the file folder marked Ms. Zoe Bakker.

Chapter Four

The building, its exterior paint peeling from the damp air and harsh sunlight due to the location near the docks, was the chosen space for 'Papillion Transport' office. Gregory Arsenault sat in the outer office drinking coffee, reviewing manifests. He wasn't usually surprised by his business partner, but the call he received earlier did. What could have caused Nazim to end his 'business' trip so early? He thought reclining in his desk chair, feet propped up onto the wastebasket.

Business for the two men was the distribution of illegal drugs from Algiers and Morocco into Europe. Nazim used his familiarity of the criminal underworld in the Algerian and Moroccan for supplying the drugs. While Gregory's secret ownership of a local shipping company allowed them to ply the Mediterranean Sea from Marseille, and it was becoming more lucrative.

Glancing over the shipping manifests and arrival logs, Gregory took notice of his freighter scheduled to arrive from Tangier later in the evening. "Who's meeting the cargo ship tonight?" asking his close friend and pseudo shipping manager, Louis Clement.

"I believe it's Franco and Hakim meeting the ship," Clement said.

"Make sure they're covered; we don't want any problems the same day Nazim returns," Gregory said. "And Louis, remind me to discuss our need to have Aziz recruit more men to keep up with the processing. I'm getting tired of our crew doing all the work with no help from him except his cousin."

"Yes, Greg, I'll remind you," Louis said.

With the direction given, Gregory looked at his watch and realized he had less than thirty minutes to meet his partner's flight at the airport. Grabbing the keys to his Peugeot sedan, he left Louis to make the arrangements for backing up Franco and Hakim at the docks later in the day.

***

While Gregory and Louis were preparing to receive another drug shipment from their supplier in North Africa, Gregory's partner in the operation was fourteen hundred kilometers away in Scotland.

Stepping into the international terminal at Edinburgh's airport, Nazim Aziz felt exposed like a first-time nudist at an unfamiliar beach, security cameras pointed in every direction. His criminal past was not well-known outside the southern coast of France and of Algeria. Constantly suspicious of individual activities by design, he still felt uneasy every time he entered a terminal, whether it was at an airport, train station or bus depot. Any place where a security camera had the means of recording his image, it was a risk to him.

Wandering through the crowd, Nazim took his place in line as the agent called the next passenger in line to move forward, assisting each traveler with tickets and luggage.

"Good morning," the agent said as Nazim stepped forward to begin his check in before boarding the flight from Edinburgh. "May I please see your identification and confirmation?" she asked. Nazim handed over his passport and the confirmation he printed out in the hotel's business office. "Mister Louis Remesy, do you have anything to declare?" asking the predetermined questions that all agents were required to do.

"No; I just have the small carry-on satchel and my work papers," Nazim said. He was confident his passport would stand up to the ticket agents' review.

The travel document was genuine since the name he was using was of his mother's uncle who had since passed away several years ago, in La Havre. With Gregory's help and five thousand francs to a clerk in the La Havre hospital, Nazim was given the documents from his uncles' stay, including the death certificate. From there it only took another thousand francs in the hands of the public administration clerk to see the passport created. Once this was accomplished it allowed Nazim to become 'Louis Remesy' and use it on occasions such as this.

After a few minutes inputting his information into the computer, the agent declared handing Nazim his ticket and passport back. "You are all set. Please continue to your left, and gate A14."

"Merci," Nazim said walking away from the counter and proceeding to his gate.

After an uneventful flight, including a brief stop in Paris, his flight touched down at the Marseille Provence airport with a brief chirp as tires contacted the tarmac.

Glancing out the window, the sky was cloudy along the horizon of the Mediterranean Sea was visible off in the distance. Moments later, Nazim's gaze was interrupted by the crew announcing the gate number they would exit and the area they could claim their luggage.

Nazim strolled through the terminal exit and into the baggage claim area, looking for his friend and business partner, Gregory Arsenault. Hearing the arrival announcement over the speakers, Gregory had joined the other patrons gathering to meet family members and friends exiting into the arrival lounge.

"It is good to see you my friend," Nazim said grasping Gregory's hand firmly and receiving a warm embrace.

"You appear no worse for wear; how was the flight?"

"The flight was as expected, relatively boring but pleasant as the children who were traveling seemed well behaved," Nazim responded as they walked out to the car park. Walking into the elevator, Nazim told his partner of the call he received from Ewan Sutherland, his Scottish contact, before boarding the jet.

"Detectives from Scotland Yard know about you? How could they learn about the meeting?" Gregory asked. "Who could know of our activities that they might have said something to the authorities?" His mind swirled thinking through the possible leaks to his partners' travels.

"First; let's return to the office and make sure we are set for today before we worry about tomorrow," Nazim said.

"What do you suggest we do about this?" Gregory asked. "I mean, what'll your next step be if it turns out the authorities having identified you?"

Gregory wanted to know everything, but he likewise knew most times, a hasty reaction only leads to greater troubles. Getting off the elevator in the parking complex, he pulled out his keys, thumbing the lock release just as Nazim and he approached his sedan.

After tossing his bag in the back, Nazim slid into the passenger seat. "Later this afternoon I'll call our young Scot to see if he can place names to our problems."

***

Meanwhile, a delivery truck sat outside the entrance to the receiving area of the port, the figure of Hakim Talib slumped in the passenger seat of the Volvo. Although his eyes were closed, he was far from being asleep as his mind was going over the shipping manifest for tonight's pickup.

"Hakim, how can you sleep in such a position, it hurts my back?" his partner for the evening said. Raising, the Algerian grabbed the handle bolted over the door and pulled himself upright.

"Is this more to your liking Franco?" Hakim said looking at the Frenchman, himself leaning on the trucks' steering wheel. The seat barely confined the hulking frame of the driver as the small truck's interior was not meant for individuals over two-and-a-half meters in height.

Closing his eyes, Hakim thought, this was the fifth time his cousin, Nazim, had trusted him to handle the receipt of the hashish shipment at the docks. I owe a great deal to Nazim, considering the circumstances he'd fallen into while growing up in slums of Algiers.

In his late teens, Hakim exercised poor judgment, requiring Nazim to step in and persuade one of the principles in the Algiers drug trade to spare his cousin's life. Hakim had learned a hard lesson in the underworld when it came to trust when one of his 'friends' had double crossed him on a transaction. Losing half-million Algerian dinars, equal to three and a half thousand British pounds was a princely sum to the crime syndicate. To this day, Hakim swore an allegiance to his cousin he would honor until his death.

"How many pallets will we be accepting?" he asked, looking out into the harbor. The horizon was dotted with freighters and luxury pleasure craft making their way into or out of the busy French port.

"Six; four originated in Algiers and two from Tangier," the burly driver said.

François 'Franco' Laurent was the muscle behind Gregory Arsenault's shipping operations around the Marseille docks. When called upon, he would conduct "a cleaning" as he liked referring to the elimination of any member that became trouble for his boss.

Shifting back to Hakim, he saw his partner going over the custom documents they needed to pass along to the inspection personnel before picking up the shipment. The documents were opposite of ones used by the ships quartermaster when the vessel had docked at Algiers two days earlier. These would be correct, allowing Hakim and Franco to take possession of the fake cargo containing the hashish and cannabis resin were switched dockside.

Franco's boss made sure documents would pass the scrutiny of customs officials, including the police in the event they were singled out for inspection after leaving the docks.

While growing up in Algiers, Hakim's cousin learned putting things in plain sight made it far easier to protect. This was true when trying to hide the drugs from customs officials. His mentor had taught him if you place a viper in the middle of the road, people will always walk on the sidewalk. It was this metaphor and lesson Nazim recalls when they are moving shipments between the ports.

In this case, a legitimate shipment of olive oil had left Marseille bound for the Algerian capital, complete with proper importation documents. While in transit, the quartermaster switched the original documents with a second set of documents with errors for use when unloading the contents at the port. As the custom agents and port authorities noted the errors, the legitimate cargo would be placed aside in a holding area waiting to be returned to the ship.

With the flurry of movement at most ports, the ability to control a few pallets is often overlooked. It is during this period when oversight by a customs agent, well paid by the Algerian drug cartel, would look the other way. Then similar pallets, which now contained illegal narcotics, were brought forward for loading. The legitimate cargo with erroneous documents, would be removed. After being taken to a separate warehouse where the bottles with olive oil replaced ones containing the altered cannabis resin and raw hashish, they were brought back to the docks.

With this 'sleight of hand' completed, the pallet was readied for placement back on the freighter for its return trip to France. No one had been aware the contents of the pallets which now contain the illicit drug product bound for a return trip to Marseille.

Two of the multi-purpose tugboats were escorting the *M/V (motor vessel) De Gaulle* into the harbor mouth. She was the regularly scheduled vessel for 'Papillion Transport' sailing the "Maghreb" route in the Mediterranean between France and the North African countries of Morocco and Algiers.

"I see our friendly harbor pilot is safely aboard," Franco said spying movement on the ship's bridge, as the vessel inched closer to its berth in the harbor.

"Let's get the truck in line," Hakim said, pointing to the terminal entrance becoming crowded with other trucks and drivers arriving to pick up their designated cargo.

As Franco maneuvered the truck into position at the dock, Nazim and Gregory sat down at the table in a non-descript office building across from the harbor.

Pacing back and forth in the office, the Frenchman took a drink from his coffee cup before speaking. "If the British police suspect you, then we need to find this person who spoke to the police; or worse, to INTERPOL," Gregory said, alluding to the international police agency in Europe.

Staring across the table, the French-Algerian drug dealer questioned his partner. "Who knew of my trip to Scotland?" though he knew the answer on how this trip had been arranged.

"Here in Marseille? Let's see, there was Louis, Hakim, myself, oh and Sophia," Gregory said mentioning the young Frenchwoman.

Relaxing with his hands folded and resting at the table, his eyes closed, he next asked. "And do we know who Sophia used to make my arrangements?" once again knowing the answer but making the query.

"She did as she always has; using a common computer at the local café to access the airline website," Gregory said, disliking the direction of the question. Sophia was Gregory's niece, the daughter of his deceased brother.

"Relax Gregory, I'm sure she used every precaution," he said sensing the tension in his friend's response. "It's possible the DCJP was looking for someone, passed the information to the British and I fit their profile." Nazim had considered this possibility while sitting on the flight from Edinburgh. Nevertheless, am I still safe allowing Gregory's niece access to my activities? The French authorities can well access information about my earlier criminal activities in Algiers as he continued thinking of possible instances where he might have been found out.

"If that's the case, maybe it is time we shifted our focus and place of business elsewhere?" Gregory asked, gulping down the rest of his cold coffee.

"I'm not ready to concede that I've been completely compromised," Nazim said, standing to refill his own coffee. "As for Louis; the two of you have known each other for how long now?"

"Well, we've been business partners for over twelve years now," Gregory said. "And we've been at each other's side for nearly sixteen years." He considered his friend more a brother than a business partner. He had first met Louis Clement during their induction into the French Foreign Legion as troubled youths. After leaving the Legion, both men became involved in various criminal activities while establishing their presence in the seaport of Toulon over 12 years earlier.

It was just before their dismissal Gregory assumed control of the shipping firm, 'Papillion Transport' for dispatching two members of the Legion during a training exercise in French Guiana. It was made known to Gregory that one victim he and Louis dispatched was heir to the shipping company, and as payment, granted ownership of the four-vessel fleet.

Nazim thought for a moment, taking his time pouring more coffee into his cup. Is it possible a slip of the tongue, maybe a careless word by someone in Aberdeen caused the two officers from Scotland Yard to appear at the docks? These questions were just the beginning that would plaque him as he stood silently in the room.

"Your contact in Aberdeen; are we sure he's not playing both sides?" Gregory asked, interrupting Nazim's train of thought.

"Possible; yes, but not probable since I directed him to contact the boat workers after picking me up at the airport, and before driving to the docks," Nazim said. "But, it will be a point to take and exercise greater caution in the event I need to make another visit."

"And what of this 'Mr. Higgins', the Irishman you met five months earlier in Algiers who wanted this transaction?" Gregory once again asked his friend. "Doesn't your gypsy blood tell you something suspicious about this man?"

As he watched a freighter being led out to sea, the drug-trafficker contemplated their current position. Nazim thought about his friend's question. "I understand your concern, and its mine too," he said returning to the table. "I have thought it could be possible the Irishman would create a 'set-up' or 'sting' to have our operations exposed. But by doing so he accepts risks of his own; because his man, um..., Ewan, would have been caught by the police," struggling to remember the young Scotsman's name.

It was just over five months earlier in a café outside Algiers; a business associate of Nazim Aziz's was approached by a European gentleman looking to conduct a 'drug' transaction for his employer in the British Isles. He introduced Nazim to the gentleman who referred to himself as 'Mr. Higgins', an Irishman whose employer wanted to end the influx of South American influence in what he referred to as 'his pitch'.

During this meeting, the European outlined his demand for a 'marketable product.' In this case, the product was hashish, and cannabis resin, distributed to specific vessels supporting oil rigs in the North Sea. It was a suspicious inquiry, but after several hours of discussion and a healthy fee transferred into a shadow account in a Moroccan bank, the men agreed to the arrangement.

Nazim's associate in Algiers, who knew him by his alias 'Louis Remesy', made the arrangements to help move their product through France. Learning of this new avenue to expand their effort at a minimal risk, Nazim directed Gregory to use his police contact and have this Mr. Higgins vetted as best as possible.

Through a series of inquiries and the passing of several thousand euros to the right police clerk, Gregory found 'Mr. Higgins' had no record with French authorities or INTERPOL. This news made him suspicious and uneasy, but with transferring 250,000 euro's into Nazim's account in an Algiers bank from Rabid, the transaction was set in motion. Assisted by his contact, Nazim made the agreement to have the first 'trial' shipment to Aberdeen Scotland in ninety days.

Chapter Five

In the Police Municipale' building located in the Sainte-Marthe district of Marseille, Detective Geneviève Benoit was reviewing her notes from a surveillance effort they were working. She focused on the scant information they had on local smuggling operations between Marseille and North African locations. "Claude; do you see any patterns in the ship movements on this manifest?"

"Other than the routine cargo ships we've already accounted for, I'd say no," glancing at her list. "But we're still waiting on Berger and Masson to provide information on their surveillance of the freighters arriving from the eastern Mediterranean ports," mentioning the other two officers of their unit.

Peering at his partner over his cup of coffee, the senior could see the frustration mounting. "Remember, you need to look in the 'not so obvious' locations and the obvious ones," Claude declared. Setting his coffee down, he picked up the listing of arrivals and departures from the terminal servicing the cruise lines.

"The cruise ships?" Geneviève asked rather quizzically tugging at the end of her ponytail.

"Of course. Drug smugglers try to avoid the obvious shipping vessels, and they'd also try to disguise their activities as best they could," he said pointing out to the harbor.

"But, passengers and their luggage are checked, scanned, and sniffed," she said alluding to drug-sniffing dogs and their handlers walking amongst the tourists and their belongings.

"Ah, yes they are supposedly inspected; but what about the crew members?" Claude asked raising a finger to the office ceiling in a comical gesture.

"Some crew may never leave the ship because of the tempo of operations, especially during the summer months," Geneviève said in a matter of factual tone.

"That's true, but even crew members receive visitors during port calls, who may or may not be legitimate family members or guests," Claude said. "So; we need to look in all areas, not just the obvious ones." With that, Claude grabbed his now-empty coffee cup and walked out of the office, leaving Geneviève to ponder her dilemma alone and in silence.

With a small piece of a much larger puzzle handed to her, Geneviève began reviewing the cruise ship port of call listings, looking to create a clearer view. "You must look in the 'not so obvious' places'," she said to herself, comically mocking the term used by her partner earlier.

With her list of cruise lines that made port calls in Marseille, Detective Benoit sat quiet as her partner maneuvered their patrol car towards the harbor. Standing in front of Terminal 2, the two detectives, began discussing crew activities with the first officer from one of the major cruise lines operating in the port. "We respect our crew member's privacy," the first officer replied to Claude's question about on shore activities.

Studying the First Officer for a reaction, the female detective posed her question to him. "When they return, though, do they get inspected like the passengers?" Geneviève asked.

Pointing out to the line of crew-members being inspected. "Of course; we must follow the law like everyone else for customs and regulations," the first officer said.

Composing a note of the officer's responses, they continued to discuss what could be considered 'normal' activities for the crew before completing their inquiry. It was the third such response to their investigation and questioning that day as Geneviève and Claude thanked the first officer. "So where does this leave us?" she asked as they walked past several busloads full of Scandinavian tourists preparing to board the luxury cruise liner.

"Everyone has a price," Claude said pointing at the porters handling the luggage of the tourists for a fist full of euros. "I am sure the crew members are checked. But as they say 'who is watching or overseeing whom' is the question," the detective continued. "Just look over there," singling out the uniformed cruise ship agent checking a handful of employees at a separate gate from the tourists.

She could see what her partner alluded to as the action gave the appearance of organized chaos. "If that's the case, it means finding the dishonest agent and the crew members," Geneviève said.

"Yes; it does," Claude said. "And don't forget. It's not just dishonest crew-members getting a kick-back, we need to consider the cartel controlling this area too," alluding to criminal syndicates controlling the harbor.

She shook her head in disgust knowing they were looking up very tall mountain needing to be climbed if they were to find answers to their drug trafficking question. "So, we follow one or more of the crew members that we identified earlier?" she asked.

"Yes. It's a start and I recommend we focus on the cruise lines that recently docked at the more 'questionable' locales," the senior officer said. "Which includes the ones along the Mediterranean coasts, both on the European side and the African side," Claude said.

***

A thousand meters from the cruise ship terminals, a bustle of activity was taking place as trucks loaded with merchandise were inspected then released. "Sign here," the customs agent pointed to Hakim passing the customs document to him. Hakim did, signing his name in Arabic script in the spot identified by the agent out of habit.

"Could you please print your name; our agents do not read Arabic," the customs agent asked Hakim.

Looking annoyed at the customs agent, Hakim spelled out his name on the form under his signature. With that done, the agent pointed to one of the forklift operators and the stack of pallets to be loaded onto the waiting truck. "Franco wake up! We are getting our pallets loaded," Hakim shouted pounding on the side of the truck.

Startled by the sudden thumping against the cab, Franco's elbow slipped off the edge of the steering wheel and struck the horn, letting out a loud blast. Looking around and embarrassed, Franco exited the truck and helped Hakim open the rear doors, "You're an ass!"

"And you complain about how I can sleep in the truck," Hakim said pulling open one side of the delivery truck doors.

As the last of the pallets were loaded, Hakim closed and locked the containers doors, watching as the customs agent applied the security seal over the latch.

"Are we set?" Franco asked as Hakim pulled himself into the cab.

"We are free to leave," he responded. After nearly six hours at the docks watching the goods come from the various ships at dock, they could finally leave with their 'cargo'. "Mind the speed limit as we leave," Hakim said. Removing a cell phone from his jacket, Hakim dialed the number to his cousins' office, "We are cleared and, on our way," he said in Arabic.

"They are on their way," Nazim said to Gregory putting the phone down on the desk.

"Good; I'll tell Louis to prepare the warehouse to receive them in an hour," Gregory replied pulling out his own cell phone to contact his business partner. The drive from the docks to the warehouse on the eastern outskirts of the city was not long. But the circuitous route was always taken to make sure the product was never compromised. The former appliance warehouse off the expressway in the northern part of the city had been in Gregory's control for over five years and served their operation well. There was always truck traffic coming in and out of the area so their vehicles were never suspected or considered out of the ordinary to the casual observer.

"Some days I wish we could drive through the tunnel," Franco drawled making his way through the traffic in the Les Olives district.

"I hate the tunnel," Hakim replied, not wanting to let on to his partner of his claustrophobic fear. "Plus, driving this monster of a truck, we would never pass the entrance without scraping the roof on the sides with your driving skills," he joked with Franco. Hakim knew he would trust no one other than Franco when it came to driving. He had reflexes of a Formula 1 driver and the foresight of a gypsy fortune-teller, recalling several of the other instances where Franco exhibited his driving skills.

In the warehouse, Nazim and Gregory were observing the work crew Louis had assembled. Half-dozen men were walking about the floor, clad in blue chemical suits, each one wearing a respirator. Looking down onto the floor below the office, they could oversee the preparations to process and transfer the raw hashish and cannabis resin from the olive oil bottles. These bottles were like ones that had been packaged in the boxes from the six shipping pallets collected by Hakim and Franco earlier.

Early afternoon soon became evening as the men working within the warehouse toiled over their tasks. The process of extracting the drugs was simple, but laborious. A dozen bottles were opened and lowered into large pots of boiling water, liquefying the drugs making it easier to pour into new containers. While heating the hashish, it was producing an addictive vapor, which is why Gregory's men always wore the protective masks. "How much more needs to be extracted?" Nazim asked.

"We have three pallets already emptied and extracted, with one near completion, and two remaining to start," Gregory said, looking at the workers below in their safety suits.

"Very well," Nazim said. "We've forty-five days left to have the delivery prepared for the Bonaparte before its scheduled departure," the drug smuggler said recalling the agreed upon schedule with the mysterious Irishman.

"Louis and his people will need fourteen days to finish processing the hashish and cannabis resin before we can return it to the shipping crates."

"I know; but the weather can turn foul in the Channel, and I don't want any reason to delay making this shipment if we can help it," Nazim said. "We've been paid to make this transaction happen, and with luck, it'll lead to many more of the same."

"Once Louis is done, that still allows the shipment thirty days to transit from here to the North Sea," Gregory said.

"Weather in the Channel during the coming months is fickle," the French-Algerian said. "And I'm not confident with the Irishman's demand to transfer this much product in the manner he suggested. We haven't attempted something like this before," Nazim said. I don't want to risk things just because this mysterious Irishman says it can be done, reminding himself to follow his version of the plan and not 'Mr. Higgins'.

***

At the same time Nazim and Gregory were discussing the plans to ship, Franco Laurent was sitting in a café' in the Villette district of Marseille, awaiting his guest.

Several years ago, Franco parlayed his association with Gregory and Louis Clement to secure his own supply of narcotics. Having established himself as a 'reliable supplier' with local drug dealers, he began distribution of narcotics to specific individuals' through-out the city, in tonight's case; it was a senior steward from a 'Nordic Cruise Line' vessel frequenting Marseille.

Looking at his guest entering, Franco rose from his seat to greet her, "Good evening Grace," he said leaning down and placed a brief kiss on each cheek.

"Hello Franco," Grace said in her usual heavy Philippine accent.

"How was your trip?" asking in a polite tone.

"It was hectic, too many passengers always wanting more," the steward said. "I'm always on my feet," she replied, lifting one of her legs to show off her swollen ankles. It also provided Franco a glimpse under her uniform skirt, showing him, she was prepared for the evenings activities.

Waving his arm towards the door, he said, "Well then, may I suggest a night in a comfortable room and a hot bath."

"That would be most enjoyable," Grace said giggling like a teenager.

Reaching into his pocket, he pulled out several 10-euro notes and left them on the table to pay for his drink, which he left half full.

In the shadows of several buildings, Detective's Benoit and Lemieux sat in the unmarked car keeping a watchful eye on several members of the cruise ship, but one in particular had drawn their attention. Even though they'd identify a handful of workers, their suspect for the night had been joined by a local man. Watching the diminutive steward and the taller Frenchman leaving the café, Geneviève said, "Well, there goes our target for the night."

"And it's safe to say, we know what they'll be doing in a few moments," Claude said. Lifting the night binoculars, the detective observed the Frenchman sliding his arm over the shoulder of the woman, cupping her breast.

Geneviève's skin tightened as she thought of being manhandled by a stranger, fighting back the horrors of past encounters from her youth in Cherbourg. Just the passing thought caused an involuntary shiver to course through her body.

With surveillance of the street dealers growing cold, Detectives' Benoit and Lemieux focused on several crew members from the cruise ship line, conducting a weeks' worth of surveillance while their ship was in port.

"Do you suspect she knows she's under surveillance?" Geneviève asked. It was an easy task to follow the steward since she still had her service uniform on from the cruise ship. The greater problem was the fact she was just barely five feet tall, noting her height.

"Not likely, even though the cruise ship docks here, she's still a foreigner and doubtless knows nothing of our laws, customs or our mannerisms," Claude said. "And let's not lose sight of the fact we're taking a stab in the dark by selecting the members we have," he reminded his colleague. "For all we know, she's completely innocent."

"But if she's innocent, does that make her companion innocent as well?" Geneviève asked.

"It's possible; so, at our next opportunity we might want to photograph each of them to see if he's in our database." Some senior detective you are, forgetting to grab a camera for the surveillance, he thought chastising himself. "Did our analysis not show she was a possible target because of her 'questionable' activities in other ports?" Claude asked.

"Of course, it showed a trend," Geneviève said. "From what we've learned, this steward makes a habit out of visiting restricted areas of the cities they dock at," alluding to the cruise lines documentation.

"And in that case, as they say in America, we've 'probable cause' to conduct our surveillance," he said. Without a trace of evidence to show for it though, he thought his frustration growing at the lack of movement on cases centered around the drug dealers in the city.

***

Two naked bodies reclined on the king-size bed of the darkened motel room, the sheet covering their lower torsos. Lying against the muscular and tattooed body of her guest, Grace draped her arm across his chest, running her fingers through his coarse hair. "Franco, several of the younger crew wanted to buy more of your product from me, but I didn't have enough for the entire trip," she said.

"Is that so?" he asked. The product he supplied Grace for sale to the other members of her ship was prescription-grade amphetamines and barbiturates, originally developed for a German pharmaceutical company.

Circling her fingernails across his penis, tugging at his foreskin, Grace asked "Can we discuss a new deal for more of the products?"

"We either discuss business, or you offer pleasure; not both," Franco said. How can I concentrate on both business and pleasure when she's doing things like that? his eyes closed enjoying the brief foreplay she provided.

"In that case, let's call room service, I'm hungry," she said bouncing herself off the bed and prancing to the desk like a gymnast.

To Franco it was a sign she was pressed for the product and time. In past encounters, they wouldn't handle any transactions until the next morning, however this evening looks to be a different case.

"Shall we have a simple plate or something more?" Grace asked.

"Something simple, and don't forget my Heineken this time," he said walking past her on his way to the bathroom to wash himself.

***

As the evening wore on, Hakim entered the office where Nazim and Gregory were discussing the next step in supplying their drug cocktail to the mysterious Irishman, 'Mr. Higgins'.

As the door opened, Gregory glanced up from the notes laid across his desk. "And what have you and Franco been up to since you dropped off the truck," he asked with a hint of anger in his tone.

"We did as we usually do; we returned the truck to the yard near the velodrome," Hakim said looking at his uncle's partner with a disconcerting look. "And then I returned to my apartment for the night."

"And what about Franco?" Gregory asked.

"He mentioned going back to his apartment so he could clean up and meet a woman from the cruise ship."

Nazim sat, taking in the exchange between the two men before voicing his concern to his partner. "Gregory, you might want to have a talk with Franco when he returns," he said.

Gregory rubbed his hands across his face. Having François Laurent as part of their organization, was his and Louis' doing. Tonight, made the third instance Franco broken from his routine Nazim had demanded each set of drivers adhere to, to insure their operation was not brought under police scrutiny.

"I'll have Louis and one of his men go and pick him up as soon as they complete transferring the hashish from the bottles," Gregory said. It was becoming clear Franco was wearing out his welcome. And any level of trust Nazim once had for him was waning. Since Franco continued to think of his own well-being above the operation, angered both he and Nazim at the Frenchman's lack of loyalty.

Nazim looked at the clock hanging on the wall and then down to the floor of the warehouse. Based on his calculations the men would finish the transfer of the hashish and cannabis resin in another day if all went well.

Shifting back to Gregory, he gave the Frenchman his view on the matter. "Have Louis and one of his men go look for Franco as soon as it's morning, and you take over the transfer," Nazim said. Walking next to his cousin, he added, "Hakim, you'll help Gregory with the transfer as well; pay close attention, you might be called upon to lead this effort one day."

"Of course, cousin," Hakim said, getting up from the chair and going to change into a 'clean suit' like the rest of the workers on the warehouse floor.

After Hakim, had left the office, Gregory turned to his partner, "Don't you trust me to make the right decisions anymore?"

"I trust you with my life Gregory," Nazim said placing his hand on his shoulder. "But I also believe it's time for Hakim to learn more of the operation, and who better to teach him than you."

"I appreciate the fact you're entrusting me to guide Hakim, but I sense you're more concerned about Franco," Gregory said.

"You're correct, I am; he's shown a lapse in judgment which could jeopardize our whole operation. Meeting a woman, a foreigner no less, who works on one of the cruise ships can't always be expected to be the innocent laborer," Nazim said.

This statement made Gregory think of events he hoped wouldn't happen again. During their earlier years in Toulon, he and Louis killed a former 'helper' when they discovered the local police had turned him just before they completed an exchange for guns and explosives with an Italian family from Milan.

And that wasn't the first time they had to kill to maintain their anonymity, recalling the steamy jungle of French Guiana. From that point forward, Gregory and Louis had been particular about the individuals they brought into their organization. Even when they determined an individual was worthy of their trust, they still showed patience before they exposing the new members to the full scope of the operation.

***

As the last of the drugs were transferred from the bottles to other containers, the men were given a reprieve from their tasks. With little rest, two of the men left the warehouse and began the drive towards the harbor. As sunlight broke through the clouds over Marseille, Louis and his subordinate, Phillip Gaston parked their car near Hotel La Joliette just a few blocks from the cruise ship docks.

"Phillip; you head towards the cathedral and I'll go north towards the post office," Louis said. "When you arrive at the cathedral, go toward the docks, walking back to the Terminal 2 entrance. We'll meet up there," he added, pulling out his personal protection, a vintage Colt .45-caliber pistol.

"Oui," Phillip said. Stepping away, he reached under his jacket and behind his back, ensuring his own pistol was secure.

Louis walked in the opposite direction, thinking of the last time he had to be involved in 'disciplining' a subordinate worker. This was different though, he recalled, strolling past the various shops and looking at the few patrons working in the early morning. Was Nazim being cautious, or has Franco broken his trust with the organization and gone too far, questioning the decision. Moments later, he saw the distinctive figure of François Laurent and a diminutive Asian woman exiting the hotel parking garage across from the post office.

Louis picked up his pace, continuing along the sidewalk, taking a more direct path, allowing him to approach the twosome without being confrontational.

"Bonjour Franco, mademoiselle," Louis said coming up from behind on the Frenchman and the Filipino woman.

Surprised by Gregory's trusted friend, Franco stole a glance over his shoulder for another member coming up from behind him. "Louis, what are you doing here?" he asked. "And who else is out there?"

"I'm looking for you, my friend," he said pulling the jacket aside allowing Franco a glimpse of the pistol. "And yes, I've another member in the area," alluding to Phillip.

The diminutive steward clutched her companions' arm as she saw the weapon. "Franco, I don't understand, what's going on?" Grace said.

Swallowing nothing but his own saliva, Franco tried to clear his throat before answering. "My dear, this is a friend of mine," he said, not taking his eyes off Louis. "Louis Clement, I'd like you to meet Miss Grace Mendoza of Santa Rita, Luzon, Philippines," he said gesturing toward the woman.

"Monsieur Remesy needs to talk to you," Louis said using Nazim's alias. "He's concerned for your well-being."

"Fine. As soon as I see my guest safely back to her ship," Franco said nodding towards the entry point for the cruise ship terminals.

"Then we'll both see to her safe passage," Louis said stepping to the opposite side of Grace, placing the gun muzzle against her side.

Feeling the cold steel of the gun's muzzle press against her, Grace grasped Franco's hand tighter and leaned heavily against him.

"Louis, don't act like a fool," Franco replied pleading for the gunman to be civil.

"I suggest we take care of the lady and go about our business then," the former Legionnaire said coaxing the woman along the sidewalk.

As the threesome were making their way towards the docks, Phillip turned the corner near the cathedral and walked towards the agreed upon rendezvous point Louis suggested earlier.

Chapter Six

Stopping near the small coffee shop frequented by members of the police force, one was commenting on her order. "I'll never understand Americans taste for this style of coffee," Detective Benoit said to her partner while the barista was handing them their orders.

Removing the top off his coffee to add what looked like an extra cup of creamer, Claude replied, "You owe me six-euro for that by the way."

Taking out a bill from her pocket, Benoit set the money on the counter. "Here; I don't want you to starve today," placing a ten-euro bill in front of her partner. "And keep the change," Geneviève said walking out the door of the coffee shop and onto the sidewalk.

Snatching the money from the counter he replied, "You know I will," talking to the back of her head.

Sipping her coffee, Geneviève turned back to her partner. "This morning's routine is simple, right?" Scanning the busy street full of tourists making their way to and from the cruise ship docks. "Now; we're looking for an Asian woman no taller than a postal bin in a sea of golden-haired European's on holiday," the female detective said.

"Oui, and a muscular Frenchman at her side," Detective Lemieux said, sipping the still hot beverage.

As the two police detectives discussed the probabilities of finding their small 'Asian needle' in a large 'European haystack'; the two subjects appeared across the street. Louis, Franco, and Grace had reached the intersection across from the terminals.

Scanning up and down the boulevard, Geneviève spotted a familiar figure in the crowd. Is that the woman from the earlier evening with two other men? I recognize the Frenchman from the café, but I've never seen the shorter man. What does he have to do with the other two? she thought confused by the presence of Louis Clement. "Claude, the far corner of the intersection, would you say that's one of our targets?"

"Oui; I'll call for backup," the senior detective answered pulling out his cell phone.

Moving in opposite directions, their coffees were forgotten as they tossed them in the trash bin.

Approaching the intersection, Louis continued noticing Grace having trouble walking at the pace he and Franco were accustomed. "What is your problem? Do you think you're at a pageant displaying fancy clothes? Walk normally why don't you?" he demanded.

"I can't. Not with the drugs placed where they are," Grace stammered, fighting back tears from the discomfort the cylinder was causing because of its size and location.

Louis looked at Franco with an incredulous stare. "What in the devil's name were you thinking? Is this how you repay Gregory and I, by jeopardized the operation?"

Turning to Grace, Franco pleaded with her "Just a few more meters and you'll be back on board."

"I'll try," she said. "But it won't be easy after leaving you at the gate," knowing she'd be on her own walking the last 100 meters to the ship's stairway.

The trio strolled up to the intersection, joining the growing crowd of vacationers trying to make their way to the various cruise ships. While doing so, Louis glimpsed his associate Phillip Gaston walking up the street from the direction of the cathedral.

The young Frenchman looked at his boss along with Franco, who he knew only from brief encounters within the organization. However, he was not sure who the woman was standing between them and appeared to be having trouble in keeping her balance as they walked toward the intersection.

As Phillip was watching his boss at the intersection with Franco and the unknown Asian woman, Detective Benoit was standing across the street on the opposite corner. Staring at the short stranger with the Asian woman, Geneviève spotted his hand on the pistol grip hidden under his coat.

Glancing to her left, she looked at Claude closing the gap to the intersection, the faint sounds of sirens growing louder. Geneviève sensed the possibility of an awkward experience and worked her way to the front of the crowd waiting anxiously to cross the boulevard.

"We have to get Grace to the ship," Franco said, the sound of panic creeping into his voice.

Nodding in agreement, Louis relaxed his grip on the pistol, allowing him to guide the Filipino steward through the pedestrians.

Franco and Louis used their bulk, forcing their way to the front as the signal changed, releasing the mass of vacationers crossing the boulevard from every direction.

As he stepped off the curb, Louis recognized Phillip a half a block away and gestured toward him to keep his distance.

Staring at his boss and noticing the gesture, Phillip halted. *It wasn't like him to call me off, but I'll do as I'm told*, retracing his steps back to the cathedral. Glancing over his shoulder every so often, he kept an eye on his cousin as he walked up the boulevard.

Detective Benoit had made her way to the front of the crowd when the signal changed and rushed forward. She kept herself in a position to confront Louis, who she knew had the only visible weapon.

Claude was rushing to the opposite corner when the signal changed and stepped off the curb, while a tour bus was beginning its turn onto the boulevard. The bus driver glimpsed the police detective and laid his full weight onto the horn. This action was startling not only Claude but the many tourists waiting for their chance to cross the boulevard. Damn, I almost became a traffic casualty in the line of duty, at the hands of a stupid bus driver no less, looking through the massive windscreen.

With a loud hiss, the bus driver slammed on his brakes barely missing Detective Lemieux jumping back onto the curb, narrowly missing the bumper of the monstrous Prevost vehicle.

Geneviève heard the horn, but kept her focus on the target, now just 5 meters in front of her. Pulling her windbreaker aside, she drew her weapon, trying desperately not to alert the men walking toward her.

The commotion stemming from the tour bus and crowds on the opposite corner of the intersection caused Louis and Franco to shift their focus away from getting Grace to her ship.

Louis turned back to the task at hand. I've got to get Franco back to meet Nazim and Gregory before things get too far out of hand here, he told himself. Pushing forward, he caught a woman pointing a handgun at him. If I pull my weapon away, I'll be placing myself, Franco, and the woman at risk of being shot. As Louis considered his options, a Danish couple stepped in front of him, obscuring him from the woman he took to as a police officer.

In a brazen move learned while a Legionnaire, Louis stepped away from Grace, placing himself between a Danish couple while bringing his weapon to bear on the officer before him.

Just as he positioned himself between the couple, two separate police cars converged on the intersection adding to the chaotic scene unfolding before everyone's eyes.

Geneviève followed the movement of Louis at the same time the backup officers had arrived on scene and took his action as a provocative move. In a swift and well-rehearsed action, she raised her weapon, firing twice.

The hours spent at the pistol range proved invaluable as Geneviève's aim was true to form. Her first shot caught Louis in the right arm just above the elbow rendering it useless while the second one hit him in the leg.

With his weapon drawn, Claude heard the action his partner had taken. While rushing to her aid, he was confronted by one of the uniformed patrols responding to his appeal for back-up officers.

"I'm Detective Lemieux " -holding out his credentials for the officer to look at- "and she's my partner," he exclaimed, desperately trying to de-escalate the situation.

With cautious steps, the detective kept her weapon pointed at the fallen suspect. Standing over Louis, Detective Benoit secured his weapon and then looked for the man and the petite Asian woman he was with earlier. Locating the other two will be nearly impossible with these tourists circling the victim, and me, she knew.

Through the crowd, she heard Claude making his way toward her when she shouted, "Look for the other two, they're somewhere in the crowd."

Claude shouted an acknowledgement and motioned for two of the officers to follow him towards the opposite side of the street.

As the scene unfolded before him, Phillip watched the woman shooting Louis in the street. I need to leave and contact Gregory, struggling with the idea he would leave his partner behind at the hands of the authorities. Torn by allegiance for his boss and the need for self-preservation, the young Frenchman turned back to the cathedral and away from the police. As he walked away from the chaos, he realized he had no way to return to the warehouse; Louis had the car keys, noting he had no means of retrieving their vehicle.

The instant Louis moved away from Grace's side, and the shots rang out, Franco picked Grace off her feet and hustled across the boulevard toward the terminal gates. "Go; get on the ship, I'll contact you at your second stop," he said putting her back onto her feet.

"I'm scared Franco," Grace said clutching her companion.

"Hurry, I'll contact you at your second stop on this voyage, I promise," the Frenchman told her kissing her on the cheek.

With that gesture, Grace walked awkwardly to the crew gate and the customs inspectors.

"Are you ok?" the inspector asked her in French.

"I'm sorry, I don't understand?"

The inspector repeated his question, this time in English for her.

"Yes, ah, just shaken because of the accident at the intersection," Grace said looking back over her shoulder.

"Do you have anything to declare?"

"No, not today," she said pulling her passport and ship's credentials from her purse.

Watching from the gate, Franco prayed she could board without incident.

"Very well, you may board miss," the customs agent said.

"Thank you," taking her documents, and walking awkwardly toward the gangway and the crew's entrance. She never looked back as she entered the ship, not wanting to place her French lover at risk of being identified or questioned.

Chapter Seven

An hour or so after Clement and Gaston left the warehouse to get Franco Laurent, the remaining men in Gregory's crew working to complete each load of drugs. Each pallet was labeled and banded before placing them into the shipping container. The rattling of bottles caught everyone's attention as two pallets came together on the floor of the warehouse. "Be careful, we don't need any more bottles broken," Jean-Claude yelled over the forklift's engine.

Completing his inspection of the hashish transfer process, Gregory entered the office in the corner of the appliance warehouse, to the ringing phone on his desk. "Hello?"

"Monsieur Arsenault? It's Phillip Gaston," the young man said over the traffic outside the small market.

He was surprised to be getting a call from the nephew of his associate Clement. "Yes Phillip, what is it?"

"It's Louis. He's been shot. And Franco is nowhere to be found," the young Frenchman said. Having a deep breath, he continued explaining over the next six minutes what he'd seen happen to Louis on the boulevard opposite the docks.

"All right, I understand your concern, you did the right thing Phillip," Gregory said. "Can you make it to the safe house?"

"Oui, I can take a bus."

"Good, I'll have someone contact you later today or tomorrow," Gregory said. "You'll be fine Phillip, don't worry." Just as he was ending the call, Nazim entered the office.

"Something's gone wrong?"

"Yes. It seems Louis has been shot by the police and now Franco is nowhere to be found." Gregory spent the next ten minutes relating to Nazim what he had just heard from Phillip.

"Do you have someone who can present us with any information?" Nazim asked.

Gregory looked out the window at the harbor knowing who he needed to contact but was reluctant to name the person to Nazim. Shifting back to look at his associate, he said, "Yes, I know someone who can obtain information for me. By the way, the last of the shipment is ready to be moved," alluding to the hashish meant for the local gangs Nazim was supplying with the drug for their own sales.

***

As Franco was watching Grace being cleared at the customs inspection, he hurried away from the terminal and the police activity. How did this all happen? he thought taking another glance back at the scene, now crowded with many police cars and medical vehicle. Wandering along the waterfront, he hailed a passing taxi, "8 Rue Moustier," he said to the driver climbing in the backseat.

As the taxi maneuvered through the narrow city streets, he considered his next step. Sending Louis, that was Nazim's idea I'm sure. I'll need to contact Gregory before they send someone else, he thought not seeing the towns folk through the windows of the taxi.

"We're here," the driver said pulling up to building matching the address he was given. "And the fare is 12 euros."

Getting into his pocket, Franco pulled two 10-euro notes out and handed them to the driver. "Thank you, keep the change," he said exiting the cab.

"Merci," the driver said pocketing the cash.

Turning toward the entrance to the apartment building, Franco unlocked the gate and proceeded to his third-floor flat before deciding he should contact Gregory.

Resting in his apartment above the pharmacy, Franco contemplated how he would explain what had just happened this morning to Nazim and Gregory. There must have been a reason for Louis to be near the docks, he asked himself while finishing a now cold cup of coffee. But, why did he force himself on Grace? continuing to piece together the events from earlier. And now, the authorities are questioning Louis, trying not to envision what the injured companion was enduring at the hands of the police. Sensing he had no other choice, Franco picked up the phone, calling the warehouse, where just a day earlier, he and Hakim delivered the cargo of hashish.

***

As the scores of police officers secured the crime scene outside the gates of the cruise ship terminal, medical workers were treating the wounded suspect, Louis Clement. All the while, a police officer waited over him as he lay on the gurney.

51

As she kept an eye on the suspect, Detective Benoit was answering questions by several of her colleagues, wanting to know how the events transpired and then escalated. "What led you to suspect this man was a danger Detective Benoit?" one detective from the department's Internal Affairs asked her.

"Detective Lemieux and I were continuing our surveillance from last night on a cruise ship member, who we considered, was involved in drug trafficking. After we returned to vicinity this morning, I spotted our target being escorted by two men," she concluded.

"And the man you confronted, and shot was the same one you saw with the crew member from the cruise ship?" the second detective from Internal Affairs asked.

"No; the cruise ship member was a diminutive Asian woman," Genevieve said. "The man she was with from last night was a Frenchman. He's well over six and a half feet tall and about one hundred ninety pounds, with a close-cropped haircut."

"And the one you shot?" the second detective continued.

She let out a sigh before answering. "This morning was the first time Detective Lemieux, and I had seen him; but I watched him holding the gun to the woman's side," Geneviève added.

"Very well, we'll continue this back at the station. Until such time; you're being placed on administrative duty Detective Benoit," the senior officer present added before getting into his car to leave the crime scene.

"Understood," she said reluctantly clearing the chamber of her pistol, removing the magazine before surrendering her firearm to the second detective. The wail of the ambulance's siren pierced the air as the vehicle left the scene, several police cars following close behind.

"Detective Benoit? Detective Lemieux asked that I take you back to the station," a uniformed officer said motioning to the waiting patrol car.

"All right," she mentioned glancing around at the chaos she created.

***

The hospital's emergency entrance was crowded with uniformed officers sent to guard the shooting suspect. Several detectives stood in the hallway outside one of the operating rooms waiting for word on Louis Clément's condition. Walking out of the operating room suite, the senior surgeon, wearing a bloodied surgical drape looked at Detective Lemieux and the other police detectives as he removed his mask. "He's stable, but you won't be able to talk with him for several hours."

"Officer Fournier see at least one officer is posted outside the suspects' room at all times," Claude instructed the uniformed police officer.

"Oui, Detective," the officer said moving off to instruct the uniformed members assigned to watch the suspect.

The detectives gathered around, their focus on Senior Detective Lemieux. "What are you considering Claude?" a fellow detective asked crushing his empty coffee cup.

"I suspect either the man or woman who were with our suspect will come back," he said. "I've an idea this is something much bigger than just the three of them." On the other hand, it might involve someone of more importance, Claude thought to himself as he tossed out his coffee.

***

Resting in the warehouse office, Gregory was alone to consider Franco's actions and his disappearance. I was a fool for allowing myself to be persuaded to allow Franco to peddle his own drugs. And Louis was right when he said it would be trouble, but I thought otherwise, recalling the conversation he, Louis and Franco had three years earlier. The shrill ring-tone from his cell phone interrupted his thoughts. Pulling it up he saw there was no description of the caller or number, which made him wary of answering, but he did.

"Bonjour?" he said with caution.

"Gregory? It's Franco," the fugitive said.

Hearing the voice of his problems, Gregory became more animated. "Where are you?" he demanded. Why did I hear from Phillip before Franco? he thought.

"I'm at my apartment, why do you ask?" Franco answered being defensive.

"You know you shouldn't have gone out after the delivery," Gregory said. "We've measures in place to safeguard our activities. Do you not realize your actions put that in jeopardy?"

"I had business to attend to," Franco said. "Plus, Hakim said he could handle everything."

Gregory had his own thoughts about Nazim's younger cousin and his role in the organization but kept them to himself. "Still, you need to return, Nazim would like to speak with you," directing the Frenchman's next step.

53

"I can be at the warehouse in several hours," Franco said. That should give me time to call my contact and prepare for a departure, still contemplating his escape from the city.

"Very well, be at the warehouse by two o'clock and no later," Gregory said. "And Franco, don't force my hand by doing something foolish," issuing the warning.

With the call finished, Franco knew he needed to ask a favor from a person indebted to him from years past during an earlier transaction. Picking the phone back up, he dialed the number to a textile merchant who lived in the Saint-Julien district of the city.

Wassif Bassir was sitting at his home desk reviewing the last month's inventory listing when the phone rang. Taking it up he answered, "Atlantic Textiles, how may I help you?" in French, but with a heavy Moroccan accent.

"I need to place an order for an Italian fresco," Franco said.

The description the caller used caught Wassif off guard. I'd forgotten about the promise I made to furnish aid when called upon, to the young Frenchman many years ago, surprised by the caller's request.

"I need it by 1300 today," Franco said.

"An expedited order such as this comes with an added fee," the merchant said. The young Frenchman will pay for this service, he thought. Just four years earlier, he'd provided the first set of identification papers to Franco in exchange for eliminating a threat by a member of an African gang.

"I can pay any extra fee for the proper item."

"Very well," Wassif said. "Your items will be ready by 1300."

"Merci," Franco said hanging up. With his second call completed, he went into the small kitchen where he opened the cabinet above the stove.

With the doors opened, he could see the small metal flue for exhausting smoke and fumes from the stove, plus a small piece of metal secured with two screws.

Utilizing the tip of a knife, Franco removed the screws and the plate they held to expose a cloth-wrapped package. Putting on a pair of surgical gloves he kept in a drawer next to the sink, he removed the package from its hiding place.

Franco placed the bundle on the table, unwrapping and exposing four bundles of 500-euro bills, each worth fifty-thousand for over two-hundred thousand euros in drug money.

Taking one bundle of cash at a time, he wrapped it in a fresh cloth, placing it in a worn satchel he used for transferring the money. He told himself, I need to make sure I don't leave any fingerprints on the old wrappings. Now to set the next step in motion I need the city directory and thumbed through the pale-yellow pages. Pausing at the listing for travel offices, he picked up his phone and dialed the number of an agent nearby.

"Global Excursions," the female voice said after the second ring.

"Good day, I need to book passage to Tunis, with the soonest departure possible please."

"Yes, Sir, just a moment," the agent said.

What seemed like an hour but was just a few minutes, Franco heard the woman come back on the telephone call. "Sir; I've located an available cabin on the *M/V Marine-Convair*. It's scheduled to leave from Terminal Three at 1930 tonight."

"Very well, I'll take that cabin," Franco said writing the information down.

***

While Franco was planning his departure, Gregory and Nazim were discussing the actions they would take upon his arrival to the warehouse later that day. "From what Phillip described, Franco, and the woman left Louis to deal with the police, making his allegiance to the woman more important," Nazim said.

"But what made him disappear in the first place; the woman?" Gregory asked. He already knew of one motive for Franco's action, recalling the criminals' thirst for money and gambling.

Nazim rocked back in his chair, staring at the Frenchman across the table. "The woman is a pawn to Franco, since you and Clement let him deal drugs on his own," he said. "This morning just proves he was never one to be vested in our operations."

"How long have you known about that? And who told you?" Gregory asked realizing he needed to be more careful making comments in front of the others or be confronted by Nazim.

Getting up from the table, Nazim paced around the office before answering his business partner. "Early last year, Clement came to me one day to voice his displeasure at what you allowed," he said. "But he likewise said he supported your decision because if something were to

55

happen, you would handle it," alluding to Franco being Gregory's problem and not his.

Gregory closed his eyes, trying to block out what he knew would be the inevitable task of killing the Frenchman. "And once again, it suggests that time has come."

"I trust you'll handle this and do so that the others will understand they have a specific role in our operations," Nazim said.

Staring at his business partner, Gregory said, "Of course, Nazim, I'll do what's necessary."

***

Exiting his apartment with a satchel bag across his shoulder, Franco hailed a passing taxi "7 Avenue François Chardigny," he instructed the driver.

"Oui Monsieur," the driver said beginning the trip Franco dreaded since phoning Gregory earlier in the day.

Resting in the back of the taxi making its way to the outskirts of the city, he considered the outcome of his meeting with Gregory and Nazim. "Driver, I've changed my mind," Franco blurted out through the window. "Take me to the harbor and Terminal Three."

"Oui Monsieur," the driver responded, shaking his head hoping his fare was done thinking.

Observing the shops and pedestrians move past the taxi's window in a blur, his nervousness eased up. Franco thought, I'll just bribe the quartermaster and board the freighter earlier than planned, avoiding the inevitable confrontation with Gregory and Nazim.

As the taxi carrying Francois Laurent sped towards the harbor, the two drug smugglers sat waiting in the warehouse, preparing for the fugitive's arrival. Glancing at the clock above the office door, *it's 2 pm and I still haven't heard from Franco yet*, Gregory thought wondering what was delaying the Frenchman. Walking out of the office and pointing to a group of armed men. "Jean-Claude; you and Emile prepare to find Franco," he said ordering two of his trusted subordinates he and Louis had recruited.

"Do you consider Franco would leave the city?" Nazim asked walking up behind Gregory.

"Possibly; but where would he go?"

"That my friend is for you to find out," Nazim said. "You and Louis recruited him, I recommend you start looking for him where that took place," leaving the Frenchman to consider his next step.

56

It was five years ago when he and Louis came to recruiting Franco into their organization. He'd proven useful at making adversaries disappear, which included the head of a South Chad gang in Toulon. The brutal murder won Franco a position in the fledgling criminal organization. "I know someone I can call upon who owes me a favor," Gregory said. "If Franco returned to his familiar habits and surroundings, we should be able to find him there."

***

As the taxi entered the terminal parking lot, Franco looked about trying to decide if he saw anything out of the ordinary.

Completing the circuitous route from the apartment to the docks, the ride finally ended. "Thirty-five and five," the driver announced behind the squeal of worn brakes bringing the car to a halt in front of the customs building.

With his drug-money satchel in one hand, Franco opened the door, exiting the cab in a rush, but not before tossing a fifty-euro bill at the driver. "Keep it," he said before slamming the door behind him.

Striding briskly to the customs building entrance, Franco was already pulling out his papers and passport for the official. Standing in line with a handful of others waiting to board the various vessels tied to the docks, he felt a sense of calm come over him. I don't guess I'll be back anytime soon, looking at the skyline behind him.

"Next in line," the customs official announced motioning to Franco. "Papers and passport please?"

Franco presented his documents to the customs official.

"Which vessel are you boarding this morning?"

"The *M/V Marine-Convair* at Terminal Three," Franco said.

The customs agent thumbed through the boarding document, stopping on the last page. Glancing up at Franco, his demeanor took a serious turn. "I see you will disembark in Tunis, what is your business there?"

"I'm meeting my lady friend there; she's a steward working on the cruise ship *Nordic Constellation*," Franco responded hoping his nervousness didn't come through in his answer to the officer.

Taking one last look at the documents, the customs agent grabbed his stamp, marking the passport as departing France, initialing the booklet, before handing everything back to Franco.

"Merci," he said. Taking his documents and stepping through the inspection zone, Franco Laurent looked at the city one last time knowing he'd never see Marseille again on his own terms.

Chapter Eight

Just completing the transfer of hashish and cannabis resin from the last pallet, Gregory sat in the desk chair gulping down his water, before retrieving his phone from the drawer. Wiping his brow with the back of his hand, he swept aside the pool of sweat which had been building up under his breathing mask. Recalling Nazim's desire to inquiry about Louis Clément's condition, he dialed his contact's number from memory.

At the end of the second ring a woman's voice answered, "Bonjour, Police Municipale-Marseille, how may I direct your call?"

"I'd like to talk with Officer Dubois, if you please?" Gregory asked the switchboard operator mentioning his sister-in-law's name.

"Just a moment monsieur, I'll forward your call."

"Oui, Records Administration, Officer Dubois speaking," a stern female voice answered.

"Good day Officer Dubois," Gregory said. "This is Monsieur Arsenault; I was hoping you could track down a file I need for an appointment with the judicial magistrate's office?"

Getting a call her former brother-in-law and hearing his voice, Officer Claire Dubois stiffened in her chair. *It's been six months since I last talked with Gregory,* she said to herself. She glanced over at her co-worker, Julia who was engrossed with a pile of arrest records from a group of English soccer fans.

"Oui Monsieur, what is the name and court number?" she asked.

Gregory provided her with the information he needed to know; mainly which hospital and room they were keeping Louis at, what his condition was, and how many officers were guarding him.

"I'll see you have the information by the morning," Claire said.

"Thank you," he said hanging up. *How many more times do I have to place my niece's mother at risk to satisfy Nazim's plans,* he thought. Taking a drink from another water bottle, Gregory was getting a sense that his role was becoming less of a partner to Nazim and more of a pawn.

In every instance where there was trouble, he and his associate Louis were always the ones' expected to resolve the matter. And, so it would be again today. Remaining at the desk, Gregory contemplated the next call he had to make.

Continuing their earlier criminal activities in Toulon, Gregory and Louis encountered an Italian struggling to make his mark, peddling drugs, and weapons in the eastern part of the city. As he and Louis were completing their transaction, a sting operation by the police was sprung on the unsuspecting Italian in a nearby restaurant, spilling onto the street near them. In a rare instance of 'honor amongst thieves' Gregory and Louis prevented the young Italian from being apprehended, hiding him while the police conducted their search of the neighborhood.

Because of this, the young Italian Giuseppe Ricci vowed he'd be in their debt and would repay them when the time came. Over the years, the three developed a mutual bond, cooperating in and around the docks of Toulon until Gregory joined up with Nazim, moving his shipping enterprise to Marseille. Now, picking up his cell phone he dialed a number for a restaurant in Toulon.

"Pizzeria La Italia, how can I help you?" a young man answered.

"Monsieur Ricci if you please," Gregory said.

"Oui, one moment please."

In the background, Gregory could hear the familiar sounds of a harried staff working in the restaurant. Orders being taken while servers received direction on what food was ready for delivery to a customer. In moments though, a familiar voice came on the line. "This is Giuseppe; can I help you?"

"Yes, you may Giuseppe, this is Gregory Arsenault."

Hearing the Frenchman's voice, Giuseppe said, "Gregory, it's been a long time since we last spoke."

Gregory leaned back in his chair, relaxing for the moment as he talked with his friend. "Yes, it has 'Geno' my friend," using the Italians' nickname.

"So, what can I do for you?" Giuseppe asked

"I don't mean to impose on you Geno; but there's an associate of mine, and I'm having trouble locating him and I could use your help in finding him."

"And this 'associate' he owes you money I presume?" Geno asked.

"No, it's not about money, the Frenchman said. "He's irritated my business partner with several activities he's undertaken," Gregory said. "And we'd like to have a 'conversation' with him."

"I see. Is there anything you can tell me about your 'associate'?" the Italian asked grabbing a server's order tablet and pen to write the information from the Frenchman.

"His name is François 'Franco' Laurent. I recruited him in Toulon, about, of say five years ago, and I suspect he'll return there; he's just over six feet tall and 200 pounds." Gregory said taking another drink. "Oh, and he has a 'fleurs de Lis' tattoo on his left arm above the wrist," he added. "He used to have an apartment on Boulevard de Collines if I recall."

The Italian wrote what Gregory was telling him, picturing the fugitive in his mind. "Can I use this number to contact you?" Geno asked.

"Oui, you may call this number," Gregory said. "And if there's anything else, please call me as soon as you can."

"Yes, of course," Geno said. Now, the most important part of their conversation, the Italian told himself, the cost for accepting this favor. "And the fee for this favor?"

"100,000 euros," Gregory said without hesitating. "For the information on his whereabouts and an added 50,000 euros for his safe return." I don't need to remind Giuseppe the importance of having Franco returned to Marseille alive to face Nazim, he thought.

"Agreed my friend," Geno said. I know several men who would gladly hunt down this man for less, the Italian thought.

"Very well my friend, I'll let you go then," Gregory said. "Au revoir," completing the call.

***

Hakim was just finishing the last check of the repackaged drugs when he saw Nazim wave him up from the office window.

As his cousin entered the office, Nazim began his inquiry. "How did it go with Gregory?" motioning for Hakim to sit down as he passed a bottle to him.

"He's well versed in doing the refining," taking the offered seat at the table. "But, I sensed the trouble with Franco has him concerned," Hakim said taking a healthy swig of water.

"Yes, and he should be. It's a hard lesson to learn when a person must punish another for placing themselves above the group," Nazim said. "Gregory must handle Franco for the good of the organization."

"So, Franco will be made an example of?" Hakim asked. I've so much to learn, sensing the importance of following his directions and guidance, considering what his cousin had said.

"Yes, in a fashion he'll be used as an example to remind the others the importance of their loyalty to the organization," Nazim said. I wish this wasn't necessary, but it must happen if I'm to keep control, he thought wondering who would be next to betray the organization.

***

A mix of workers from the docks and warehouses crowded the small tables surrounding Franco Laurent as he was finishing his meal at a dockside café at Terminal Three. Glancing out the window he gazed upon the row of various freighters docked at the port. *Now, to contact the ships' quartermaster to see if it's possible to gain entrance ahead of the scheduled boarding time*, he told himself paying the bill for his lunch.

Unknown to the him, the two men sitting a few tables away were Detectives' Berger and Masson, keeping a watchful eye on four dockworkers identified as part of the Maghrebi gang. Word from the Gang Enforcement unit mentioned they were responsible for passing small bundles of marijuana off the freighters.

With his satchel full of drug money over his shoulder, Franco was soon exiting the café, strolling towards the pier where the *M/V Marine-Convair* was secured. Stopping a hundred meters from the ship, he spied the gantry cranes hefting containers of cargo, placing them on the ship as gently as a cat grasps its kitten.

Mindful of the chaos created by the giant cranes, trucks pulling trailers and the odd container set on the dock, Franco kept his eyes open. Continuing to walk toward the gangway secured to the upper deck of the cargo vessel, he was suddenly called to a halt by one of the dock workers.

"Hey, where the hell do you think, you're going fella?" the dock worker screamed above the noise of cranes and tractors moving about.

The Frenchman was surprised by the dockworker who'd come around one of the stationary cranes. "To see the quartermaster, so I can board the ship?" Franco replied in French, handing over his documents.

The dock worker looked over the documents, "just a minute." Stepping aside, the dock worker pulled a two-way radio from the back pocket of his dirty and oil stained aqua-colored coveralls. Talking into the microphone, he looked up to the head of the gangway, waiting for a person to emerge. "Quartermaster, this is Dock One."

A woman's voice with a heavy Texas drawl came over the radio, "Go for Quartermaster," the reply came.

Covering his eyes from the sun, the foreman of the loading crew looked along the railing of the freighter for his supervisor as he spoke. "Rose, I got a Frenchman who wants to board six hours early; his papers look clean, but I want to pass it by you first though," the dockworker said.

The woman's silhouette was visible looking over the side of the ship, watching cranes move the multi-colored boxes from trailers to ships' deck with precision and speed. "We're essentially done on the aft deck, go ahead and let him up, I'll meet him on deck," she replied.

Getting the reply of the quartermaster, the dockworker gave a quick, "Ten-four, copy all," responding to the woman in charge.

Gesturing back to Franco, the dockworker said, "You can go ahead," - adding -, "but watch your step going up the gangway," as he pointed out the steeply inclined ramp.

Having given permission for her passenger to board, the full bodied, muscular-figure of the quartermaster named Rose walked to the end of the gangway to meet the Frenchman.

Staring up at the top of the gangway, Franco noticed her, wearing the same color coveralls as the dockworker, just cleaner in appearance. Besides the company attire, he noticed a grey t-shirt sporting a Houston Texans' logo visible under her coveralls which were un-zipped just below her breasts.

Though winded from climbing the extreme incline of the ramp, Franco could still offer a greeting. "Bon jour mademoiselle," he said reaching the top step of the gangway hung over the side of the vessel.

With a wary eye, Rose watched as the Frenchman neared the top of the gangway, giving him a curious up-and-down examination. "Howdy Mister?" the quartermaster said more than a question rather than a greeting.

"Oh, I'm sorry," Franco said apologizing for not presenting his documents to her. Reaching back into his satchel, he pulled the papers out, handing them to the woman.

Reading over the papers, Rose saw her passenger was scheduled to disembark at their first stop, Tunis. She wasn't surprised to have a guest, but she was at the fact he was only going to their first scheduled stop on the 2,000-kilometer journey.

"We don't normally allow passengers aboard during the loading, ah, Mister Laurent," she said, looking at his passport. "But since we are essentially done, I'll be making an exception this one time."

"Merci, ah, thank you I mean," Franco said, offering his hand as a polite gesture, which included five neatly folded 500- euro bills together to help conceal the bribe.

Feeling the paper against her palm, Rose looked down, saw the money, and happily said, "Welcome aboard," smiling at the sudden addition to her pocketbook.

***

The evening shadows grew longer across the desk piled with various documents. It was shortly before six o'clock, and Gregory was reviewing the manifest his freighter would use for the hashish destined for the British Isles, part of this mysterious 'Mr. Higgins' order. Looking over the counterfeit papers used in the event the vessel was inspected at sea, his cell phone rang. Peering at the number displayed, he punched the 'on' button and spoke. "Hello, this is Monsieur Arsenault?"

"Monsieur Arsenault; this is Officer Dubois with the Records Office at Police Municipale," the woman said.

Peeking over his shoulder, Gregory said, "Yes, Officer Dubois. I didn't expect your call until tomorrow morning," cautious of someone eavesdropping on the call.

"The records you requested were much easier for me to find then in the past," Claire said. "It turns out your client records were obtained with the help from the 'French Armed Forces Hospital' record number 231-1."

Sliding his notepad out from the desk drawer, he hurriedly wrote down the information. "Merci Officer Dubois," Gregory said.

"You're welcome Monsieur."

Seeing the line disconnect, Gregory put the phone down and looked at the note he'd written, 'French Armed Forces Hospital', room number 231, one officer. More than likely the police would have at least four officers. And each one standing a four to six-hour shift, he thought walking to the sparsely furnished break room to discuss the information with Nazim.

Watching the handful of men who had completed the task of transferring the hashish from their clandestine containers to new ones, he waved at the French-Algerian. "Nazim; I've something I'd like to discuss with you in private," he said.

"Oui, we can go into the office and discuss it there," the head of the drug smuggling group said walking between the tables.

Spinning around, Gregory walked the few paces back to office and held the door for his partner who walked in behind him.

"What is it you need to discuss with me, but not in front of the others?"

Holding his notepad up, Gregory spoke. "The information you asked me to get on Louis, it was given to me just a few minutes ago," relating what his sister-in-law had passed to him. "He's being held at the Armed Forces Hospital. And for the moment, he's being guarded by just one officer, though I suspect they rotate on some schedule," he added.

"Good, now we know where Louis is, and how many police are guarding him," Nazim said. "It now becomes a question of whether we can move him without complicating his wounds."

Nazim took a seat in front of the desk and drummed his fingers on its surface. "What are you contemplating my friend?" Gregory asked reading the expression on Nazim's face.

"Call Sophia; I wish to speak to her about contacting Louis," he said.

"I don't think we should place her in harm's way; especially including her in something as dangerous as this," Gregory said. I'd hoped to keep Sophia at arm's length from Nazim and his criminal activities, recalling a promise made to Claire.

"Not to worry my friend; I've a plan that will keep her safe," Nazim said.

"Very well; I want to be here when you talk to her though," Gregory said.

"I would have it no other way my friend."

"When would you like to see her?" asked Gregory looking at his watch.

"Tomorrow, say around 2 pm or so. At the office building near the docks will be fine," Nazim said. Examining the paperwork on Gregory's desk, he picked one up. "And now, how do the documents look for this shipment?"

Chapter Nine

Under glowing floodlights, all mooring lines were cast-off, and tugboats took up the task of moving the container ship, now loaded with goods, out to open waters. Leaving Marseille as scheduled, the *M/V Marine-Convair* was soon steaming on a southeastern course towards Tunisia and the port city of Tunis. Franco Laurent stood in the shadows of the containers, watching the city fade away, before retiring to his cabin for the evening.

With nearly one-hundred eighty kilometers of sailing completed, there was a sudden shudder felt throughout the ship. Within minutes, a warning siren wailed on all decks, waking Franco from a dead sleep.

"Bridge; Deck watch #3 reporting water in number 1 hold," the excited voice of a Malaysian seaman said.

"Stand by #3; damage control party is being dispatched," the Second Officer said, from his position on the bridge.

Getting up from the bed, Franco hurriedly got dressed and ran out to the exposed deck to see what was happening. Stopping a passing crew member, Franco hurriedly asked, "What's happening?"

The startled sailor responded, "Not to worry sir, everything is under control," immediately rushing off to his station under the shadows of the towering containers.

Not satisfied, Franco turned and made his way up two decks along the outer stairway until he came across the familiar figure of the female quartermaster exiting the bridge. "What's happened?" he asked the woman, standing before him with a powerful flashlight in one hand and a two-way radio in the other.

"Mister Laurent, please return to your cabin," she said not wanting to tell him they were checking to see what hit the ship near the bow.

"Of course," Franco said

Returning to his stateroom, Franco could sense the ship's movement shift ever so somewhat as if in a turn. Settling back into the bunk, he quickly dozed off, but never fully asleep.

Once again, the sudden shudder vibrating through the vessel woke Franco from his sleep as it did earlier. Still wearing his clothes from earlier, he left the cabin, making his way on deck, now illuminated with the early rays of the rising sun reflecting off the waves.

Looking down at the water, he saw the reason for the shuddering; it was a harbor tug coming alongside to offer aid to the damaged vessel.

For the second time, Franco found himself encountering the quartermaster, Rose, appearing more worn out and fatigued instead of just waking from a restless night's sleep.

"The ship; it is ok?" he asked.

"We'll know in a few hours when the divers can look from the outside," Rose said.

"Divers?" he asked.

"Yes; we're being assisted into Toulon where a team can inspect the hull," pointing to the flickering lights of the French city growing closer with each passing minute.

Leaning on the deck rail, Franco looked down at the tugboat crew working the ropes and winches pulling against the cargo ship to make guiding it into port easier.

Unknown to Franco, a crew member on the tug looked at him and then to a folded piece of paper he pulled from his work overalls. The crew member was a member of Giuseppe Ricci's organization.

Removing a cell phone from his pocket, the crew member made a quick call to his boss, informing him he found the Frenchman worth 10,000 euros. This action passed unnoticed by Franco as he was paying more attention to the approaching skyline of his former home.

"Yes, you're sure?" Giuseppe said listening to the crew man on the tugboat.

"Yes, I'm absolutely positive," the crew member said glancing back at the Frenchman.

"Very well, keep an eye on him, and call me back if there's a problem." With this sudden news, Giuseppe quickly looked at his wristwatch, deciding he needed to contact Gregory at a more reasonable hour rather than five-thirty in the morning.

***

Grabbing his keys from the desk, Gregory was about to leave his home to join him at the office when his phone rang. Looking at the number, he recognized the business number of his friend, Giuseppe Ricci in Toulon.

"Bon jour my friend," Gregory said.

"Good day to you," Giuseppe said.

"And what do I owe for this call so early in the day?"

"My friend, I've found your 'associate' in town."

"My 'associate' you say?" Gregory asked forgetting about his call for help in finding Franco.

"Yes, this man, Franco Laurent," Giuseppe said.

Upon hearing the name, Gregory's interest perked up with the news. "And where did you see Monsieur Laurent?" Gregory asked grasping the importance of the call.

"One of my men saw him on a freighter being towed into the harbor this morning," Giuseppe said. "Also; I've been told this vessel was scheduled to make port in Tunis."

Hearing Franco was on a freighter destined for Tunisia was not good news for Gregory; it meant he planned to be out of the country for an extended amount of time. It also signified Gregory would have to handle a ships' crew, including the need to negotiate a 'fee' for boarding and taking Franco into custody. All of this would have to take place without arousing the suspicion of the local police or the DCJP. "My friend, can you keep an eye on the vessel to make sure Monsieur Laurent doesn't leave?" Gregory asked.

"Yes, I can have several men available for that," Giuseppe said. This will cost Gregory more euros to cover the cost of the surveillance, thinking of the added money he'd request.

"Please do so and I'll call you later today with more information; thank you my friend," Gregory said. Finishing his call with Giuseppe, Gregory dialed the number to Nazim's office to inform him Franco had been located.

"Where did you say, he was last seen?"

"On a freighter being towed into Toulon," Gregory said. "And I've someone keeping an eye on the vessel for us."

"How soon can you send Jean-Claude, and three others to bring Franco back?" Nazim asked, his thirst for disciplining the Frenchman coming to the forefront of his thoughts.

"I can have them on the road in less than an hour I'm sure," Gregory said. "I'll be in the office in less than twenty minutes, I'll contact them when I get there."

"If we wish to take advantage of your information you'll need to move quickly," Nazim said ending the call.

With yesterday's work completed getting the drugs repackaged for the voyage into the North Sea, the two drug smugglers gather to discuss the latest developments. In their office building near the Marseille docks, Gregory and Nazim were discussing scenarios they should use to learn their companions fate, now knowing where the police held him.

"How do we insure Sophia does not come to any harm?" Gregory asked.

"The same way we handle the products on the freighter my friend," Nazim said.

"I don't understand; we hide her in the hospital?"

"Not necessarily 'in' the hospital, but close." For the next ten minutes Nazim spoke of his idea to have Sophia portray a student nurse at the hospital. Describing the type who would enter patient's rooms offering to refill water bottles or distribute magazines for reading.

Rubbing the side of his head, the Frenchman gave the idea some merit. "It sounds simple," Gregory said. Hearing the plan, he now understood what Nazim described as the routine of 'hiding in plain sight' but using the ploy for his niece. "But how do we insure she's in the proper uniform and has the correct credentials?"

"That's where you and your contact will come into play," Nazim said.

"So; I need to make contact again with my informant?" Gregory asked leery of placing Claire in danger of asking too many questions around her colleagues.

"I'm willing to hear how you would insure your niece's safety if you've a better plan," Nazim said.

Resting back in his chair, Gregory knew he'd not considered an in-depth plan to contact his injured friend lying in the hospital. "All right then, I'll call my contact later in the morning."

"Gregory, you've my word Sophia will be safe when all this is over," Nazim said.

Remaining at his desk, Nazim Aziz looked over the final documents his partner Gregory had prepared earlier in the week for their upcoming shipment for the Irishman, 'Mr. Higgins' in the British Isles.

Everything looked in order reaching for his cup of coffee. Until he looked at the second to last manifest finding an improper count of pallets being loaded on the *Bonaparte* when it docks on Friday. This will not do, he thought. Preparing a note on the manifest, he used an orange highlight pen to circle the discrepancy for Gregory to correct. A simple mistake like this could cause quite a stir if the wrong customs inspector saw it, he told himself finishing his review.

Arranging the cargo manifests in a satchel used as part of the transfer, his cell phone rang. Picking it up, Nazim saw the call was coming from the overseas exchange, which meant only one of a handful of associates could be calling.

Opening the phone, he said, "Oui, Monsieur Remesy speaking," answering the call using his alias.

On the other end of the line was Sean Gilmore, counselor to 'Mr. Higgins' and the only other person outside France or North Africa to have this phone number.

"Hello, Monsieur Remesy," Sean said. "Could you please hold?" letting Nazim know the conversation would not be taking place between the two of them today.

"Monsieur Remesy, this is 'Mr. Higgins' calling," the mysterious Northern Irishman said.

"Good morning sir," Nazim said surprised to hear from the financier of his pending drug shipment.

"I was hoping you and I could discuss a future venture for a moment?" Higgins asked.

"Oui messier, I'm listening," Nazim said. Sitting back in his chair the questions flooded his thoughts. Where's this discussion going, why has the Irishman called me directly, and why so early in the morning? questioning the timing of the call.

For the next ten minutes, Higgins spoke of his dealings with his contact in South Africa and a future delivery to Tangier. "Is it possible for you to insure the security of a container and the safe loading to one of your vessels?" the Irishman asked.

Nazim hesitated for a moment, contemplating how to answer the question from Higgins. "I'm not sure you know that I've little control of work in Tangier; nor do I own a freighter for shipping," Nazim said in a moment of honest revelation. "But, there are several associates who have dealings in Tangiers that I can discuss your offer with."

It was the Irishman's turn to pause the conversation as he thought about Nazim's comment. "If that is the case, when would you be able to present me with an answer concerning the security?" Higgins asked.

"I would need at least a week to arrange contacts with the right people in Morocco before I could present you with any details," Nazim said. I must contact Omar before I travel to Tangier to discuss this action, knowing his mentor's contacts in the region would be needed.

"Well then Monsieur Remesy; I shall expect you to be available for a call in one week's time to complete our discussion," Mister Higgins said.

"I'll look forward to it sir," Nazim said as the line went dead.

Chapter Ten

As she sat in her uncle's office listening to the plan concocted by Nazim, Sophia Dubois was, to say the least, skeptical. Expected to walk right into Marseille's largest and busiest medical center, she had visions of security members detaining her in the first ten steps through the door. "This is the craziest thing they've drugged me into since agreeing to help," she said to herself.

An hour after listening to the plan, Sophia was meeting her mother's friend, a seamstress at a local clothing shop. "Here is your package," the woman said passing the parcel to Sophia. "I'm sure you'll find it to your liking," beaming a smile of satisfaction.

"How do you know what size I need?"

"Your mother provided me with all the information," the woman said before turning away to another customer.

After getting the nurses' uniform the previous day, she still had doubts of succeeding. Now, looking in the mirror, Sophia Dubois had an expression of disdain for the student's uniform she'd be wearing to the hospital. I look like a matron for the elderly, she saw taking in the figure reflected in the mirror.

From her crisp white cap, its single red stripe designating her as a student to the white hosiery and shoes, Sophia felt 'ultra-puritan' just from the look alone. What am I supposed to do if some poor soul bleeds; speculating as she stood gazing at the image in the mirror. As uncomfortable as this looked to her, she knew Gregory and his partner were relying on her to pass the letter, held firmly inside her stockings, to their colleague Louis.

As she glanced up and down the hallway, she slipped her key out of the lock. Taking extreme care leaving her apartment, she wanted to make sure no one saw her dressed as a nurse and ask questions. Coming to the entrance, Sophia stepped out of her building and quickly hailed a passing cab.

"French Armed Forces Hospital," the young Frenchwoman spoke entering the vehicle, careful not to get her uniform dirty sitting in the back of the cab.

"Oui mademoiselle," the driver said feigning to start the meter before placing the vehicle in motion with a slight chirp of the gearbox. After ten minutes of driving through town, the driver had Sophia at her destination, which was the front entrance to the sprawling medical facility.

Sophia turned to the driver as she opened the door, "How much?" she asked preparing to pull a few bills from her purse.

With a smile that showed several missing teeth, he said, "It's free for such a lovely nurse like you."

Blushing at the complement, Sophia could barely udder her thanks to the driver as she exited the cab. Closing the door behind her, she turned looking up at the multi-storied buildings towering over her and a moment of uncertainty crept over her thoughts. Trembling in anticipation she told herself, you can do this, pushing the thought of failure aside, Uncle Gregory is counting on you to handle this, just stay calm.

Striding up the steps to the entrance, she could sense the envelope taped to the inside of her thigh rubbing against the other with each step. God, I hope the tape keeps it in place, taking the final step through the massive entrance doors of the hospital.

Tugging on the handle, the door swung open without protesting. She was now in an environment foreign to her. Watching the rest of the medical staff and family members scurrying back and forth between elevators, nurses' stations, and visitor kiosks, Sophia felt relieved. If I knew there was this much action, I mean, a person could become lost among the masses, she thought watching the hustle of people moving about.

Stepping to the directory kiosk in the center of the entrance, she promptly found the Intensive Care Unit (ICU) her uncle had said Louis was being treated in. Committing the location to memory, she strolled to the elevator entrances to begin her journey. Walking into the first empty elevator, she selected the fourth floor, recalling the ICU's location from the kiosk. Before the doors could close, though, she was joined by other medical staff who immediately dismissed her as a lost student.

Sophia was not aware nursing students were directed to use the elevators at the rear of the facility. This helped them avoid being confronted and questioned by distraught family members without a teaching nurse or doctor in residence training to answer questions.

As the elevator stopped at her floor, Sophia politely moved to the front, passing the doctors and other nurses who were going to other places within the hospital. Stepping out, she glanced at the signs in front of her. Noticing the arrow pointing to ICU, Sophia turned to her left, walking down the corridor towards the ICU section. Rounding the corner, she spied a uniformed police officer talking with a nurse on duty.

Walking into an empty waiting room, Sophia gathered up several magazines from the tables. After looking around, she lifted the bottom of her skirt, to expose the envelope she placed in her stocking. Slipping the envelope into the second magazine, she picked up the stack and arranged them in her arms.

Having prepared her props to disguise the letter, Sophia walked confidently back into the corridor and toward the police officer outside the room Louis was being held.

"One moment young lady," the officer said.

"Yes officer?" A touch of fear coursed through her standing before the police officer. *God, I wish I could expose more of my figure*, alluding to the fact most men would glance at her breasts. Sophia knew if she could display more cleavage she'd distract the officer enough to let her go about her business.

"What do you have there?" the young officer asked keeping her outside the room.

"Magazines for the patient," Sophia said.

Peering at the stack of periodicals in her arms, "Very well," the officer said, letting her enter the room.

Overhearing the voices outside in the corridor, Louis head came up from the pillow to get a better view of who it was entering the room.

"Sir, I've several magazines for your reading pleasure," Sophia said emphasizing the one containing the note from Gregory, which she moved to the top of the stack.

A surprised expression crossed the injured Legionnaire's face when he saw the young nurse enter his room. "Thank you," Louis said, keeping his focus on the door and the window facing the nurses' station and the on-duty police officer.

Sophia noticed the suspension holding Louis' right arm in a series of slings, ropes and pulleys keeping it elevated from the bed.

"Are you in any discomfort?"

"A policewoman shot me in the arm, shattering one bone; it's healing," Louis said. "And then she shot me in the thigh for good measure," he added with a feigned chuckle.

"So, she was a bad shot then?"

"It would appear so," Louis said. *But if I had been her, I would have taken aim at the same locations, so I guess she's a better sharpshooter than Sophia knows,* he told himself.

"And the doctors, they did a good job at repairing the damage?" Sophia asked.

"Yes; I'll have the use of my arm in a couple more weeks," Louis said. Suddenly, in the middle of their conversation, the nurse from the station stepped into the room, announcing it was time to check and change Louis's bandages.

"Would you prefer to watch?" she asked Sophia.

"I'm sorry, I have to complete the rest of my rounds," Sophia said. As she left the room, she passed a second officer who was drinking his coffee at the back of the nurse's station.

* * *

After getting the call from Giuseppe about the presence of Franco in Toulon and then contacting Nazim, Gregory's personal phone rang. Realizing there were but a handful of people who had access to the number, he still proceeded cautiously while answering because of the time of day. "Bon jour?" he asked indifferently.

"Hello, Monsieur Adrien Richelieu, please?" a Frenchwoman asked.

"Yes, this is Monsieur Richelieu," Gregory replied assuming the role of the nineteenth-century entrepreneur, ship-owner, and banker.

"Good morning, sir. You have a message from Monsieur Higgins."

Discovering who the message came from Gregory replied, "Thank you; I'll handle the call from here." Hanging up, he walked around behind his desk, taking a seat before he dialed the number for the Irishman. After the second ring, Sean Gilmore, the Irishman's counselor answered the phone.

"Hello?"

"Good morning Monsieur Higgins, this is Monsieur Richelieu returning your call," the Frenchman said playing his part as owner of 'Papillion Transport'.

"Thank you for returning my call so promptly," Sean said answering to his employer's alias. "There's been a slight change in plans for your next shipment."

"Oh, and why is that?" Gregory asked. "Was there a problem with the past delivery we provided?"

"No sir." the Irish counselor said. "But I've concerns about the crew handling your product after it leaves your freighter," Sean said. "So, I'm planning for my own vessel to make the next pick up from your ship."

Gregory sat back and thought for a moment before answering. Is the crew on the service boat skimming some of the drugs? It had been agreed upon by him and Louis to use oil-derrick service vessels to transfer the drugs from the freighters in the first place. It had cost Gregory 50,000 euros to have the crews of the *Standard-Apollo* and *Standard-Hercules* vetted before the first transaction. Nazim would not be happy if that were the case, electing to keep his thoughts to himself for the moment.

"And this 'new' vessel; my freighter captain can trust them?" Gregory asked.

"Yes, the captain has been working for us for several years and we trust him to conduct himself accordingly," Sean said. For the sake of the movement, I needed to reassure the Frenchman to make this change happen as planned, the barrister thought.

"Very well Monsieur Higgins; I'll agree to have this one transaction occur; but just this once," Gregory said. "And for the inconvenience, an added hundred-thousand euro, paid in advance," seeing an opportunity to recoup his earlier fee.

Sean knew he would be asked for more funds, so his next answer was simple, "We agree to the fee, and I'll see to the transfer personally. But, there is one last item I need though," the Irish lawyer said. "And that's the radio frequency and call-sign to pass to my captain, allowing him to contact your freighter."

"Of course," Gregory said. Pulling the dog-eared notebook from the drawer, he turned to the page labeled 'Bonaparte' reading the radio frequency and call sign used by the freighter during that period.

Reading the information back, Sean received assurances he had copied the numbers and code phrases correctly. Satisfied everything was correct, he bid his farewell and hung up the phone.

Gregory closed his eyes and considered his next course of action. Should I tell Nazim the crews on *Standard-Apollo* and *Standard-*

Hercules were possibly taken a share of the drugs and selling it themselves? If this was the case, why haven't the Germans alerted him as to the tampered containers? If there's a problem this time, I'll let Klaus discover it and then I'll let Nazim know about the demand to change tactics, he decided.

With no further disturbances, Gregory made his way out of his house and to the office, where he found his partner making notes on a blank ledger. "Is everything in order?" he asked.

"No; I found a mistake on the last manifest on the number of pallets for transfer that's needing corrected," Nazim said, handing over the incorrect documents.

"I'll see they get changed at once."

Glancing up from the ledger book Nazim asked, "Have you heard from Sophia yet?"

"Not yet; but she should be attempting to see Louis today," Gregory said.

"As soon as we know how he is, the better I'll feel."

"As will I." You don't owe your life to him like I do, Gregory told himself.

"Now; from what I can see, we need to create two sets of dummy and genuine documents for this upcoming shipment," Nazim said.

"I don't understand, why?" Gregory asked. "Do you believe there's a possibility the Bonaparte will need to stop in Portugal or Spain?"

"No, but it's important that we plan for the possibility, even if it doesn't occur." If we didn't plan for an event, Murphy's Law will surely pay the vessel a visit and ruin everything, Nazim thought not wanting to leave everything to chance.

***

Shortly after having the experience in Louis room with the nurse, Sophia found herself outside near the back entrance of the hospital desperately trying to hail a cab.

Since drivers weren't stopping, she scurried to the eastern side of the hospital where she finally hailed a taxi to drive her to the office where Gregory was waiting.

Giving directions to the driver, Sophia relaxed and took note of what she had learned of her uncle's friend laying in the hospital bed just 20 minutes earlier. Louis was recovering from a serious injury which needed several more weeks to heal. He further mentioned he was not expected to lose any movement in his arm based on the injury. Moreover, Sophia noticed there were two police officers standing by the room on each shift, not one.

Shortly after picking up Sophia, the taxi driver pulled to a stop in front of a non-descript building just blocks from the waterfront. Getting a twenty-euro bill from her clutch, she paid the fare and exited the cab.

Going in the building, she saw the faded notice identifying her uncles' office on the third floor and walked up the stairs. Stepping onto the landing, she heard voices coming from the office to her left. Walking the dozen steps, she came upon the office and entered without knocking.

"Sophia, what are you doing here?" Gregory asked surprised by her appearance.

"I did as you wished," she said. "And you have two weeks to liberate him." She spent the next few minutes relating to her uncle and Nazim the extent of Louis injuries, and the doctor's prognosis for recovery.

"Then we'd had better begin to make the necessary plans," Gregory said.

"You're correct, we better begin planning before the police move him," Nazim said.

Chapter Eleven

As the bus came to a stop outside the central police station, half its occupants exited, making their way up the granite steps to the entrance. Entering the Police Municipale building was not a foreign act to Detective Benoit but doing so without her weapon was. She was beginning the third day to her 'Administrative' posting for the incident at the docks where she shot a suspect and endangered a crowd of unarmed civilians.

Walking up the stairs two steps at a time, she entered the small office shared by herself and three other detectives conducting counter-surveillance on Marseille's drug traffic. She noticed that her regular partner, Detective Claude Lemieux, had yet to arrive this morning.

Relaxing at her desk, she began the mundane task of looking over various reports showing vessel movements in and out of the French port for the last six months. Cruise ships, freighters, and pleasure craft, every one of them with somewhere to go with someone or something of importance onboard. Each was a link to the mysterious Frenchman and the young Asian woman at his side. Lost in thought, Geneviève did not hear the door open or notice her partner Claude enter the office.

"Still looking for the 'needle' I see," Claude said.

Startled by the sudden intrusion, she practically fell from her chair. "Damn you Claude, you scared me, again."

"I'm so sorry," he said an apologetic look on his face. "Here, allow me," helping her to her feet.

"With nothing better to do, yes, I'm still looking for the woman. And, I've come across a peculiar series of events between one of the cruise lines and several freighters," Detective Benoit said.

"Which cruise line?" Claude asked.

"Let's see, oh, here it is, the *Nordic Cruise Line* (NCL)," handing Claude the printout.

Glancing over the listing, Detective Lemieux could see the anomaly Geneviève had identified. Every time a ship under the NCL flag made port in the Mediterranean, it was following or preceding a freighter that called Marseille its home port.

"This 'coincidence' is becoming all too frequent based on the reported activity of docking records for us to ignore," he said. "We've a cruise ship, like the *Nordic Constellation* and a freighter like *M/V De Gaulle* using the same port hours apart from one another," Claude said.

"Correct. Each one operating from Marseille, which lends itself to something happening between them, right?" the police officer said, referencing the map outlining the Mediterranean and its known ports and routes.

"Maybe; and then again, maybe not," Claude answered.

"And it shows the *Nordic Constellation* is the one constant in each of the scenarios," Geneviève said. "Studying this movement, do we need to consider the owners of the *M/V De Gaulle* and their relationship with *Nordic Cruise Lines* as conspirators in some illegal scheme?"

Resting in his chair, and sipping his lukewarm coffee Claude said, "Now you're getting to tangible clues in the case."

"Well, if that's true, we need to verify the Asian woman from the shooting is aboard the NCL cruise ship and investigate them for drug trafficking," Geneviève said.

"And that's where your involvement will end," Claude said. "You have your competency hearing in two days."

She slammed the report onto her desk. "Damn bureaucrats," forgetting she was still waiting for the Internal Affairs investigation into the shooting to conclude and give their findings.

"Until then, you need to mind yourself and behave," the senior detective said in a fatherly tone.

"You've no idea how difficult it is for me to sit in this office all day? I'm going nuts," Geneviève exclaimed.

"Oh, I most certainly do understand young lady," Claude said. "About, oh, six years ago, I was part of a team trying to apprehend a group of bank robbery suspects," he added. Seems like yesterday when I was a member of that a police squad, he recalled. "I came across one suspect in an alleyway; he pulled his gun, and I pulled mine. In an instant; we both fired and each of our shots hit the other," opening his shirt to expose the scar left from the bullet wound to his upper chest.

"It was fortunate for me, that the aim of the robber was not so good," Claude continued. "But my aim was better since my bullet caught him below his left eye," wincing at the memory of seeing the round impact, exploding against the suspect's skin. "I too had to wait out an Internal Affairs investigation because of it. So, my recommendation to you is accept what the investigators send to Paris; you'll be a better officer in the end," Lemieux said walking out of the office.

Claude went straight to the men's room where he stood before the sink, splashing icy water against his face. Damn, I hope she never brings that memory up again, pushing the ghostly image of the young seventeen-year-olds ashen and disfigured face from his vision.

***

Sitting in his office, Nazim finished his review of the corrected manifest Gregory had fixed the previous day. Peering up at the clock above the window, he realized he would need to make his call soon to avoid disturbing his contact during evening prayers.

Pulling out his cell phone, he searched through the list of contacts until he found the right one. Choosing the 'phone' icon displayed, he launched the call to his associate living in Algiers.

"Good evening?" the gravelly voice asked.

"Good evening my esteemed brother," Nazim said.

The face of Algiers most notorious criminal syndicate lit up hearing the younger French-Algerian's voice. "Nazim, it has been too long since we last spoke," Omar Khalid answered.

Beginning early into Nazim's sojourn into crime, it was Omar Khalid who accepted the French-Algerian into his syndicate, mentoring him on the illegal business of drug trafficking. It was likewise this relationship which helped save Nazim's younger cousin Hakim Talib from sure death at the hands of a rival, but less powerful syndicate as well.

"I apologize if I've interrupted your evening," the drug smuggler said.

"Not so, you're always welcome to call me," Omar said. "Now; what is it that I can help you with Nazim?"

"I need your help in apprehending a man in Tunis," Nazim said. "I believe he's taken passage on a freighter scheduled to dock there tomorrow evening."

"All right; does this man travel alone?" Omar asked. I'll need to decide how many men to send to Tunisia. The trip from Algiers to Tunis is over ten hours by vehicle, and the men need to be ready before confronting the Frenchman, calculating the time needed for the journey.

"Yes; he's traveling alone, but it's possible he might join an Asian woman from a cruise ship," Nazim said.

81

"Very well my friend, telex his likeness to me and I'll see what I can do."

"Thank you," Nazim said. "I'll send it to you shortly."

***

In the growing darkness of the Police Municipale offices, Detective's Benoit and Lemieux continued analyzing the cruise-ship and freighter connections throughout the Mediterranean Sea ports of call.

"Here, this came from Detective Berger," passing a note to Benoit.

Reading the paper, Geneviève looked up at her partner. "So, Nic and Guy have a lead on dock workers handling marijuana, so what?"

"The dockworkers have been seen at every freighter except those belonging to 'Papillion' according to their surveillance," Claude replied. "Seems a little strange don't you think?"

Before Geneviève could answer there was a knock on the outer door as it swung open.

Entering the detectives' small office, Captain Julien Duval, announced, "Detective Benoit and Detective Lemieux, I've good news."

"Yes, what is it?" they both asked.

"Because of the proximity of the shooting to the docks last week, and that we can't seem to find the Frenchman or the Asian woman," Julien said. "We passed information to the other districts along the coast. And we received a notice this afternoon from the station in Toulon about your suspect being spotted," the captain concluded.

"Is he on a ship?" Geneviève asked.

"Yes; seems he was seen on a freighter, the *M/V Marine-Convair* as it was towed into port for repairs. Unfortunately, from what we've learned, the vessel made the necessary minor repairs and then set sail two hours later," Julien said.

"Do we know where the next port of call is?" Geneviève asked.

"Yes, it's next scheduled stop will be Tunis."

Detective Lemieux set his coffee down before pulling a stack of papers toward him. Rifling through the myriad of listings, he found what he was looking for. "The *Nordic Constellation* will make a port call there tomorrow as well," beaming at his partner.

Duval swiveled his head back and forth between the two detectives. "And this means what to your investigation?" the captain asked.

Geneviève spoke about their hypothesis of crew members from specific freighters and the cruise ships working as a team to transport and distribute illegal narcotics through-out the Mediterranean. "And the

Frenchman and Asian woman from last week were seen walking toward Terminal Two, where the *Nordic Constellation* was docked."

Leaning against the file cabinet, the senior officer digested what his officers were saying. Gently shaking his head Captain Duval said, "It can likewise be just a mere coincidence."

Having the reports in his hand, Claude spoke. "True sir, but we've a reasonable doubt as to the possibility," taking up the cause to persuade his captain that they had a tangible lead.

Seeing the conviction of his two detectives, Captain Duval relented. "All right, you may continue with your investigation." Looking at Geneviève he added. "And you are re-instated, Detective," handing her the letter from the review board, clearing her of any wrongdoing in the shooting of Louis Clement. "You may go down to the armory and retrieve your service weapon before going home too," leaving the office.

Geneviève sat there in silence, the shock, and suddenness of the condition hitting her like a blow from a hammer. "Merci sir," she said, hoping Captain Duval nor Detective Lemieux could see the tear forming in the corner of her eye, happy in the knowledge her service record would stay untarnished.

Chapter Twelve

The waning light of day reflected off the Mediterranean against the container ship. As harbor tugs came out to meet the *M/V Marine-Convair*, a series of horn blasts echoed across the water. Assisting the vessel while navigating the narrow waters surrounding Tunis's harbor, the tugboats led ship toward its berth at the concrete pier.

Watching from the deck, Franco Laurent saw the white superstructure of the *Nordic Constellation* sitting tied to the pier opposite the commercial docks where the freighter would be secured.

"Monsieur Laurent?" the twang of the South Texas drawl interrupted his thoughts.

"Yes, madam?" he said looking upon the robust figure of the woman.

"I hope your brief stay on board was pleasant?"

"Yes, it was most enjoyable, thank you."

"Once the ship is secured to the pier, I'll see you're allowed off," she said just as her ever-present radio squawked with orders from the bridge.

"Standby to receive tug boats on the starboard side," the order echoed as she strode across the deck and away from Franco.

Within an hour, the large cargo vessel was secured against the concrete pier. In the growing darkness settling over the harbor, a bustle of work took place under the glowing beams of light that illuminated the pier and the ship.

Walking down the gangway to the firmness of the concrete pier, Franco hastily looked about to decide if there were any officials he should present with his passport and documents.

Seemingly from nowhere, a uniformed customs agent walked up to him and asked for his documents of travel. Pulling the passport and travel visa from his duffel bag, Franco again skillfully allowed several fifty-euro notes to fall to the feet of the inspector.

Sight of the money caught the agent's attention, who promptly stooped down, picking up the bills, placing them in his pocket. All this was done without taking his eyes off the Frenchman.

Franco stood and smiled at the Tunisian customs official, not making a commotion about the money now in his pocket.

"Welcome to Tunisia, you are free to go," the customs agent said, applying the stamp and his initials across Franco's passport page.

"Merci" he replied and walked to the gates visible in the distance where he studied various workers entering and exiting the docks. Leaving the dock's security, Franco found himself besieged from all directions as several of the local poor came begging for money from any foreign sailors leaving their ships.

Catching a cab coming down the road, Franco quickly stepped off the curb and waved his arm. Following the European, the driver applied his brakes, bringing the ancient Russian sedan to a halt, a plume of dust rising a scant five feet from where Franco stood.

"Where to mister?" the driver asked in broken English.

"To the cruise ships please," the Frenchman replied.

"One hundred euros please?" the driver demanded holding his hand out, with no attempt to place the vehicle in motion until paid.

Sitting back in the seat of the sedan, Franco reached into his pants pocket where he pulled three twenty-euro notes out. "Sixty now, and forty when we are at the dock."

"Thank you," the driver said taking the cash, placing the sedan into gear and speeding up in the direction of the cruise ships. Unknown to Franco, the average fare between docks was equal to twenty-euros, but he showed little concern as long as he had the chance to see his companion again.

Sitting behind the driver of the speeding sedan, Franco wondered if he'd survive the ride as they weaved through traffic which was entering and exiting the port facilities. Just as soon as the fare began, it suddenly came to an abrupt halt as the driver pulled into the parking area reserved for the taxis. Shifting back to look at Franco, the driver proudly held out his hand, saying "Forty euros please."

With a chagrin look to his face, Franco handed over two more twenty-euro notes knowing he'd just been skimmed of extra money by the shrewd taxi driver.

"Shukran," Franco said exiting the cab and stepping toward the security gate outside the large cruise ship.

Forcing his way to the security gate amongst a growing crowd of locals and Scandinavian tourists, Franco finally got the attention of one of the cruise ship workers. "I'm trying to get in touch with a steward, her name is Grace Mendoza?" he said shouting over the crowds to the worker. "Tell her it's Franco," he added.

"One moment sir," the worker said, reaching for his two-way radio, speaking a language Franco didn't understand. "Where is Chief Steward Mendoza?" he asked in Tagalog, the native language of the Philippines.

"She's off-duty Gomes; you know that," came the response from the cruise ship.

"Go tell her that there's someone here looking for her," the crew member said. "He says his name is Franco."

"Stand by," the voice said from the radio.

"If you'll please wait here for the moment, they're trying to locate her," Gomes said, pointing Franco to the wooden benches just inside the security checkpoint.

"Merci," Franco responded setting his pack down but keeping it within arm's reach, settling onto the weathered and warped wooden seat.

Sitting on the bench, Franco observed a growing number of youths, mostly males gathering outside the checkpoint. They were keeping a close eye on the many tourists getting off buses, which had taken them into town to shop and visit the ancient city. Several of the older ones were paying close attention to a group of older Scandinavian gentlemen, who by all appearances sampled too much of the locally brewed liquor. Strange that a country with predominate Islamic population tolerates public drinking and drunken behavior? he mused.

While worrying about what might happen next, Franco felt the soft touch of a woman's hand upon his face. Turning, he met the petite figure of Grace standing before him. "I missed you," Franco said, reaching down, and lifting her off the ground in a ferocious hug, making her squeal to the delight of those nearby.

Setting her back on the ground, Grace's right hand slapped his face, "Damn you; I still hurt for the last two days," reminding him what she endured as they parted ways in Marseille earlier in the week.

Several of the crew members and guests looked on anxiously, wondering what Franco's response would be. Feeling the sting of her slap, he rubbed the tingling flesh of his cheek and said, "I'm sorry; I deserved that for what happened," bending down to kiss her on the cheek.

As the two lovers reacquainted themselves, a melee started where the local youths and the drunken tourists had merged. Soon the air was filled with shouts and the slap of skin on skin as the youths took the fight to the inebriated men from the cruise ships. But in true fashion, the inebriated Scandinavians fought back and through sheer size and strength, caused the local youths to disperse.

Soon the local authorities were on the scene, asking everyone outside the gates to present their papers, establishing a barricade to prevent anyone from exiting or entering the docks.

"What am I supposed to do now?" Franco asked. "I need to find a room for the night." My passport won't let me step on the cruise ship without a proper ticket, he told himself feeling stranded now.

As if answering his prayers, the cruise ship had catered a local produce provider to deliver fresh vegetables and fruits and the truck was being allowed to exit. Acting on the fly, Franco asked the driver for a ride to the local hotel near the docks.

"Yes, of course," the driver said, allowing Franco to climb into the cab.

"I'll meet you first thing in the morning," he said to Grace as the truck pulled through the security blockade. Looking back, he watched the local police trying to discuss the events with patrons of the ship, some sober and some not so much.

Shortly after leaving the docks, the driver stopped outside a local hotel near the docks and allowed Franco to get out of the cab. Reaching into his pocket, he took one of the remaining fifty-euro bill still loose from his duffle bag and handed to the driver "Shukran" he said.

Walking into the small but surprisingly clean interior of the hotel, Franco greeted the young couple at the front desk. "Good evening, I would like a room for the night please?"

"Yes Sir, we have several rooms available," the young Tunisian man said.

Surprised at the response, Franco relaxed and smiled thanking them for their hospitality, handing his passport over to them as collateral for staying in the hotel. Pocketing the key to the room situated on the second floor, Franco climbed the stairs and found the room overlooked the nearby beach and waterfront. With the stress of his journey over, he collapsed on the bed, still clothed, drifting immediately asleep, sounds of waves crashing in the distance his companion for the night.

***

It was just after midnight when a weathered Land Rover carrying three men arrived in Tunis. The men, having driven across the desert from Algiers, made the perilous journey of 820 kilometers as hastily as the vehicle allowed.

Each man had a photo of Franco Laurent and a note stating they would be paid a sum of 100,000 dinars for the capture of the European. The note also alluded to an extra 50,000 dinars if they apprehended the Asian woman with the Frenchman.

Driving through town, they found a hotel that could offer them a room for the evening. Paying the fare, the three men entered their room, setting their belongings down. Before turning in for the night, they faced east, offering prayers for their safe arrival and for the events to come in the following days.

The oldest and leader of the three spoke, setting the tone for the evening; the youngest being directed to keep watch and stay awake while the other two rested. Soon, the only light in the room was of a candle burning to allow the youngest Algerian to read his Koran.

Staring at the picture of Franco, the young criminal etched the image into his mind, determined to earn his part of the bounty the elder Algerian had promised. Closing his eyes, he pictured himself giving the bounty to his ailing mother so she could have a better life than the slums where Khalid had found him. "Insha alla," he said to himself praising Allah, as he returned to his Koran.

Chapter Thirteen

As the morning sun crested the horizon to the east, the shrill sound of the 'muezzin' and his recorded call to prayer for the Muslim faith filled the air. The beginning of the 'adhan' brought the young Algerian to his feet as he stepped to his two companions to wake them so they could join him in prayer.

Soon after the morning prayer, the three Algerian members of Omar Khalid's syndicate joined the other guests of the hotel to eat in the small café. Sitting at one of the small tables, they enjoyed a meal of bread, yogurt, helpings of mixed fruit such as apricots, melons and dates and strong black coffee. Sitting quietly, they dare not speak of apprehending the Frenchman, they knew discussing the topic in the open would only invite questions which they couldn't answer.

The sun cast a warm orange glow against the drab walls of the hotel room that Franco had sought refuge in the evening before. Getting up out of the bed, the French fugitive walked into the bathroom to relieve himself and wondered what the day would bring for him and Grace.

Finished, he washed himself, and realized he'd not packed toiletries such as a comb, a toothbrush or a razor. Peering at the growing stubble that was becoming obvious by the reflection in the mirror, this look just might serve me well in the coming days. Franco was unsure of what Nazim and Gregory might have planned for bringing him back to Marseille, but he didn't want to take any chances.

Now dressed, Franco walked down the stairs to the lobby where he found a buffet style breakfast waiting for the few guests already awake. Bowls of boiled eggs, mixed fruits, sweet cakes with honey and an urn of coffee awaited him. Taking a plate, he served himself some of the fruit, a slice of sweet cake and a cup of coffee. Sitting at a table which allowed him a view of the entrance, he soon became more aware of the need to preserve his security in the foreign land.

Soon after finishing their morning meal, Khalid's men left the hotel and drove to the docks where they saw the faded blue hull of the *Marine-Convair*. The large container ship was tied fast to the concrete pier, its upper deck still piled high with the multi-colored containers.

Pulling off the road, they parked their car. The oldest instructed the youngest one to stay and watch over their vehicle, less it become a target for the local thieves. Pulling the photo of their prey from his pocket, the eldest Algerian walked up to a group of cab drivers standing around and smoking cigarettes, waiting for a fare. As each driver was shown the picture, there was a shake of the head. That is until the third to last driver looked at it.

"Yes; he paid 100 euro to be taken across the harbor," the driver answered. The driver began laughing with a near-toothless grin, knowing he made 80 euros from the fare. "I took him there," pointing at the large white vessel across the water.

"Shukran" the Algerian said politely, walking back towards the car and his two companions. Reaching the car, the older man spoke to the other two about their target being taken to the cruise ship across the harbor.

***

Franco waved down a taxi as he stood outside the hotel, squinting at the bright sun as it continued its ascent into the morning sky.

"Where to sir?" the young Tunisian asked in crisp English.

"The cruise ship if you please," Franco said in French. I can't let others know that I'm fluent in several languages until it became necessary.

"Oui Monsieur," the driver replied placing the vehicle in gear, joining the morning commuters heading in the direction of the port facility at the western edge of the city. Clutching the satchel containing his money, Franco wondered if Grace could hold the money onboard.

After a short drive, the cab glided to a halt into the parking area where passengers could exit. Staring anxiously through the window, the scene outside the customs screening area was drastically different than it was last night.

"How much do I owe?" Franco asked.

"Twenty-euro sir," the young Tunisian said.

Pulling three ten-euro bills from his packet, he handed them to the driver through the security window separating the back seat from the driver, "Shukran."

As Franco Laurent exited the cab, the three Algerian men working for Omar Khalid stepped out of their car across from the customs check point in the car park.

Walking through the crowds, they scanned the faces of those of European descent, immediately eliminating the locals from their search. Walking to the edge of the boulevard separating themselves and the customs gate, the middle henchman noticed the man from Marseille they were sent to apprehend. "There," he said, pointing to the Frenchman who was a head taller than the others making their way to the security check point.

Checking both ways at the flow of cars, trucks and bicyclists and the few camels, the senior man scurried across the boulevard, to the dismay of his two companions. The youngest, bolder than the other man, took a wary step off the curb following the older one, weaving between vehicles with drivers blaring horns at the careless youth.

Peering back at the sound of the raucous and noisy scene, Franco saw the older and younger Algerians making their way across the busy roadway. Any other time I would find this funny as shit but knowing how bad Nazim wants me returned to France makes this much more threatening, he muttered to himself.

Walking to the customs agent, he held out his passport and announced he was meeting a guest onboard the cruise ship. "My lady friend works as a steward on board," he said working hard not to turn and see just how close the two men were getting to him.

"Very well, stand at the visitor's area," the agent said, pointing to the small block building inside the security zone. The agent handed Franco back his passport allowing him to enter the port and away from the threatening three men, who had made their way outside the security checkpoint.

As Franco looked through the chain-link fence separating himself and the men from Algiers, the oldest one shouted, "We'll meet soon my friend," pointing in his direction. This manifesto made Franco uneasy, now having an idea he would not be left alone at the docks from this point forward.

Following his quarry behind the wire fence, the leader of the Algerian syndicate team smiled, his teeth a blaze of white against his dark complexion. Staring at the cornered Frenchman, he pulled out a cell phone and pushed the redial button to start his call.

"Hello?" Omar Khalid said answering the call.

"We've found the infidel, and I can see him," the older Algerian said.

"Can you seize him?"

"No; not at this moment, but we'll not lose sight of him, we will succeed."

"Contact me if you need help," Omar said ending the call.

***

In a gated, private home in the Saint Julien district, Gregory Arsenault was sitting in his study looking over the transit documents for his vessel in the Caribbean Sea. Reading the report, *M/V Cousteau II* was in transit from Cayenne of the former French colony, Guiana to Santa Domingo in the Dominican Republic, loaded with sugar cane and Brazilian mahogany. This was the largest of the four freighters that Gregory owned, which was listed under the ghost corporation named after a French industrialist from the 1800's.

Louis Clement, his trusted partner from their time in the French Foreign Legion, and the older brother of Louis, Yves, only knew this fact. That Gregory was the owner of the vessels transporting the hashish and cannabis resin throughout the Mediterranean for Nazim Aziz and his blossoming drug cartel.

Unknown to anyone, including Louis and Yves, was the secret alliance that Gregory had made with a drug cartel operating out of the Dominican Republic. His agreement was to be granted a legitimate business enterprise for two years throughout the Caribbean Sea. This allowed him to establish clientele, after which he agreed to allow the Cousteau II to transport drugs across the Atlantic Ocean four times a year to be distributed on the continent.

If all works out, I'll retire to a sun-drenched island the *'Cousteau'* sails past as she plies the seas, putting the reports back in his safe.

***

Sitting in her apartment along Boulevard Leau in the Bonneveine district, Geneviève sat in her easy chair drinking a cup of coffee. Taking her cup in one hand she, re-read the letter from the Detective General for the fifth time that evening. *'The Internal Affairs council, having reviewed all documents and heard interviews of all parties involved in the shooting incident on 02 June, in the 'Villette' district find Detective Geneviève Benoit cleared of all wrongdoing in the shooting of Msr. Louis Clement.'*

Wrongdoing, she said to herself recalling the events of the day as if it happened moments before. I saw a man holding a gun to a woman and when I confronted him, he showed his weapon and I shot him, there's no wrongdoing anywhere. Given the circumstances, I'm sure any of my fellow police officers would have done the same thing, except for making sure they hit his arm to deliver it useless. Geneviève knew one in the department was as skilled as her when it came to firing their pistol and hitting what they intended. The next step is to find the other two, she said to herself, walking into the kitchen to place the now empty cup in the sink.

Grabbing her purse, she checked for her weapon before leaving the apartment. Heading outside, she caught the bus that would take her to police headquarters and a new day looking for the drug dealer and fugitive.

***

Sitting alone in the office, Detective Lemieux looked over the interview notes from the investigators after they had spoken with Louis Clement at the hospital. Nothing appeared or looked out of place, which by itself seemed out of place. Disconcerting to note for the detective was the valid permit the victim had for carrying a concealed weapon.

Just as he was finishing his last thought Detective Benoit entered the office, with a smile that denoted a sense of relief to the wearer. Looking at her partner, she asked, "What's troubling you now Claude?"

Passing over the interview report to his partner, Claude said, "It appears your shooting victim had a permit to carry his pistol."

"And this allowed him to have it pointed at the woman?"

"No; but it makes me wonder why he had a permit in the first place?" the detective asked holding his coffee close to his lips.

"He expected trouble from the big Frenchman and was using the woman as leverage," Geneviève said thinking along the same lines as her partner.

"Correct; but there's nothing suspicious in his background check other than he was a member of the Legion early in his youth," Claude said.

"And you believe there's more to him than what was found in the records?"

"Yes; which means I'll ask him a few more questions," Claude said. "While I'm doing that, you question the hospital staff about anyone else who paid him a visit," grabbing his jacket and coffee as they left the office.

After a short drive through the city. the two detectives were entering at the hospital. Walking through the lobby always gave Geneviève a foreboding sense of uncertainty. Some days I wish I could put a finger on why I've never felt at ease amongst these doctors and nurses, she said to herself.

Getting off the elevator on the floor where the Intensive Care Unit was located, Benoit and Lemieux walked to the nurses' station. Here they found one of the police officers assigned to keep watch over the patient, Louis Clement.

"Who has seen the patient in the past few days?" Claude asked the young officer who suddenly was becoming more attentive seeing their credentials and who they represented.

"Only the doctor, the nurses at the station, the other officers on duty," the police officer said answering the detective's question. "Oh, and a trainee nurse too."

"A student nurse, here in ICU?" Geneviève asked. "Are you sure?"

Turning to the lead nurse behind the desk, she asked her question again, only this time directed at a member of the hospital staff. "Is it standard practice for student nurses to be in the Intensive Care Unit?"

"No; it's not common, unless they're with a staff member on rounds," the lead nurse said, answering the question, a worried look upon her face.

Geneviève and Claude both exchanged a look that said they were just given a piece of a puzzle that needs further scrutiny. "We need to talk with the hospital security director," Claude said turning away from the nurse's station.

"We'll need to look at their security film as well," Geneviève said walking back to the elevators and the ride to the main floor.

After asking a volunteer at the information kiosk for directions to security, the two detectives walked in to the outer office to find the director preparing to leave.

"Can I help you?" he asked.

"Yes, my name is Senior Detective Lemieux; we need to see your security films for the ICU ward for the last 5 days," he said, holding out his credentials for the director to see.

"Is there a problem?" the director asked returning to his office.

"We believe there might've been someone posing as a student nurse visiting ICU and one of our prisoners there," Geneviève said.

Showing the officers through a security door, the director escorted them to the command center where five members sat watching over twenty video monitors. Each screen with a different view or set of views of vital hospital spaces.

Walking to a locked cabinet that he promptly opened, the director pulled a series of computer discs from a file and placed them in a vacant computer station. Putting the disc in the drive, he selected the video program and scrolled to the date in question.

"This is the recording from the ICU ward; the machines capture images every forty-five seconds," he said pointing to the display on the screen.

As the recording played out on the computer screen, nothing appeared out of the ordinary. It wasn't until after forty-five minutes of viewing did the display show a nurse carrying magazines come into view.

"There; stop it," Claude said.

"She's not dressed like the other nurses on the ward," Geneviève said.

"Play it forward, but slower," Claude said.

The security director rolled his hand across the controls allowing the image to move forward, frame by frame. Each image showing the nurse being stopped by the officer on duty and then entering the room where Louis Clement was being treated. As the frame moved forward, it went black, coming back into view as the figure of the nurse walked out of the picture heading toward the elevators.

"We need copies of all your footage for this day and for all floors," Detective Lemieux said to the security director.

Turning to Geneviève, he said, "We'll have a break in the case if we find this woman," pointing to the screen. Peering at the video, he noticed the image of a gentleman walking towards the nurse's station, then turning away, trying to avoid being seen by the police officer. "It seems there might be more than one person trying to visit our suspect as well," he pointed to the screen speaking to his partner.

***

After the uneasy experience with Omar Khalid's men at the dock entrance, Franco Laurent was finally reunited with his lover, Grace Mendoza. The Frenchman stood mesmerized at the sight of the Filipino woman in her crisp white steward's uniform walking the one hundred-fifty meters from the gangway to security.

"Bonjour Monsieur Laurent," the steward said wishing her lover good morning walking passed him and into the air-conditioned space of the Security and Customs office.

"Good morning to you as well," Franco said following her into the office as she strolled right past him.

Standing at the counter with her crew credentials, Grace spoke briefly with the security and custom supervisor, signing the release form, and exited the office joining her French lover.

Staring at Franco, she spoke confidently. "You're now in my custody Monsieur Laurent," taking him by the arm and beginning their walk back to the cruise ship.

This action was not lost on the three men working for Omar Khalid as they watched their prey walk up the gangway with the diminutive woman in white. This unexpected turn of events caused the older one to turn away from security and pull the cell phone from his pocket for the second time this morning.

Dialing the number, he waited for the call to be answered before speaking.

"Qayidi, we have a new problem," he said.

"And what is that?" Omar asked.

"The Frenchman has gained access to the ship, we can no longer seize him," he said.

"Not to worry, you will standby in the event he leaves the ship."

"As you wish," the older Algerian said.

Walking through the opulent passageways of the cruise ship, escorted by Grace, Franco felt very much like a celebrity. Each crew member they passed stood aside for them as they walked along each deck, making their way towards Grace's quarters.

Soon they were at the doorway to her private quarters, which she unlocked allowing them to enter. "Welcome to my home," she exclaimed. It was the 3-meter by 4-meter space Grace shared with another steward, a Malaysian woman, still on duty at the Ambassador's level of the ship.

Pulling the only chair in the tiny cabin out from under the desk, she offered it to Franco so he could sit. "So; what do you think?" she asked pulling her skirt up above her waist and straddling the Frenchman, kissing him on the mouth.

"It seems so small for a person of such importance," Franco said. I can't believe she and another woman share this space for weeks on end, appalled at the size.

"This is a palace considering we've spaces where six girls share a room this size," Grace said squirming lower onto her lover's lap. "Also; we've several hours before Carmen is off duty," alluding to the fact she expected to be naked in his arms, and soon.

"I've a small problem we need to discuss first," Franco said. She doesn't understand I'm being pursued by three Algerians, trying to decide what to tell her.

Lifting her off his lap and pulling her skirt down, Franco spend the next twenty minutes relating to her what had happened since they parted company in Marseille; from his decision to leave Gregory and Nazim, gaining passage on the freighter, to joining her in Tunis.

"And you see, I need your Captain to grant me immunity so I can avoid the criminals that have been sent to take me back to France," Franco said.

As she sat on the edge of her ship-board bunk, Grace shook her head in disbelief. I can't believe my French lover could be in such trouble as to need asylum onboard the cruise ship, sensing her dream fading away. "Captain Rolfson cannot give you asylum," she said. "He's not the owner of the boat."

"I know that; but he's the captain, and when a captain is at sea, he has the authority to do many things," Franco said. "It's just like in the old sailing days. He could discipline the sailors, provide last rites, he even would have the authority to marry people at sea."

Understanding the term 'marriage' brought Graces' doubts to rest, as she heard Franco was ready to marry her. And in her mind, it meant she would no longer be confined to working on the cruise liner. "Yes," she said jumping into his arms, the thought of being wed to the Frenchman dancing through her head.

"Grace, it was an example, I wasn't proposing to you," Franco said pulling her arms from around his neck and placing her gently back on the deck.

With a sudden realization, hearing that the man in front of her had not proposed, Grace broke down in tears. "How can you say such things?" her thoughts of living a life away from the daily grind of servitude vanished in a mere second of dialogue.

Looking at the young Filipino woman in tears he bent down and gave her a hug. "Grace, I care a great deal for you," Franco said. "But today, I need to be sure we can both be safe, and with those men on the dock, it won't happen," he said calming her down with the logic of his request.

"If you get your asylum from the captain, then we can talk about settling down together?" Grace asked with a typical Asian demand to her voice.

"Yes; we can discuss it after I know we're both safe."

Chapter Fourteen

Shortly after receiving the call from his follower in Tunis, Omar Khalid called Nazim Aziz to give him with the information about Franco Laurent. "Our mutual friend has found solitude on the cruise ship," he said, relaying the information from his man in Tunis.

"I see, thank you for calling," Nazim said. What should I do next? I want this person to be dealt with for the good of the organization, but does it mean being returned to France?

Sitting at his desk, he contemplated telling Gregory to involve his Italian friends from Toulon in the attempt to apprehend Franco and bring him back to Marseille. But could the Italians make that possible? Or is it time to turn my back on Franco and let him continue to think we are after him, making him look over his shoulder each day? As he continued to think through the information, Gregory entered the office holding the completed documents for moving the drugs to England on the *M/V Bonaparte*.

"My associate from Algiers has found Franco," Nazim said, as Gregory placed the packet on the desk.

"Where specifically did he find him?"

"In Tunis; he's aboard the cruise ship," Nazim said. "So how do you think we should continue?"

"Your associates can't apprehend him?"

"No, there are too many innocent people, which also mean too many witnesses," Nazim replied. I was hoping you would offer other options on how to handle the fugitive member of the organization you recruited, he thought.

Sitting at the table, Gregory stared at the wall with a blank expression. But behind the unfocused eyes, his mind raced through the possibilities of getting his hand on Franco Laurent. And, more important, how to make him an example of what not to do against the organization.

"I know there's a freighter which sails between Marseille and the African coast," Gregory said. "It's the *M/V De Gaulle*, and it is preparing to deliver goods to Naples. They could be given instructions to put into port behind the cruise ship, it would give your Algerian supporters a place to take Franco if they apprehend him," Gregory said. *I need to be careful, I don't want Nazim to know about owning the freighters or 'Papillion Transport' less he demands I turn control over to him*, he thought.

"Is that so; and you know this information to be legitimate?"

"Yes; I've worked with the captain of the vessel in the past when Louis and I were working in Toulon, and he owes me a favor," Gregory said.

"Then we should prepare to request that they offer their help if it can be arranged in time," Nazim said. "Meanwhile, I want to have Sophia go back to the hospital and give some information to Louis about our plan to free him from the police."

***

Sitting in her apartment, Sophia was reading the instructions her uncle had written for her return trip to the hospital to visit Louis Clement for the second time. As she read the description, she was pleased to see it would not include wearing of the nurses' uniform again, a garment she considered very unflattering for her figure. For this visit, I'm to work as a kitchen worker delivering meals to the patients in their rooms, seems simple enough she told herself.

Just like before, she would have the information Nazim prepared hidden on her. And while passing the tray of food, she would pass along the envelope to the bed ridden man.

The instructions were simple. Based on information from Gregory's source, they would liberate Louis upon his transfer from the hospital to the central jail's infirmary. This was scheduled to happen in three days' time and would involve a minor traffic accident with the ambulance before it reached the jail compound.

The following morning, Sophia went to the hospital, only this time she wearing food service scrubs and would enter the facility through the rear service entrance, not the main lobby. Walking past several custodial staff responsible for the cleanliness of the wards, she briefly stopped one worker and asked for directions.

"Where's the kitchen?" she asked the older gentleman getting his cart ready with cleaning supplies.

"Down that hallway, first door on the right," the older Frenchman said. He didn't pay close attention to her or her features, which this time she could put on a brief display if the need arose.

100

"Merci," Sophia said making her way toward the kitchen area. The closer she came to the food preparation area, the stronger the scent of cooked eggs, bacon and coffee became. Getting to the door, she spied the delivery carts filled with meals, ready to be moved to their respective floors. Glancing carefully at the instruction sheets taped to each side of the tall warming carts, she came across the one labeled for the ICU.

"Go and deliver the food," the kitchen supervisor said. Without hesitation, Sophia pulled the cart destined for ICU from the line and pushed it towards the service elevator.

Entering the elevator by herself, she slid her hand along her thigh, pulling the taped envelope away and placing it under the tray identified for Louis. As the elevator doors opened, Sophia pulled the cart out of the lift, looking in both directions to insure she did not hit a patient or staff member.

Starting at one end of ICU, she skillfully delivered each tray to the selected room, greeting the occupants then departing, making her moves look as routine as possible. Nearing the room Louis was in; she saw the police officer walking towards the bathroom, knowing this was the perfect time to deliver the message unopposed.

Pulling the tray containing the envelope, she walked confidently into the room, a beaming smile on her face only to encounter the second officer walking from behind the privacy screen.

"Excuse me," the young officer said apologizing as he missed upsetting the food tray held by Sophia.

"You startled me officer," she said, side-stepping the young policeman who she caught glancing at the open blouse of her uniform and her exposed cleavage.

Setting the tray down and looking at Louis Clement, she asked if all was well with him.

"Oui, mademoiselle," he replied, happy because she didn't appear to have been recognized by the officer.

"Enjoy your breakfast. I'll return in one hour to collect the tray," she said exiting the room. Pushing the warming cart back to the service elevator, Sophia's heart was racing fifty-times faster after the experience in the room.

Choosing the second floor and basement, she prepared herself for an uneventful exit from the hospital, while the warming cart rode the unaccompanied elevator back to the kitchen area.

Getting off the elevator at the second floor, Sophia bypassed any of the added security staff that was in place in the main lobby since her first visit. Dashing to the end of the hallway and into the stairwell, she could finally discard the kitchen staff clothing that she wore into the hospital. Pausing on the mid-level landing between floors, she undressed. Unbuttoning the blouse, she pulled it off and hung it over the handrail while sliding the small satchel she wore beneath it off her shoulders.

As she reached in and pulled out a thin t-shirt and a pair of shorts, she listened for any noises. Pulling on the shirt, she undid the clasp on the front of the work pants, sliding the zipper down so she could step out of the legs without tripping. Pulling off her shoes, she kicked one leg of the scrubs off, then the next until she stood with nothing more her t-shirt and socks covering her body. Grabbing the shorts, she hastily stepped into each leg opening, pulling them until they sat snugly between her thighs.

Just as Sophia finished dressing, a door leading from the fourth floor opened above her, as men walked down the steps in her direction. In a mild panic, she hurriedly grabbed her running shoes and satchel and proceeded down to the first-floor exit, leaving the kitchen garb behind on the landing.

Taking a moment at the closed door, Sophia reached down and pulled the running shoes on her feet so as not to arouse any suspicion as she exited. With the voices growing louder, she opened the door, walking into the lobby, filled with what looked to be the same doctors, nurses, and patients from the other day.

The two officers patrolling the stairwells finally turned the corner from the second-floor landing, proceeding to the first when they came across the discarded uniform. Running across the garments, one officer used his radio to report the findings while the second one continued down the stairwell until he exited the first floor.

Hearing the call from the two patrol officers, the security office sounded the alarm, alerting all the staff in the hospital to a possible threat. As the warning was passed, security personnel emerged from the various corridors and established a barricade at the main entrance forcing a stop to all foot traffic.

As this occurred, Sophia reached the exit within the gift shop where she made a hasty departure from the building, walking straight to the first taxi on the street.

"Taxi!" Sophia shouted, waving her arm at the closest one making its way to the curb.

"Oui mademoiselle," the driver said as she slid into the back seat. "Where to mademoiselle?"

"201 Rue de Rouet," she said directing the driver to take her to a friend's apartment. Sliding into the backseat, Sophia noticed a police car pulling in ahead of them behind a white sedan, causing her to slouch down in the seat to avoid being seen.

***

Pulling the police car into an empty space outside the hospital ahead of a departing taxi, Detective's Benoit and Lemieux were again returning to the last location hoping to find a potential suspect.

"You take the photo of the woman to the taxi stand and ask the driver's if they have seen her or picked her up," Claude said. "I'll go into security to see if they have any images of her or the Arab gentleman."

"Certainly," Geneviève replied walking toward the line of waiting cars and their drivers.

Reaching a group of drivers near the lead taxi, Detective Benoit greeted them while flashing her credentials. Carrying a photo of Sophia Dubois in the nurses' uniform, she showed it to the men and asked, "has anyone of you seen this woman?"

Each one looked at the photo, and one by one they all shook their head, except one.

"Yes, I've seen her," a middle-aged driver said smiling as he recalled the woman's curves under the outfit.

"Did you bring her here or take her away?" Geneviève asked.

"I picked the woman up here and dropped her off in the 'Spinning' neighborhood," the driver answered.

"Thank you," she said walking toward the entrance to inform her partner of this new detail to their investigation.

Claude Lemieux was sitting in the security office, looking over another series of images showing a woman working as kitchen staff, before making a hasty exit in a stairwell.

"You're sure this is the same woman as before?" Claude asked.

"Yes, I am sure," the director said. "She fits the profile image perfectly."

Geneviève entered the office; "We've a possible location for the woman."

Just then a security officer said "Inspector, you need to look at the screen," alerting them.

Glancing at the video feed for the main lobby, they saw an image of the same man who entered ICU a few days before and then promptly left. Unknown to the officers, it was Hakim Talib, making notes on the layout of the hospital to prepare for liberating his friend from the police officer's custody.

Turning to Geneviève, Claude instructed her to make her way to the gift shop area while he and the security director would walk across the lobby toward the suspect.

Following his direction, she took a security officer with her, making their way to the hallway near the gift shop while waiting for Claude and the director to meet in the lobby.

While Detective Lemieux and the director rounded the corner and walked toward Hakim, he noticed them and promptly turned away, heading for the side hallway by the gift shop. In doing so, he walked into Detective Benoit and the other security officer.

"Just a moment, sir, we want to talk with you?" she said stepping in to his path.

"Who are you?" Hakim asked trying to push past the woman.

Geneviève produced her police credentials and showed them to him, just as Claude and the security director arrived in the hallway.

"I did nothing wrong," Hakim said.

"As I said; we wish to ask you a few questions?" the female detective said turning to her colleague for a sign as to what they should do next.

"Director, do you have a private room we could use for a few minutes?" Claude asked.

"Certainly, this way," the director said motioning down the corridor.,

With three security members and the two police officers surrounding him, Hakim walked toward the security office to be questioned by the detectives.

Sitting at the table across from the police woman, Hakim felt uncomfortable. He was not use to having a woman in a dominant position over him, so for the moment, he felt weak and alone.

"Why were you trying to visit a patient on the ICU floor?"
Detective Lemieux asked the suspect as he leaned against the wall of the
small room.

"I thought the patient was a former colleague from the shipyard,"
Hakim said.

"And what's the name of your friend?" Geneviève asked.

"His name is Julien Clerc."

"Where does he live?"

"Le Delorme district, if I recall, but I've never been to his home,"
Hakim said.

It was Claude's turn to make Hakim uncomfortable, sliding next to
the suspects' side of the table, while producing the grainy photo of
Sophia from the security cameras.

Jabbing his finger in the center of the photo, Claude asked, "Have
you ever met the woman in this picture?"

"No; I have not," Hakim said, looking directly into the face of the
policeman leaning on the side of the table.

Claude looked at Geneviève and motioned to her to go with him
outside the room.

As soon as they were outside, and the door closed, Claude spoke.
"We've nothing on him to explain keeping him, I'm afraid."

"He's hiding something though."

"Still, we can't connect him to anything today, so we have to let
him go. At least for the moment," Lemieux said.

Opening the door, Geneviève spoke. "You're free to leave."

Learning this, Hakim stood and walked past the two officers,
hurriedly leaving the hospital, not turning around to see if they followed
him as he left.

***

While the police held Hakim for questioning, Nazim and Gregory
were discussing the movement of the drugs to the harbor for loading
onboard the *M/V Bonaparte* for transport to the mysterious buyer, Mr.
Higgins.

"Who did you select to make this delivery?" Nazim asked.

"Julien and Hector can handle this, they've done it before," Gregory
said.

105

Before Nazim could ask another question about the shipment, his cell phone rang on the table. Getting up from the sofa, he walked over and picked up the device, seeing the number for Hakim.

"Sabah alkhyr Hakim," Nazim said.

"I have bad news cousin," Hakim said spending the next several minutes providing Nazim with his version of what had just happened at the hospital. He also informed his cousin they asked about his knowledge of Gregory's niece, Sophia.

"Where are you now?"

"I am at the 'Cafe Fresco', and I am sure I was not followed," Hakim said.

"I'll have one of Gregory's men pick you up and bring you to the warehouse. Stay in plain sight, you'll be safe," Nazim said before he hung up.

"What's happened?" Gregory asked.

"Hakim was detained by the police at the hospital," Nazim said, telling his associate about the police questioning his cousin about Sophia.

Gregory looked at his business associate, debating on what his next course of action should be. I swore to Claire I wouldn't allow anything to happen to Sophia while she was living in Marseille, knowing he needed to do something to protect her.

"Send one of your men to pick up Hakim," Nazim said. "I'll have him join my friend in Algiers for the time being." An hour later, the older French-Algerian was finally reunited with his cousin.

"The police now have an idea you and Sophia are associated with Louis," Nazim said.

"But you asked that I go to the hospital to see if Gregory's plan was sound."

"True; but I wasn't aware they had information that included you." Looking at his cousin, Nazim spoke. "It's because I'm more concerned for your safety and the role you have with the operation. I've decided you should return to Algiers and Omar Khalid."

"And I'm going to do what there?" Hakim asked.

"First; you'll aid Omar and his men as they apprehend Francois Laurent in Tunis," Nazim said. As Nazim provided the details of his plan to help Omar Khalid, he also explained his plan to have the young Algerian prepare for the shipment arriving in Tangier from Cape Town in the coming months.

"I've always been loyal to you cousin, and I'll do as you wish," Hakim said. I know in my heart Nazim would not place me in a position if he couldn't trust me to handle all the possible circumstances that went along with it, thinking of his exile to Algiers.

"You'll sail on the *M/V Bonaparte* with the product being prepared for the Irishman, but you'll disembark in Algiers after the ship has refueled," Nazim said. "You've a day to prepare before the ship departs."

Chapter Fifteen

With his cousin safe, Nazim was explaining his reason for having Hakim join his mentor Omar Khalid, and when he would leave France. As this was taking place, Detective's Benoit and Lemieux were leading a police raid on the suspected apartment of the nursing student.

As police vehicles blocked the intersections at Rue de Benedetti and Boulevard de Louvain, the detectives placed theirs behind the apartment minimizing traffic in front of their target building.

Walking together around the corner, Geneviève and Claude made their way to the suspects' apartment when a young woman stepped out of the building. As she turned to lock the apartment entrance, she noticed the police barricade at the end of the street and turned away from it.

As soon as they noticed the young woman exit the building, Geneviève picked up her pace, not wanting the woman to re-enter the building she had just vacated. "Police, keep your hands away from your bag," she yelled at the young Frenchwoman.

The sudden command from the policewoman caused Celine to drop her purse on the sidewalk, spilling its contents in front of the officer. "What do you want with me?" she asked, as the officers stood over her with their weapons drawn but pointed down and away from her for the moment.

Geneviève looked at the woman and said, "Where are you headed?"

"I am late for work," the young woman said.

"And where do you work?"

"At the 'AC Hotel Marseille' near the velodrome."

"Can you or someone else verify where you were three days ago, say, at around 8 am?" Claude asked getting a sense this was not their suspect.

"Yes, my partner can; I was working an extra shift," she said. "I missed our breakfast date she arranged."

By this time, other officers assigned to the raid were advised the woman being questioned was not the suspect they were searching for and could remove the barricades, returning to their posts.

"You'll need to come back to the station with us," Geneviève said. "We'll need to verify your statements."

***

Soon after talking with Hakim, Nazim returned to the appliance warehouse where he found Gregory discussing the procedures for transferring the container at the docks with Julien and Hector. "The customs agent will demand you open the container to inspect it, and have the dogs go through it."

"Are we confident the dogs will find nothing to alert them?" Nazim asked walking towards the men.

"Of course; I'm very confident things will go well," Gregory said letting out a whistle. Unknown to Nazim, he had solicited the help of a former Legionnaire who trained the drug and bomb-sniffing dogs used by the DCJP and the Police Municipale' handlers.

Just as Gregory had whistled; a large German Shepard came bolting from around one stack of empty pallets toward the container. Running back and forth, its tail wagging furiously, the canine worked its way around the container until its handler came to his side, placing a leash on the collar.

"How do you recognize if the animal senses something in the container," Nazim asked.

"Romain, please show my associate how the dog alerts on the drugs," Gregory said.

"Oui, Greg," the handler said, "Elise' open the bag with the drugs," he shouted informing his partner to open her bag with the test item. "Hunter; seek," Romain commanded the canine.

Soon the dog was wandering the open spaces of the warehouse, moving amongst the pallets, boxes, and containers until it came upon a large box set to the side. At this point the dog barked and took a more aggressive stance towards the box.

Getting a whistle from his pocket, Romain blew it three times and the German Shepard laid down, still targeting the box. Getting to the dog, Romain again placed the leash on the collar, leading the animal a few paces away from the box, before calling his partner to show herself. Standing in the box, Elise held the test packet of the cannabis resin, the same drug held in the container being placed on the Bonaparte in the next day.

"My friend, you're full of surprises," Nazim said. "I shouldn't doubt your resolve to think of all the possibilities."

"Romain; thank you and Elise' for helping once again," Gregory said handing over a plain manila envelope.

"Merci, Greg," Romain said thanking his friend. "Good luck my friend."

***

After seeing his partner's demonstration at the warehouse, Nazim made his way home in the Chateau-Gombert district, where he recounted the events of the last few days.

Relaxing back in his chair, he reflected on each event. A policewoman wounding Louis, Franco leaves the country to protect a foreign woman, and then Hakim is identified by the police because Gregory's niece was identified passing information. He likewise thought back to the experience he had while in Aberdeen, trying to secure the added sale and transfer of hashish for the Irishman.

Is this just a run of poor luck, of all the events happening in the last few weeks, or are they a coincidence? As Nazim recalled how each event took place and who was involved, he still remembered needing to prepare for his discussion with Mr. Higgins about some transaction happening in Tangiers.

Before I discuss what, I can and can't help with, I need to discuss this with Omar, he reminded himself. He realized if he tried to tackle something of this degree without consulting his mentor in Algiers would lead to a great deal of trouble. He also needed to inform Omar about Hakim joining him in Algiers to insure his younger cousins' safety. All because he recognized the police having reason to suspect him as an associate of Louis Clement.

Getting up from his chair, Nazim walked to his desk and opened the side drawer and retrieved a cell phone. This was the same phone he used while in Aberdeen and could be disposed of in the case of an emergency.

Searching through the list of contacts, he soon came upon the number he was looking for and selected it. While making the connection, he contemplated on how much extra time he should negotiate with the Irishman so he could make his case to his mentor in Algiers.

"Hello?"

"Good evening Mr. Gilmore; it's Monsieur Remesy calling," Nazim spoke using his alias.

"Good evening; may I ask the reason for this contact?" Sean asked as it was out of character to receive a call from the French-Algerian drug trafficker.

"I would appreciate it if you could pass along a message to Monsieur Higgins for me."

"Go on Monsieur Remesy," the counselor said.

"I would like Monsieur Higgins to consider postponing our meeting until the following Monday. This will allow me time to discuss his request with my associates in Tangier," Nazim said lying to the counselor.

"I will pass along your request Monsieur Remesy," Sean said. "Is there anything else?"

"No; that is all, have a pleasant evening, Au revoir."

***

Waking up with the sun, Gregory walked into his kitchen and prepared his coffee. Standing by for the machine to finish brewing, he gathered several items that had become his stable for each morning meal; bread, butter, fruit preserves and several pieces of fresh fruit.

With the coffee brewed, he poured a cup before sitting at the table. Writing a few notes to himself, he listed items he'd try to take care of later in the day. The first was to contact Henri Levet, captain of the *M/V Bonaparte*, letting him know to be vigilant while transporting Hakim Talib to Algiers.

His next note was arranging for his niece, Sophia Dubois, to be moved out of Marseille, avoiding any further interaction with Nazim or being arrested by the police. I know I need to include her mother in this discussion since they lived in the same building, just doors apart from each other.

As he was considering his third action for the day, his cell phone rang in the front room. Striding out of the kitchen to fetch the phone, his lover Giselle came out of the bedroom, wearing a camisole and tap pants, looking fatigued from the previous evening. "Hello?" Gregory asked, knowing who the caller was by the number displayed on the screen.

"Good morning Gregory," Nazim said. "Last night I was thinking through our current events and I believe we need to close ranks with our current crews," he said. He'd secretly been considering this for several

111

weeks, but the last few days only cemented his resolve to minimize those in the inner circle of knowledge.

"I understand," Gregory said sliding his arm around the waist of Giselle, drawing her closer, enjoying the feel of the soft satin and lace fabric covering her body. "I'd also want to discuss our current arrangement with the men."

"Fine, we also must work out the plan for liberating Louis from the police," Nazim said.

"I'll meet you at the office in one hour," Gregory said trying to keep his composure while Giselle moved her hands across his body towards his crotch. "Make it an hour and a half."

***

Showing up at the office, Nazim sat behind his desk and like Gregory, made notes of what needed to be accomplished as the date for shipping the narcotics approached. His first concern was ensuring the safe passage of Hakim to Algiers and protecting Omar Khalid. He still needed to communicate this to his mentor, so he could present his cousin with a clearer idea of his role within the Algerian's organization.

As he contemplated the plan to free Louis Clement from police custody, his partner came through the office door just as his cell phone rang. Staring at the device, he saw the number for the international exchange, which caused him to look at it with a sense of concern and trepidation. He motioned to Gregory to sit and stay quiet as he started the call.

Picking it up, he answered, "Hello?"

"Good morning, Monsieur Remesy if you please?" came the requestors statement in a heavy Scottish accent.

"Yes; I'm Monsieur Remesy, can I help you?" Nazim said apprehensive as to whom he was conversing.

"Aye, Monsieur, my name is Mister Hunt," the head of the crime syndicate in Glasgow said feeling somewhat optimistic he was talking to the genuine 'Mister Remesy' in France.

The name of the Scotsman sent a mild shock through Nazim, since he'd never spoken with the gentleman who he only learned as an acquaintance of Ewan Sutherland. Having been called by the Scotsman, he paid closer attention to what was being said. Listening to the caller, he motioned for Gregory to close the office door and sit while he completed the call.

"I'm calling to pass along your friend has taken ill and was transported to the hospital," Hunt said, not offering too much detail lest the call was being recorded.

"I see; and how did this take place?" Nazim asked.

"It turns out our friend was involved in an altercation and now is resting in the hospital under constant supervision," Hunt said hoping Nazim would understand.

As Nazim was conversing with Alistair Hunt, Gregory continued to sit on the chair opposite his partner, eager to hear what was being said by the other party.

"I understand, please let our friend know I wish a speedy recovery and a quick release back home," Nazim said. "Is there any other news?"

"No; not at this moment, but if there is anything of importance to discuss, I'll be the one to pass it along," Hunt said. The Scotsman once again hoping Nazim understood he'd be doing all the communication concerning future drug transactions and not Ewan.

"I see, then I'll let you go about your duties, goodbye," Nazim said ending the call.

Gregory leaned forward from his chair looking at his business associate waiting to hear the details about the call.

Closing the cell phone, the French-Algerian's expression was one of concern and mild shock. "It seems our Scottish contact in Aberdeen was hurt in an altercation and is in police custody," Nazim said, considering yet another incident affecting his organization.

"Well; does this affect our shipment at the end of the week?" Gregory asked, needing to know what instructions to give the freighter's captain.

"No, we continue on as planned. There'll be at least one-weeks' sailing time before we need to make the transfer," Nazim said. Wringing his hands, he considered a change in strategies for future tactics in moving drugs to the British Isles, unsure what the impact of Hunt's call would bring about.

***

As Nazim and Gregory were learning of Ewan Sutherland's injuries and arrest from Alistair Hunt, Detective's Geneviève Benoit and Claude Lemieux were just beginning their day. This included filing their report of their interrogation of the hotel clerk, mistaken for Sophia Dubois' as the nursing student.

"We look to be no closer to finding this woman today as we did three days ago," Geneviève said turning through the transcripts of their interrogation of Hakim Talib. "And we don't even know if she's involved in any drug dealing either."

"Patience is a virtue, 'mon Cheri'. We must treat this case like the onion, peeling back each layer until we get to the middle seed," Claude said slurping at his lukewarm cup of coffee. "And it's important that we focus on one situation at a time, or we'll miss something important."

As they both considered each statement looking for subtle nuances or inconsistencies in what each suspect said concerning their stories, the phone on their desk rang.

"Police Municipale', Detective Benoit speaking."

"Detective, this is Officer Cleric from the hospital," the young security staff member said.

"Yes, what is it you want?"

"We've detained another gentleman trying to visit your suspect, Monsieur Clement," the officer answered.

"All right, Detective Lemieux and I will be there in a few minutes," she said hanging up. "Our suspect has had yet another visitor," she said to Claude grabbing her purse before stepping out the door.

Having detained the suspect from the hospital, police detective's Benoit and Lemieux were sitting in the police interrogation room facing Phillip Gaston, the partner of Louis Clement.

In a reversal of roles, Lemieux took the lead, asking the suspect questions about his relationship with Clement. Benoit meanwhile stood to one side, letting the suspect gaze upon her physique and alluring looks from across the room.

"So, you say he's a friend you heard had been injured?" Claude asked.

"Oui Monsieur," the young man replied, stealing a glance at the policewoman in the corner of the room toying with the buttons to her blouse.

"And how did you come to know of your friend's location?"

Gaston felt the strain of being in confinement of the integration room. This hampered his ability to answer promptly and confidently to the detective's questions, which were coming slower and less assured.

"We were supposed to meet a friend at the docks for breakfast," he said, grasping for any statement which sounded logical for the moment.

Watching their suspect growing uncomfortable, the female police officer recognized it was time to assume the interrogation duties. "Excuse me Detective; can I please have a moment?" Geneviève asked, preparing to play her role in the integration session.

As both stepped out of interrogation, Gaston rested his head and hands on the table, contemplating his answers to the questions to be asked again when the police returned.

Geneviève said looking at her partner, "I believe I can get something from him."

"Be careful mon Cheri. You're walking a thin line with what you're planning," Claude said, knowing Geneviève would use the oldest trick, her femininity, to coax Phillip Gaston to talk.

Strolling back into interrogation alone, Geneviève already undid two buttons of her blouse, exposing the black lace bra and her tanned breasts for Gaston to view. Sitting across from their suspect, Geneviève leaned onto the table, her breasts nestled between her arms stressing the deepness of her cleavage. "So, my partner is not convinced you're being truthful," she said in a low, sultry tone, beginning her interrogation.

"I am, I swear," Gaston said, keeping his eyes focused on the tanned skin of the policewomen's bosom.

"If I'm to convince him you're telling the truth, you need to be honest with me," Geneviève said altering her position so her breasts shifted upward. "You said you're meeting your friend for breakfast," she said. "And, this friend had a young lady with him, no?"

"Yes; a Filipina from the cruise ship," he said realizing what he had just spoken.

With this information, Geneviève shifted her arms again, making the fabric of the bra move, exposing a tan line of golden hue and soft white skin for him to admire. "And the woman was a problem to you and Louis Clement, wasn't she?" she asked bobbing the bait in front of Gaston to take.

"Franco was the problem we were sent to attend to," he said, the sudden realization he'd just condemn himself and Louis because of their association with Franco.

"And Franco's full name, what is it?" she asked, seeing she could get the name of the tall Frenchman from their earlier surveillance activity.

"It's François Laurent, of Toulouse."

"Thank you; that will be all," Geneviève said, standing, and buttoning her blouse before leaving the interrogation room.

Walking out of the observation room, Claude walked up to Geneviève and congratulated her on getting another connection to their investigation.

Chapter Sixteen

Several hours after the police interrogation session with Phillip Gaston, Gregory and Nazim were sitting in the office discussing their next steps for transporting the drugs. The discussion was based on the news concerning their connection in Aberdeen from the earlier phone call. As Nazim outlined his intentions to Gregory, the latter's cell phone rang.

Removing the phone from his pocket, Gregory looked down at the number and saw it was originating from police headquarters.

"Hello?"

"Monsieur, I wish to inform you Monsieur Gaston's presence in court has been confirmed for 0800 today."

"Oui and you were able to confirm this already?"

"Oui, court number 231-1," Sergeant Claire Dubois said.

Gregory listened to his sister-in-law and thought; this is the same number she gave regarding Louis Clément's detention at the hospital, recalling what she'd passed along.

"Thank you, I'll contact the courthouse if I have any more questions," Gregory said ending the call.

Nazim looked at his business associate, who had a puzzled and concerned look upon his face having been told one of his men had been taken into police custody.

"Phillip Gaston is in custody," Gregory said.

"How in Allah's name did this happen?" Nazim asked angrily.

"All I know is he was caught at the same hospital as Louis," Gregory said, standing and walking toward the door.

"Where're you going?" Nazim asked.

"Outside," yanking the office door open, "I need some fresh air."

Stepping out of his partners' presence, Gregory took the time to gather his thoughts. He too was seeing his part of their organization crumble around him. First, Franco and the woman, then Louis gets shot and now Phillip being detained. Wandering in the early afternoon sunlight towards the harbor, he could make out the superstructure of his vessel, the Bonaparte, as it stood tethered to the pier. Cranes swung back and forth, the last of its cargo being removed and placed on the waiting vehicles for transport to the holding zone for inspection.

Maybe it's time to consider cutting ties with Nazim, as he came upon a concrete barrier and sat upon the top. In the beginning of their relationship, it was easy to move a pallet or two of the narcotics. But it now seemed Nazim wanted to venture out beyond his means. And he was willing to sacrifice the people he and Louis had assembled to achieve his own goals. Do I let Nazim know about my ownership of the vessels? he asked himself, knowing if he did, he might open himself to black-mailed or coerced into doing something more drastic beyond moving drugs.

***

On the outskirts of Tunis, with the sun sinking and the tide rising, small harbor tugs began the laborious task of pulling the cruise ship into open water. Gradually, with lines taunt and engines belching exhaust from each tug, the cruise ship finally relented, easing through the muddy water, the propellers churning it brown.

Peering at the city from the upper deck, Franco Laurent felt a sense of relief. He noticed the three Algerians standing behind the security fence knowing their prey was slipping casually away and out of reach.

"So; now we can talk about getting married?" Grace said leaning against the arm of her lover.

Glancing at the perky diminutive figure of the Filipino steward, Franco spoke. "As soon as we're away and I know nothing will happen when we step ashore, we'll discuss marriage," noting he needed a plan if Nazim and Gregory continued pursuing him.

The leader of the three men working for Omar Khalid looked at the cruise ship as it moved further and further out of sight. Recognizing he had failed his master, he further knew that it was his responsibility to inform him of his shortcomings at the assigned task.

Removing the mobile phone from his shirt pocket, he selected re-dial and pushed the lighted button, waiting for the response to come.

"Hello?"

"Qayidi, I have failed you," the leader spoke shamefully as his companions watched him. "The infidel; he sails on the tide on the cruise boat."

"Do not concern yourself. Return to our home, you will be welcomed," Omar said, knowing his men's effort were not wasted knowing he could make arrangements after the ships' return to Marseille.

***

Northwest of the North African nation, across the waters of the Mediterranean, a similar scene played out in the harbor in Marseille. "Let go the aft lines," Captain Levet commanded at the direction of the harbor pilot standing aboard the *M/V Bonaparte* while beginning its voyage towards the British Isles.

"Tug 21, back one-third," the pilot spoke into his radio handset as he sensed the container ship ease away from the dock.

"Back on-third, aye," the response came crackling over the two-way radio from the captain of the harbor tug acknowledging the order.

"Tug 44, ahead one-third, 5 degrees' right rudder," the command came as the pilot began the task of bringing the freighter about so it could sail out of the harbor.

As the choreographed dance played out on the water, Hakim Talib looked over at the churning waters as the vessels worked in unison to achieve the common goal. Glancing back at the skyline of the city, Hakim wondered what the next few days would bring, returning to Algiers to work with Nazim's mentor, Omar Khalid. It was Nazim striking a deal with this notorious leader for my safety from a rival gang, knowing it was time to repay the debt.

"Captain; the ship is yours," the harbor pilot announced turning control over to its registered master now that the freighter was in open waters.

"Thank you, Henri'; always a pleasure having you on board," Captain Levet said shaking the pilot's hand having signed the release ticket for the maritime office records.

Withdrawing from the bridge, the pilot walked down the ladder to the deck, throwing his leg over the rail and crawled down the rope ladder tossed over the side. The ladder hung precariously over the churning water as the pilot boat sped in to make its rendezvous pickup and their passenger.

With a wave, he scampered into the boat and sat in the cabin chair as the small speedboat pulled away and made its return to Marseille.

***

As the dawn broke, Omar Khalid left his bedroom, shared with his 'mahzia', or concubine, a young woman of twenty years to the sixty-four-year-old syndicate head. Each day he began with a series of daily ritual exercises and yoga-like activities to keep both his mind and body sharp.

Retiring to his bedroom, Aisha had already prepared his bath and clothes for the day. Accompanying him into the bathroom, the young woman helped him undress and helped as he stepped into the large copper tub. Sitting in the soothing hot water, Aisha washed him using a natural sponge and pumice soap, scrubbing his skin, and removing the sweat of his earlier work out. Finishing his bath, Omar stood drying himself, then went into the bedroom and got dressed, refreshed and ready for the problems Allah would pose to him for the day.

Before walking into the dining space, he picked up his mobile phone remembering he need to make a call to help his young apprentice Nazim with his wayward associate. Opening the phone as he sat at the dining table he scrolled through the list of names until he found the one he needed. Before selecting the phone number, he placed a coffee cup in front of himself which one of his servants quickly filled with steaming and strong local coffee. Next, he turned the bowl over so his servant could fill it with a mix of granola, fruits and yogurt made from goat's milk.

Pressing the icon on his phone, he started the call to his friend and fellow crime boss in Naples.

"Hello?"

"Hello, may I speak with Mister Alberto Scuderi please?" Omar asked.

"One moment; may I ask who is calling?"

"Yes; my name is Monsieur Khalid, of Algiers."

In a few moments time Omar heard the familiar voice of his friend and part-time business partner, Alberto Scuderi.

"This is Alberto."

"Alberto, it is Omar Khalid calling, how are you today?"

"I'm well my friend."

"Alberto, I'm sorry for the early morning call," the Algerian began. "But, I need help apprehending a Frenchman from a cruise liner," Omar said describing the circumstances surrounding François Laurent on the *NCL Constellation* and the need for his return to France.

"Omar; I can do this for you my friend," Alberto said. "I propose we don't negotiate a fee since we're associates; let us settle at fifty-thousand euros."

"Alberto, it's as you wish," Omar said. It's a small price to pay the 'Don' since information about Nazim's activity in Marseille has an impact on my syndicate, contemplating ways of protecting his criminal activities.

***

As the sun continued on its ascent in the eastern sky, the *M/V Bonaparte* sailed through the waters as it neared the Algerian capital. First Officer (F/O) Pierre Bellamy scanned the horizon, looking for the slightest hint of a small boat sailing in their path. Being vigilant was necessary as the large container ship moving at a steady 21 knots was not the easiest to bring to a stop.

Below the bridge on the main deck, Hakim scurried along the outer walk way, shielded by the sun by stacks of containers coupled together three units high above him.

Staring out the bridge window, F/O Bellamy spied the Algerian making his way forward towards the bow. The first officer knew the passenger was trying to stave off his seasickness by keeping his body in motion.

"Monsieur Bellamy, the harbormaster is hailing us," the young seaman said, sticking his head through the open door connecting the radio room to the bridge.

"Thank you," the first officer said. "Slow to 8 knots, set the bow watch," instructing the crew manning the bridge. Soon a shrill whistle could be heard as the deck crew was alerted to man the rail at the bow in anticipation to receive the harbor pilot.

Hearing the shipboard intercom, Captain Levet left his half-finished breakfast on the table of the mess and made his way to the bridge. Making his way through the passageway, crewmembers in his way quickly made themselves as small an obstacle, allowing the captain immediate access to wherever he was headed.

"Captain's on the bridge," one of the seamen on watch proclaimed seeing the ships master enter through the central passageway.

"Everything all right Pierre?" the captain asked.

"Yes Captain; we've been alerted by the harbormaster about the pilot being inbound, so I set the bow watch."

"All right then, carry on," Henri said. "I'll return at the top of the hour to relieve you."

***

In the third-floor courtroom, proceedings were underway for sentencing the latest group of felons arrested in the past week. "Phillip Gaston, you are charged with obstructing an ongoing police investigation," the prosecuting attorney declared as they stood before the sentencing judge. "How do you plead?" he asked the young man, standing between two police officers.

"Not guilty," Phillip exclaimed having not been afforded an attorney from the courts, so he knew nothing else to declare.

"Let the record show the defendant entering the plea 'Not guilty' to the charge," the judge announced to Officer Dubois, who was annotating files being prepared for the court.

"Yes, your honor," she replied finishing the notation.

Looking on from the audience, Geneviève and Claude heard what they wanted as Phillip Gaston was charged and made his plea. With the formality of the sentencing complete, they both stood, exiting the room, walking out of the court-house and towards their car.

"Now; we have to find 'François Laurent' and his lady and we can move to the next case," Geneviève declared to Claude as they pushed opened the doors simultaneously.

"And the first place to look is the exit records for the cruise ships," Detective Lemieux said maneuvering the Citroen C4 sedan into the flow of traffic.

***

After a short and uninspiring trek across the Mediterranean Sea from Tunis, the sparkling white cruise ship was being escorted in to the harbor servicing Palermo, Sicily. Looking at the skyline, Franco Laurent felt calm, having left the potential captors in Tunis, and the captain granting him permission to continue on board for the near future.

Unknowing to the Frenchman, the harbor pilot presented Captain Rolfson with papers, advising him of the fugitive Laurent, and the need to hand him over upon arrival. It was this or his vessel would be placed in quarantine for forty-eight hours with no one allowed on shore.

Not wishing to create an unpleasant scene with all the passengers over just one man, the captain agreed to the conditions. Informing the harbormaster of his decision, who in turned radioed the waiting party to apprehend the Frenchman.

Getting the news, three men dressed as police working for Alberto Scuderi, made their way to the gangway sliding into place near the middle deck of the ship.

As the ship was tied to the pier, Franco turned from the rail, only to be confronted by the first officer and two crew men. The crewmen, who by all appearances, were not to be taken lightly.

"Monsieur Laurent," the officer said. "You're to come with us; please do not make a scene," showing him the Tazer-like unit held in his left hand.

Franco glanced at the crew men, noticed they too each had a Tazer in their hands and large nylon zip-tie cuffs used by police to apprehend protestors.

"But, I've the captain's assurance of safe passage," Franco said.

"That was yesterday; today we've new information on your past activities," the first officer said, urging the Frenchman to the stairwell leading to the lower decks. As they reached the deck below where Franco had been admiring the city, the men working for Scuderi appeared, ready to take possession of the 'prisoner' from the crew.

"Monsieur Laurent; you're being detained at the invitation of the French consulate," the senior officer said as one of the junior imposters placed sturdy handcuffs on his wrists.

In just twelve hours, François Laurent went from standing on the cruise ship to sitting in the locked cabin aboard the freighter *De Gaulle*, now sailing towards Athens. Since being turned over to Captain Dubois and his crew by Alberto Scuderi's men, Franco knew he was facing a harsh sentence upon his return to Marseille.

"Oui Gregory," Captain Sebastian DuBois said. "We've got him secured in a cabin on the lower deck." The ships' captain was one of a handful of individuals who knew Gregory Arsenault was the owner of 'Papillion Transport'. And the Frenchman controlled not only his ship, but three other vessels used for moving legal and illegal cargo throughout the Mediterranean Sea.

"What is your current schedule?" Gregory asked.

"We should be back in Marseille in less than a weeks' time," the captain said. "Just after making our scheduled delivery in Algiers."

"I'll inform Nazim of the schedule, he may want you to hand over Franco when you dock in Algiers," Gregory said. "Until then, your job is to make sure he stays alive."

"Oui Greg, I'll see he's kept alive." Sebastian said, contemplating what discipline his boss was thinking.

Chapter Seventeen

Sitting in his personal office in the La Cabucelle district, Nazim was reviewing dispatches from the Moroccan syndicate supplying him with the hashish and cannabis resin. It was here the drug was being enhanced in a secret laboratory in Rabid before being shipped to the British Isles. As he turned to the last page of a dispatch, his cell phone vibrated on the desktop.

Noticing the number on the screen, he answered, "Hello?"

"Nazim, it's Gregory. I received a message from the captain of the *De Gaulle*, and he has Franco Laurent onboard with him. It appears your friend in Algiers knew someone in Sicily who could help in apprehending him after all."

A wry smile crossed his face hearing the news. I'll have to remember to contact Omar and thank him for helping bring Franco back to be dealt with. "That's good news," Nazim said. "When will the vessel return from its current voyage?"

"They foresee returning to Marseille after making their scheduled stop in Algiers," Gregory said. "Which should be a week or so from now, provided there's no issues after their stop in Athens."

Nazim thought about this revelation for a moment, considering the possibility of asking Omar Khalid to deal with the Frenchman. If Omar agrees to handle Franco, it would ease any problems having him around the activity here. Just as he was preparing to tell Gregory of his decision, the cell phone began to 'beep' in his ear, alerting him of another call. "I'll let you know something in a day or two," he said, "I've another call I need to answer."

"I'll wait for your decision then," Gregory said.

As soon as Gregory completed his call, Nazim thumbed the phone symbol to respond to the incoming call. "Hello?"

"Hello, Monsieur Remesy," the counselor to Mr. Higgins said. "This is Mister Gilmore from Ireland calling."

"Good morning Mr. Gilmore; what do I owe for the pleasure of this call?" Nazim asked.

"I've been asked to meet with you regarding 'Mr. Higgins' appeal for cooperation with a transaction in Tangier," he said to Nazim. "I was hoping to meet with you in a weeks' time."

Nazim thought for a moment, leery of the suddenness of the invitation by the Irish to meet, but again at the possibility the counselor for 'Mr. Higgins' was an informant for the police. This could be favorable as I would have Omar Khalid's men to back me if there are any problems. "Mister Gilmore, I agree to the meeting," Nazim said. "Where would you recommend this meeting take place?"

"I've a business meeting in Algiers, so I would propose there if that's agreeable to you?" the Irishman asked.

"I can accommodate this invitation," Nazim said, knowing he had acquaintances there if he needed support.

"Thank you, Monsieur Remesy. I'll send you information where I'm staying," Gilmore said. "And you can make your arrangements," the Irishman added, not fearing reprisals from the drug dealer since he had his own protection.

"Very well, I look forward to meeting again soon," Nazim said. Now to contact Omar and make the arrangements for his men, and for handling Franco, he told himself looking down at the mobile phone in his hands.

***

Looking out his office window, Nazim studied the various ships docked at the port, each superstructure painted a different hue for its respective company. Some were fresh and bright while others were fading and dulled by weather.

Angling away, he looked at his watch and realized he should call his mentor Omar to discuss his trip to meet Mr. Gilmore from Ireland, and the pending arrival of François Laurent on the *M/V De Gaulle*. Picking up his mobile phone he thumbed through the list of contacts until he found 'Khalid, O' which he selected.

The phone chirped once as it connected to the overseas exchange before ringing. After the second ring a feminine voice answered.

"Hello, how can I help you?" the young woman asked.

"Mister Khalid, if you please?" Nazim asked, envisioning the young woman, wondering what state of undress she might have been in.

Understanding the caller ask for Omar, she handed the phone to him as he lay reclined amongst the large pillows placed on the king-size bed.

"Good afternoon, this is Khalid."

"Good afternoon Omar; I hope that I was not disturbing your sleep?" Nazim said knowing the activity his mentor was performing.

"Nazim, your call came at a very opportune time of the day," Omar said swinging himself to the side of the large bed and sat upright.

"I'm calling to inform you I'll be in town in several days to discuss a business transaction with the Irishman," the drug dealer said. "And was hoping to have a moment of your time."

"Certainly, I can make myself available for you my young apprentice," Omar said.

"I'd like to discuss having your support in two matters when I am there," Nazim continued. "The first one being assistance in a transaction taking place in Tangier and the second is my desire for you to 'host' the fugitive, Franco Laurent."

"It would be an honor to discuss both matters with you Nazim," Omar said. I wonder what you're committing yourself to if you need my help in Tangier. And handling the fugitive Frenchman would be a pleasure for what it cost me to have Alberto Scuderi's involvement.

"Then I look forward to being in your company," Nazim said. "I will telex my information to your assistant so the arrangements can be made."

"Shukran," Omar replied.

"Ma'a as-salamah," Nazim said ending the call.

***

While the late afternoon sun shone through the window of an old commerce building off the highway, two men huddled in discussion. In a building near the bustling docks of Marseille, Nazim and Gregory sat across from each other, working on the next set of plans for shipping the drugs.

"With the information you received regarding Phillip, we need to take harsher steps at maintaining our anonymity," Nazim said.

"I agree; but to what extent?"

"I've a meeting with an associate next week in Algiers regarding Franco; I'd like to discuss his possible involvement with our other activities."

"We discussed the possibility of moving after your experience in Scotland several weeks ago, and you said it wasn't necessary; why the sudden change of heart?" Gregory asked.

"It's not a change, it's only a discussion," Nazim said.

"And if this 'associate' agrees to aid in the effort, then what?"

"Then you and I will have another discussion, since it's 'our operation' to control," Nazim said.

"If that is the case, I'll need to have a meeting with the members of 'Papillion Transport' to ascertain what their concerns or desires are on the matter; if you have no objections?" Gregory said. I need to remind Nazim that I'm the one controlling the freighters used to ship his illegal goods, including the narcotics.

"No, we need their cooperation in our operations," Nazim said.

"Likewise, it might be time for you to ask you associate to offer some loyal followers to help in processing the hashish," Gregory said.

"And why is that?"

"Our original agreement was for my men to maintain the security and delivery of the drugs, not to handle them."

"And you think the current work is below them?" Nazim asked irritated at the question.

"No, of course not. But losing Louis, I need to make sure I have someone we can trust to back our security, an individual not busy emptying and cleaning bottles," Gregory said.

"I understand. I'll discuss this with my associate in Algiers as well," Nazim said.

***

Leaving Nazim at the office, Gregory got in his car and proceeded to the other side of the city. He had but a few hours before an arranged meeting with associates from Toulon. Parking in a public lot, he strolled the two blocks to the location of his niece Sophia. At an apartment near the police station, Gregory was helping Sophia gather her belongings. He knew keeping his promise, getting his niece away from the growing criminal activities of his partner Nazim, was important to her mother Claire.

"How am I going to explain this to Celine?"

"Right now, it's better she not know of things going on; at least for her own safety," Gregory replied stuffing clothes into a box.

"And where am I going to stay?" Sophia asked.

"You'll go to the Pizzeria La Italia in Toulon and meet with Giuseppe Ricci," Gregory said to the young woman. "He'll see you're looked after as you get settled."

"Do you trust him?" the Frenchwoman asked her uncle.

"Yes; we have an understanding and I know he'll keep his word," the Frenchman said recalling his conversation with the Italian just a few days earlier about his niece.

***

In the growing darkness, outside 'French Armed Forces Hospital', Gregory Arsenault and Julien LeBlanc sat patiently for the vehicle transporting their friend Louis Clement to the Police Municipale' building.

"Is Hector and Pasqual ready to stage the accident?" Gregory asked.

"Oui Greg, they know what they are to do."

And with this knowledge reaffirmed, Gregory noticed a non-descript van pull out of the emergency zone carrying his friend. He knew this because earlier, Officer Dubois provided the information to her brother-in-law. In return, he made the promise to help her daughter distance herself from the French-Algerian and his criminal activity.

"Contact Hector, let him know the van is moving," Gregory said putting his Peugeot sedan into gear and speeding off after the vehicle now 25 meters in front.

Five minutes after leaving the hospital, on a narrow section of Avenue Alexandre' Alsanti the van came across an accident between two vehicles blocking their passage. Hector and Pasqual were both out of their vehicles, engaging in a staged argument, each man screaming at the other of who was to blame.

The police officer in the passenger seat of the van exited, approaching the men who quickly had the officer turning his back on the van and its driver.

Following the van ahead of them, Gregory and Julien pulled up from behind. While Gregory used hydraulic jaws to crush the door's lock; Julien pulled the door open, subduing the lone guard with pepper spray before tying him up with plastic handcuffs.

"Gregory? Hector? Am I glad to look at you," Louis exclaimed seeing his friends as the liberated him.

"Quickly, we must leave," Gregory said continuing to hear the verbal abuse being directed at the lone officer by Hector and Pasqual at the front of the van.

***

The dim glow of the light on the night stand illuminated the belongings set out on the bed. Nazim was packing his travel bag for the trip to Algiers and his meeting with Omar Khalid. Amongst the clothing and shaving kit, he packed a small leather Koran and his portfolio holding his notes for discussion with the elder Algerian.

Do I ask for his help in leaving Gregory? Going on to contemplate the latest events seeming to appear out of nowhere to undermine the drug cartel he was trying to build. Does Omar have a connection to a shipping firm discreet enough to handle our product? was another lingering thought as he and Gregory had created a level of trust with 'Papillion Transport' for moving drugs between the North African ports and Marseille. And what do I make of Gregory's request for more men? Maybe this is the time to move everything back to Algiers.

Looking about the room, he felt he'd accounted for everything he would need before leaving, apart from one item. Looking towards the open bathroom door, he noticed his companion lounging in the sunken tub, a half-filled glass of wine in her hand. As he made his way to the open door, he turned off the lights, allowing the glow of the moon and stars to guide him.

Realizing he would have no such luxury in Algiers, he stripped off his dress shirt and stepped out of his slacks, entering the warm water next to the woman. Immersing his body in the steaming water, he sensed the physical tensions fading away, though he still had many details about the trip racing through his mind.

Sensing movement next to him, Nazim watched the woman pouring a glass of wine and place it next to his hand, and then slid herself against his reclined body. Reaching across his own body he picked up the glass of wine and took a taste of the varietal from Lyon.

***

Captain Levet looked down at the main deck of his ship as his deck crews and the longshoremen began removing the chains and binders securing the stack of containers. Watching the teams of men move about the multi-colored boxes, he saw his 'guest' Hakim Talib was preparing to exit the ship. Peering down on the dock, he noticed the customs official standing with two other men, dressed in the traditional gandoura robes and linen slacks.

"They all seem rather friendly don't you think?" asking his first officer who'd joined him.

"Too friendly for my liking," F/O Bellamy replied. "I'd expect the customs official to keep the others at bay, but he's actually escorting them like they're royalty."

"I know our employer is not happy about his partner's activities outside of France," Levet said. "And if this is an indication, I understand why now," tossing his cigarette towards the water.

"Then why are we doing business with them?"

"Because making money means compromising in some circumstances," the captain said. "When do we begin off-loading?" turning his attention to the task of mastering his vessel.

"In one hour," Bellamy replied. "Just seven containers to off-load and three to take on," recalling the manifest details. "After that, we're off to Station Bravo for refueling," alluding to the floating barge located a kilometer off-shore.

Captain Levet observed as soon as Hakim stepped onto the dock, he quickly handed over his passport to the customs official who stamped it and turned away. The other two men greeted Hakim with handshakes as they led him to a waiting car. As they walked away from his view, Captain Levet returned his attention to that of his ship and cargo.

"As soon as we clear the harbor, I want a transit at maximum speed," the captain mentioned. "I want to get the drugs off as soon as we are able to meet with the British," alluding to the rendezvous.

"At that speed we'll be in the North Sea in under five days," Bellamy answered displaying his uncanny knowledge of time and distance.

Chapter Eighteen

The office fan whirled back and forth, pushing the stagnant summer air across the room. Each of the detectives were engrossed in their respective notes, piecing together clues on the drug smuggling activity of the cruise lines. "Detective Benoit and Detective Lemieux, please report to the Superintendent's office at once," the public-address system announced throughout the Police Municipale building.

Looking up from their respective computer screens, the detectives glanced at each other in the hopes the other would know what was about to happen.

"Any idea on why we're being called Claude?" Geneviève asked, rising from their desks, and heading out the door towards the senior officials' office.

"Don't ask me. I'm not aware of anything," Claude said, not knowing why they were being called upon, while turning the corner leading to the Administration offices.

Opening the outer office, they discovered their supervisor, Captain Julien Duval, Principal Detective for the Marseille office standing by the open door to the District Commandant's office. Stepping between the desks dotting the office space, they entered to meet the senior official sitting at his desk holding a communique' in his hands.

"Please sit down," he said as the two detectives entered the office.

Both Geneviève and Claude took the offered seats across from their superior while Captain Duval stood behind them.

"As I recall; the two of you have been focusing on the drug movements amongst commercial ships and cruise liners," the commandant said reading the briefing notes provided by their supervisor.

"Yes sir; we believe we've found there's a connection between a specific set of cruise ships and freighters," Claude said.

"Well, as of today; you're both off that case, and you're being re-assigned," the official said holding up the communique' from Paris. "Per Superintendent Chevallier, your new assignment is to help two members from Scotland Yard and aid in their ongoing investigation into drug trafficking," he said. "It turns out they have evidence that the drug shipments originate here in Marseille."

"And what of Detectives' Berger and Masson?" Lemieux asked about his other officers.

"They'll remain on their current assignment for the time being," Captain Duval answered.

"And the two from Scotland Yard, do we know their names and ranks?" Claude asked his superior.

"Yes; based on the information provided by their Chief Superintendent Collingsworth, you'll be working with Chief Inspector Conor McDermott and Inspector Andrew Fletcher," the captain said.

"We'll be hosting the inspectors for two days here in Marseille," Captain Duval spoke from behind them. "We believe by having them come here, we can be more aggressive in the investigation and avoid being identified as 'soft' on our home-soil with drug trafficking."

"What information does the British inspectors have which makes them think the drugs are coming from Marseille?" Geneviève asked.

"A full packet of their current evidence is being sent by courier today," the commandant said. "I recommend you finish passing your current work to Captain Duval and prepare by reviewing those documents as soon as they arrive. If there are no further questions, you're dismissed," he said ending the briefing on the matter.

Exiting the office with Captain Duval behind them, Detectives Benoit and Lemieux returned to their office in silence, each lost in their own thoughts of the task lying ahead. Going in the office, each sat down, as Captain Duval closed the door before speaking. "It's important to Superintendent Chevallier we show our British counterparts the Central Directorate is willing in our cooperation. But likewise, firm with our resolve to end this quickly, not allowing it to be a stain to our police work," the supervisor said to his detectives.

"You'll have our best efforts," Claude said. This work could catapult me to a more senior detective's position within the department over his peers.

"Oui, we'll do all that's necessary to bring credit to the department," Geneviève said. I wonder if this exposure will help me move up in rank, always thinking of advancing since joining the department.

With the direction provided by their captain, the detectives drove to the airport to meet their British counterparts. Dropping his partner at the terminals' entrance, Detective Lemieux pulled his car towards the parking structure. Standing in the arrival terminal, Geneviève held a placard with the names of the Scotland Yard detectives on it for her visitors to notice.

Reaching the bottom of the stairs ahead of his partner, Inspector Fletcher who stopped to relieve himself, Conor spotted the sign, walking up to the Frenchwoman and introducing himself. "I'm Chief Inspector McDermott."

"Welcome to Marseille," Geneviève said. "I was told to expect two of you from Scotland Yard?"

"Aye lass, my companion's in the loo, he'll be down in a wee bit," Conor said observing the tight curves and athletic build of the French detective. *Aye, if only Ailene came in such a nice trim package as this one*, he thought comparing his lover in Aberdeen to the French detective.

Just as Andrew reached the bottom of the stairs, he spotted Conor and the French detective talking when a gentleman walked up to them.

"May I introduce my partner, Senior Detective Claude Lemieux," Geneviève said.

"Chief Inspector Conor McDermott," the Scot said shaking hands with his opposite number in the French police.

While Conor and Claude were exchanging pleasantries, Andrew stood slightly behind waiting for a chance to introduce himself to the French detectives.

"And you must be Inspector Fletcher," the policewoman said taking notice of the young Londoner standing behind Conor.

"Yes; please call me Andrew," exchanging handshakes with both officers.

"I suggest we head to the hotel first so you can drop off your luggage," Lemieux said. "Then we can go to the office and begin our work," leading his two guests to the waiting police car sitting along the curb.

Soon after arriving at the Police Municipale' building, they sat in the spacious conference room. With Conor and Andrew across from Claude and Geneviève, they opened file folders with information pieced together over the last three weeks.

"This began in Portsmouth after a French freighter left the docks," the chief inspector said. "And we encountered three deaths from the same batch of drugs," Conor said taking the lead in the opening conversation.

"You're sure it was a French vessel?" Claude asked, not wanting his country to accept the blame for a British problem.

"Aye, it was the only one that left the harbor in a forty-eight-hour period after the deaths," getting a sense of animosity from the French detective. "Likewise, we'd report of the freighter making an unscheduled stop in the Channel before docking in Germany," Conor pointed out on the map which had been prepared for their discussion. "Here," tapping the spot, "with British-flagged support vessel 150 kilometers from the nearest working site."

"So, you believe the French freighter offloaded some drugs to the British ship before continuing to Germany?" this time it was Geneviève asking Conor the question.

"Yes; it appears at some point there was a transfer between the two," Andrew added feeling somewhat left out of the discussion.

"We've learned through records the freighter was the *M/V Joan of Arc*," the Scotsman said. "And it's registered to 'Papillion Transport' here in Marseille," Conor said laying one of his cards before the French in this game of high-stakes poker.

"We've heard of this company but have had no solid leads or suspicions regarding drug trafficking," Claude said recalling their investigation into the cruise ships. "At the moment, their vessels are under surveillance."

"Then I recommend that we look a wee bit closer at the people working for 'Papillion Transport' and their activities," the Scotland Yard detective said to his French counterparts.

"Oui, we can begin there," Claude said. "But is that the only connection you have to this point?" calling for the visiting inspector to share more than the freighters' name or that of the owner.

"We likewise have an interest in this gentleman," Conor said as Andrew pulled the photo of Nazim Aziz from the folder, showing it to the French officers.

"At first glance, you can understand we considered him to be of Middle Eastern descent," alluding to the photo. "But because of the freighters' origin," he continued. "We're also thinking he'd be a naturalized citizen from a country bordering the Mediterranean," Conor said going with a hunch he'd considered but never voiced to anyone until now.

"We've many nationalities here in France, Chief Inspector, as does Great Britain," Geneviève said looking closely at the photo. "This man has some of the same features as one we interviewed in the hospital," uttering in French to her partner.

"I'm sorry, but my boarding school French is rusty; you've seen this man?" Andrew asked sensing they missed something.

"Not this person, but someone who looks very much like him," Claude said embarrassed for not continuing the conversation in English.

"Could it be a brother or maybe even a close relative?" Conor asked.

"Oui, very much so," Geneviève said looking at the picture and imagining the features of Hakim Talib from the video they reviewed.

"I recommend your officers search for this man then," Conor said. "And figure out if any connections can be made."

"I agree," Geneviève replied. "Do you have the photo as an electronic file?"

"Yes; I can give it to you on a disc," Andrew said reaching into his satchel for the computer disc containing Nazim's photo.

"Then it seems we have work to do," Claude said to the inspectors in the room as he stood. "We'll take my car to the office," dropping the empty coffee cup in the trash.

Returning to the police station after their day of interviewing the staff of 'Papillion Transport', the French detectives along with their British counterparts reviewed notes, discussing outcomes of each interview.

"I got the impression they're genuine workers for the shipping company," Andrew said sitting at the conference room table. "Everything was neat, and for all appearances' sake; correct."

"Oui, the members of the office I spoke with did not suggest illegal activities being conducted," Detective Benoit said pacing around the room.

"We need to consider the possibility they're privy to the deception just like those who control the freighters," Conor said thumbing through his notebook.

"If that's the case, we need to consider the freighters too," Claude said recalling the tack they were using for the drug trafficking amongst the cruise ships and freighters.

"Can we get a schedule to see when the ships come and go?" Andrew asked mentioning how the inspectors used the schedules to track the support vessels and freighter.

"Oui, we can get that," Claude said picking up the phone and requesting the latest shipping schedules for the port.

"Let's hope we didn't miss a boat that's already sailed," Conor said thinking they were still two steps behind the drug traffickers.

Spending the better part of the day reviewing interview notes from their questioning, Chief Inspector McDermott and Inspector Fletcher now sat at an outdoor café near the hotel. Their conversation centered on the last twenty-four hours with their French counterparts.

"Do you think they know more than they're letting on?" Conor asked his younger partner.

"I've gotten the feeling they want to know more; but they've only scratched the surface in their own investigation," Andrew answered taking a sip of his Pellegrino.

"I'm nae sure they knew about the drugs and their freighters," Conor said. "They're focus has been with folks going on holiday and the cruise ships."

As they both sat thinking thru the events and information gathered over the past weeks, it became apparent they had the upper hand on the drug trafficking investigation.

"I say we let them track down this 'Adrien Richelieu' fella who owns 'Papillion Transport'," the Scotsman said drinking his beer. "And we'll go about finding the chaps who are receiving the goods," Conor said to his partner.

In a similar fashion, Detective's Benoit and Lemieux were having the same conversation as McDermott and Fletcher. The French detectives were regarding where their investigation stood and what the inspectors from Scotland Yard provided.

"I believe the English have more to share than what we've been allowed to learn," Geneviève said to her partner.

"I would agree to a point," Claude said taking a sip of his sauvignon. "They know a ship from Marseille is involved, but not the 'whom' as it were."

"What is it you propose then?" Geneviève asked, "We find out who owns the vessels and let the British worry about the drugs being brought onshore?"

"It would be reasonable to expect them to handle the ships in transit to their ports while we apprehend the parties responsible here in Marseille," Claude verbalized his theory.

The French officers sat at the table of their preferred café contemplating Claude's theory, unknowingly aligned with what Conor had proposed earlier to Andrew. As she sat in thought, Geneviève considered her role in this plan her partner proposed and how it would help or hinder her chances of promotion within the department.

"Tomorrow, I'll recommend we divide our efforts with the agreement to share all information," Claude said finishing his wine.

***

Sitting alone inside the dining room of his hotel in Marseille, Conor scrutinized the notes he and Andrew accumulated in the two days working with detectives' Benoit and Lemieux. He was once again trying to piece together the puzzle of who was responsible for the movement of the drugs, but also the death of his niece, Edna.

"More coffee Monsieur?" the hostess asked.

"Aye, thank you," Conor replied holding up his cup.

As the waitress refilled his coffee cup, Conor noticed Geneviève entering the dining room from the lobby, holding a folder under her arm.

"Good morning," he said as the French policewoman drew nearer to his table.

"Good morning Conor," she replied. "You appeared to have had a restless night."

"Aye, I've got a feeling we're not making any headway on this."

"Detective Lemieux and I've got a theory about tracking the freighter ownership."

Opening the folder, she pulled several papers out and placed them in front of Conor, each one with a list of names and events.

"It seems you've a few avenues to explore," Conor said looking at each sheet of hand-written notes. "But I dinnae read or write in French."

"I'm sorry," Geneviève said an embarrassed expression coming across her face. She took a few minutes to read off the notes her and Claude and written the earlier evening while discussing their approach to apprehending the drug traffickers.

"Claude and I agreed we'd look into the vessel owners while you and Inspector Fletcher continue tracking down the drug traffickers when they come ashore," she said.

"And our superiors will let each side take on those particular tasks?" Conor asked the woman sitting across from him.

"Oui, we believe they will because it allows you to focus on activities on your home soil while we handle things on our end, as you say," Geneviève replied. Her and Claude didn't want to divulge to the inspectors from Scotland Yard they'd yet to discuss the arrangement with their superior, Captain Duval.

Later that morning, the inspectors from Scotland Yard and the detectives with the French police sat in the conference room, explaining their joint proposal to their superiors.

"Out of mutual respect for both agencies, you all agree to share the information and credit for arrests?" Captain Duval asked the gathered police officers.

"Yes; because one can assist the others with the information gathered," Detective Lemieux said as the senior member.

"Aye, and by finding the source who's buying the drugs, we'll be able to stop them from being brought onshore," McDermott chimed in on the conversation.

"William, what do you think?" the French official asked the British officer listening in on the conversation via telephone.

"I believe we could all benefit with the collaborative effort," the senior officer in London replied. "Let's give it a go shall we."

And with that, the two police agencies forged a pact to take down not only the drug trafficker, but also the buyers regardless of nationalities. And in the process, identify and apprehend the supplier.

***

Strolling through the terminal, Nazim was optimistic he could continue traveling as he had before the situation in Aberdeen last month where he felt his cover had been compromised. Stepping up to the Air Algeria counter, he once again used his Louis Remesy passport to secure passage, with the typical questions being asked for traveling outside the country.

At the same time Nazim was gathering his boarding pass, Detective's Lemieux and Benoit were making sure their guests, Inspector's McDermott and Fletcher, made their connections within the same terminal a hundred meters away.

"Have a pleasant flight," the two French detectives said.

"Thank you for your hospitality, we'll be in touch," Fletcher replied.

McDermott heard little of the pleasantries being exchanged as he watched Nazim Aziz walk towards the entry point to the departure gates. Shaking his head, he wasn't sure if the person walking passed was the same one they encountered in Aberdeen last month, but there was something familiar about him.

Nazim had prepared himself to travel back to Algiers by wearing a traditional gandoura over his linen dress shirt and summer weight slacks. In addition, he wore a linen skullcap visible under a 'fez' if he had chosen to wear one. This was a sharp contrast to the woolen sweater and rain slicker he wore in Scotland. But his hair and beard were not of a specific length or style to allow him to have a unique appearance.

"Conor, we're going to miss our flight," Andrew said tugging on his partner's arm leading him towards the departure gate and their flight back to Scotland.

Looking back at Claude and Geneviève walking out of the terminal, Conor knew he'd have to alert his French comrades to what he saw. Shifting his gaze back to Andrew who was a few paces ahead, he resigned himself to the fact he might've just missed a potential suspect. Either that or mistaken one of many North African gentlemen who traveled throughout Southern France as a drug smuggler by mistake.

Chapter Nineteen

Nazim Aziz stepped off the Air Algeria flight into the glaring light of the setting sun. Raising his arm to shield his eyes, he looked down at the faces lining the terminal windows to ascertain if he could spot his friend and mentor, Omar Khalid.

Standing in the terminal just out of the sunlight's glare, the elder Algerian stood with one of his loyal subjects, waiting for his young apprentice to appear. "Get the car ready," Omar said to his young companion spying Nazim exit the plane.

Entering the customs zone of the terminal, Nazim gained a respite from the scorching sun and the rising temperature. Executing the stop at the customs kiosk, the French-Algerian made his way to the waiting section where he met his mentor and friend. Going up to the elder gentleman, they embraced and exchanged the token kiss on the cheek as was their custom.

"It's good to meet you again my friend," Nazim said standing back from Omar.

"As it is for me to seeing you again," the crime czar of Algiers said. "Let us go to a more private location where we can talk, and you can get settled." Walking out of the terminal, they quickly found Omar's driver waiting for them with the passenger door of a late model Mercedes-Benz sedan open for them. "Take us to the compound Ismail," Omar said to the young man driving once he and Nazim were settled into the back seat.

"Yes, your excellency," Ismail said placing the German sedan into motion and joining the mass of vehicles exiting the airport.

Showing up at the compound in the Les Tagarins region of the city, Nazim was given time to refresh himself and change before sitting down with Omar Khalid. Splashing cool water over his face, he noticed he was joined by the twin sister of Aisha who stood holding a clean towel so he could dry himself.

"His excellency will meet you when you are ready," the young woman said handing the towel to Nazim.

Accepting the towel from the young servant, he thanked her drying himself as she turned, walking back into the bedroom, her figure an inviting and intoxicating lure to him.

Having gotten dressed, Nazim made his way to where his host waited, escorted by the young Algerian woman. Stepping into the large study, he saw his mentor reclining in the large overstuffed sofa dominating the room.

"Come sit and take refreshment with me," Omar said.

"Thank you," Nazim said as each twin sister emerged carrying a tray.

Entering the salon, Aisha carried one with fruits and sweet bread, while her sister Ketifa came in with a pitcher of water and glasses for the gentlemen's use. Pouring a glass of water for both men, Ketifa offered the first glass to Nazim and then the second to Omar.

"I was actually surprised by your cousin's demeanor," the elder Algerian said, alluding to Hakim Talib. "Over the last five days, he's taken to being here very well."

"I am pleased to hear that," Nazim said. "I am hoping he can be of service to both of us while he's here in your company."

"Rest assured, he will," Omar said matter of fact like to the younger man sitting before him. "Now; you asked to have a business discussion my young friend," he said beginning the talk Nazim requested. "How can I be of service to you?"

"First; I would like to thank you for helping with the apprehension of François Laurent in Palermo."

"I saw it as a needed action to avoid a problem to both of us," Omar said.

"I would ask if it's possible, he be held here until we can dispense a just form of discipline for his disloyal behavior."

"I believe it can be arranged," Omar said.

"I also want Hakim's involvement," Nazim said, hoping his cousin's inclusion in whatever disciplinary act deemed adequate would leave its impression with the crew in Marseille.

"We'll work together when the time comes," Omar said thinking of an act deemed relevant. A wry smile came to his face. "And the second item you wish to discuss?"

Having a drink of the cool citrus flavored water from his glass, Nazim said, "I've been approached by the Irishman to furnish security for a shipment." Looking at Omar, he continued outlining what he knew. "There's a container arriving in Tangier he wishes to have protected until it can be loaded on a freighter," he said. "I was asked to insure its safety."

Looking closely at his apprentice, Omar detected in the man's eyes he wanted to show a strong proud image, but also understood his limit of what he could promise. "Do you know where the container comes from or what it might hold?" Omar asked taking a sip of water.

"I've not been told that. But, I'm meeting this Irishman's counselor tomorrow at Hamma Garden to discuss what arrangements are expected and can be made," Nazim answered. "I would also like to ask for the company of two of your men to be present when I have the meeting if possible?"

"I'll have Ismail and one other present for your meeting," Omar said. "And I'll think about assisting you with your request for Tangiers on one condition."

"What might that be?" Nazim asked.

"You must gain assurances from the Irish whatever is in the container, it will not bring harm to anyone in Tangiers or here in Algiers."

"I understand; it will be as you asked if it's in my ability to do so."

"Then I suggest we both begin our preparations for tomorrow," Omar said standing up from the sofa, making his way to his private room, followed closely by Aisha.

Seeing his mentor had finished their discussion, Nazim took his leave as well, making his way to the guest room lead by Ketifa.

"Is there anything you wish for?" the young Algerian woman asked opening the door to the guest room.

He knew too well the woman was offering herself, but now, he felt the need to concentrate on the tasks he might have to face tomorrow. "No. I will be fine," he said dismissing the young woman from her expected obligation.

After a restful night's sleep, the echoing sound of a man's voice filled the room. The sun was cresting the eastern horizon, and as Nazim lay in bed, he heard the 'muezzin' and his recorded call to prayer for the Muslim faithful. Soon the servant staff for Omar Khalid would move about the house to prepare for the new day.

Getting out of bed, he walked quietly into the bathroom and prepared himself for the coming day. Standing under the flowing water, he washed away perspiration and stickiness he felt on his body which came from flying amongst so many nationalities and their questionable hygiene.

Stepping out from the bathroom, he was surprised to be met by Ketifa who stood before him. "May I prepare something for you?"

"A simple breakfast please," Nazim said.

"As you wish sir," she said trying not to stare at his nude body and the significant disparity between his and her master's genitalia.

Having dressed, Nazim made his way to the dining room where he found Ketifa had prepared his 'simple' breakfast. Platters of fresh cut fruit and several different sweet breads were laid out with a container of honey to drizzle over it. Along with the fruit and breads, there was a large carafe of fresh brewed coffee with a pitcher of cream and sugar sitting next to it. Helping himself to the food, he noticed Omar had entered the room.

"Good morning my friend," he said walking to Nazim's side and shaking his hand. "I take it you slept well?"

"I slept peacefully, thank you," Nazim said to the elders' question knowing he would be displeased with Ketifa if he said anything to the contrary.

***

Twenty kilometers away in the dining room of the Hotel Sofitel Algiers Hamma Garden, Sean Gilmore was already awake, having a traditional breakfast of fried eggs, fruit, and toast along with tea. He had arrived earlier the previous and settled down in his room and have a restful night's sleep. He knew this was of paramount importance as he prepared to meet with 'Monsieur Remesy' regarding the weapons shipment in Tangiers. Looking about the dining room, he could hear several other Western visitors, which helped place him at ease.

Shortly before nine o'clock, Nazim Aziz walked into the lobby of the hotel to meet with the young Irish counselor. As he walked across the marble flooring, he noticed one of Omar Khalid's men sitting in a chair reading the local newspaper. Going in the dining room, he noted the Irishman sitting to the right, his back against the wall while facing both entrances from the lobby and the garden.

This man is no fool, he thought to himself walking up to the table. Yet, there's something oddly familiar about his face, staring at the Irishman.

"You must be Monsieur Gilmore or should I address you as Monsieur Higgins?" Nazim asked holding out his hand, alluding to their first meeting.

"It's Gilmore; and you are Monsieur Remesy?" the barrister said standing up from the table and shaking hands; afterward Sean offered the French-Algerian a seat at the table. Guess the wig and glasses weren't enough, recalling his first meeting with Nazim.

"How can I be of service to your employer?" Nazim asked starting the negotiations for his and Omar Khalid's services in Tangiers.

"My employer is expecting a container of goods to arrive in Tangiers the first week of September," Gilmore said. "And he wishes to have it safe guarded until it can be loaded on a vessel for shipment," sipping his tea.

"I understand. What assurance do I have that what's being shipped won't be dangerous to my men?" Nazim asked keeping his promise to find out about its contents.

"The contents being shipped is meant specifically for use by my employer," Sean said answering the question. "At his discretion and where it suits his needs."

This caused Nazim to pause as it answered his question but didn't reveal what it was or how it would be used.

Sean saw the hesitation in Nazim's face and he felt this could be cause for the French-Algerian to renege on the agreement. "I can assure you Monsieur Remesy, you and your men will not be in any danger while the container is being secured, or after it is placed onboard the vessel."

Learning this did little to ease Nazim's concerns as he felt uneasy at what he was not being told about the container and its contents. However, he also weighted the potential for Omar's help in securing a separate means of handling the drugs in the event he parted ways with Gregory and Louis Clement. "How long will my men be needed?" Nazim asked taking a calculated chance this arrangement could become something more fruitful.

"No more than seventy-two hours," the Irishman replied. "From the time the container arrives in Tangier till it departs and the vessel is safely in open waters," he added hoping to place Nazim's fear in check and secure the deal. "Afterwards; two hundred and fifty-thousand pounds' sterling will be transferred to an account you choose, no questions asked," Gilmore conceding the final point to the deal, payment.

Sitting back in his chair, feigning to take a drink of coffee which had been brought to him, he considered the offer and what it would mean. Not seeing a substantial risk in what he or his men would be involved in, he decided. "Then I agree; I'll offer this service to you and your employer," Nazim said knowing he was committing Omar Khalid to the deal as well.

Standing up from the table, Sean reached across the table offering his hand as a conclusion to the deal which Nazim accepted, consummating the arrangement. What he didn't notice was Ismail moving closer to the table. The Algerian, a knife sliding out from his sleeve, was anticipating the Irishman doing something harmful. But in the end, nothing more than the handshake took place.

"If you'll excuse me then, I must contact my employer and complete the arrangements," Sean said taking his leave from the French-Algerian crime boss. As he walked out of the dining room, Sean let out a visible sigh of relieve knowing he was cutting the negotiation close. Looking at his watch, he saw he had just under an hour to make his way back to the airport for his flight back to Belfast.

Watching the Irishman walk out of the dining room, Nazim motioned to Ismail to the table. "Move the car to the front, it's time to return to the compound," directing the young Algerian. Three days of surveillance of a container for two hundred fifty-thousand pounds, he told himself. Much of the fee he would turn over to Omar for helping provide the men, not to mention paying for bribes to the Moroccan's involvement.

***

Returning to Khalid's compound, Nazim was relaxing on the veranda shaded from the African sun, cooled by the breeze emerging off the waters of the Mediterranean Sea. Taking a sip of his chilled water and watching the lithe figure of Ketifa float in the pool, he contemplated the deal he had just made with the Irishman. Averting his gaze from the young woman floating in the pool, his cell phone rang breaking the silence.

Picking up the cell phone Nazim answered, "Oui, Monsieur Remesy,"

145

"Herr Remesy, it's Klaus Schmidt," the German said hearing his business partner.

"Yes, what is it?" Nazim asked annoyed at the distraction of the call from his enjoyment of watching the woman swimming naked in the pool before him.

"The vessel arrived without the drugs last night," Klaus said alluding to the *Standard-Apollo* making contact at the gas derrick in the North Sea.

Hearing this caused Nazim to bolt upright in his chair, the movement startling Ketifa who had exited the water, walking toward the seat next to him under the veranda. "What do you mean it didn't have the container onboard?" Nazim said, standing up, pacing back and forth, his mind reeling at the news. Weeks of preparation creating the hashish and cannabis-resin cocktail with a street value of nearly one million-euros was now gone, his anger amplified hearing the news.

"The *Apollo* captain said the freighter gave the cargo to another boat earlier that morning," Klaus said relating what had been told to him by the Scot, Captain McKenzie. "Also, there was a British warship nearby just after the support vessel departed. However, we made the transfer of the drugs from the past shipment, but now we've nothing to prepare," the German said.

"I understand Klaus, plan for you and your people to return to Hamburg; I'll see what this is all about," Nazim said ending the call.

As the conversation was going back and forth between Nazim and Klaus Schmidt, Omar walked outside to see why his young associate had raised his voice. "What was that all about?" Omar asked sitting down at the table where Ketifa, still naked and wet, poured him a glass of water.

"My current drug shipment, all twenty-five thousand kilos worth, appears to have been stolen, pirated at sea," Nazim said, his mind reeling from the loss of the narcotics.

Watching his young apprentice struggling to comprehend the situation, the older man asked questions necessary to begin the search for those responsible for this action. "So, what do you know at this moment?" Omar asked in a calm fatherly tone of the young man still pacing back and forth.

"The crew leader working the derrick was told a different vessel encountered the freighter, taking possession of the container," Nazim stated, becoming calmer seeing his mentor was relaxed and in control.

"And who might control the actions of this service vessel?" Omar asked, making Nazim think through the possible scenarios.

"The normal routine was arranged by my partner, Gregory Arsenault when we shipped the narcotics out of the area," he said. Is it possible my friend and partner of eight years is behind the theft? Nazim thought.

"Has he led you to believe he has not been truthful throughout all your dealings?" Omar asked, formulating his own plan to learn who deceived his apprentice.

"No; most certainly not," Nazim said not recalling any instance where Gregory might have concocted a ploy such as this.

"The Irishman has been very distant in his dealings though, has he not?" Omar asked planting a seed of doubt as to the legitimate nature of the arrangement made nearly four months earlier.

"What do you mean by 'distant' Omar?"

"He always sends his counselor to conduct his business; so, you need to ask yourself, who else has the gentleman met?" Omar asked continuing to paint a picture of the mysterious 'Mr. Higgins' as the culprit behind the deceit.

Thinking to earlier this morning, Nazim finally realized his meeting with Sean Gilmore took place in Algiers, not Marseille which would have given him the advantage. But he wasn't given a reason. "Are you saying the Irish meant to steal the drugs while they negotiated for our help on a different matter?" he asked, trying to understand the 'why' behind the action.

"Deception is a strong negotiating tool if used in the right manner," Omar said looking out at the pool catching Aisha and Ketifa swimming in the transparent waters. "The magician's skill in 'sleight of hand' tricks make him worth watching," Omar said, once again reinforcing the notion the Irish were behind the theft.

"What does it benefit the Irish if they use deception to conduct one act and negotiate to partake in another?" Nazim asked still unsure of which direction to vent his rage towards, blind in the fact he didn't know what parties were responsible.

"That is what you and I will try to find out," Omar said. And I know just the person who needs to be contacted to look for that information. Turning he watched the glistening figures of the sisters walk past him so they could dress and prepare for the midday meal.

"I must get back to Marseille and find out what happened."

"No. Stay one more day; let me make a few phone calls so we can begin our plans to find the responsible parties together," the elder Algerian said. "Then, when you are of a calm mind, you can return to Marseille," Omar said.

"As you wish," Nazim said, hearing a hint of wisdom in what was said. I can't afford to let this anger cloud my judgment, struggling to free the anger he felt from his thoughts.

***

Just as Klaus Schmidt was notifying Nazim about the missed shipment, Henri Levet was calling his boss, Gregory Arsenault to inform him of the same action. "Gregory, this is Henri onboard the *Bonaparte*," the French captain said hearing his friend answer the phone.

"Is everything all right Henri?" Gregory asked hearing the defeated tone in his friend's voice.

For the next ten minutes, Levet recounted everything that had happened over the preceding two days. From making the delivery to the *Nordic Supplier* who he thought was the *Standard-Apollo*, to meeting the actual support vessel and his discussion with Captain McKenzie.

"First, I'm glad you and the crew are safe," Greg said wanting to assure the captain he and crew were more valuable than Nazim's drug shipment. "Second, I need you to finish offloading your shipment in Hamburg so the British won't suspect you in anything."

"And what of the cargo?" Levet asked feeling responsible for the loss for the drugs.

"Allow me to worry about that; you worry about the crew," Gregory said. "It turns out I've been deceived by a skillful magician," the former Legionnaire said to his captain.

***

Leafing through a stack of printed reports for the third time, the female detective let out a sigh of disgust. "Have we established a date when the cruise ship will return?" Geneviève asked looking through the manifest listings.

"Not until next Monday," Claude said.

"Has Captain Duval contacted the cruise line office for the ships roster?"

"I'm not sure, why don't you call him."

Picking up the phone, Geneviève dialed her supervisor's number, only to hear the irritating sound of a busy signal in her ear.

148

"It's busy, so I'll just take a stroll and see if I can catch him."

"You do that. I'll sit here and pore of these manifests by myself," Claude said, a distasteful look on his face. Scoffing at the woman, he picked up a dozen pages of shipping manifest from the pile stacked between their desks.

"I'll be back before you know it, so don't complain or I'll find some excuse to be gone longer," Geneviève said in a playful tone.

Sauntering through the front halls of the police station towards Captain Duval's office, Geneviève walked past two patrol officers as they recounted the story of their prisoner escaping.

"I still don't understand how someone knew of our route, we didn't know until morning," the first officer said.

"Still, how did they know that Gilbert was the only one guarding the prisoner?" the second officer asked.

"I'm willing to bet, someone said something at the wrong time and to the wrong person," the first officer said.

"Excuse me, but what prisoner escaped?" Geneviève asked joining the conversation.

Recognizing who asked, the first patrolman said, "Oh, excuse me Detective Benoit. I didn't notice you standing there."

"So, which prisoner was it?"

"It was the one you shot several weeks ago," the second officer said.

"Why the hell didn't someone let Detective Lemieux and I know about this?" as she turned away and made her way to Captain Duval's office.

Reaching her supervisor's office just as he was exiting, Geneviève asked, "Our prisoner escaped?"

"What are you talking about Detective Benoit?"

"I just overheard two patrolmen talking about Louis Clement escaping during transfer from the hospital."

"Yes, two men created a diversion, and he was liberated from the van, they used pepper-spray to subdue Officer Gilbert," Captain Duval said. "Thankfully, he wasn't harmed in the escape."

"But why wasn't Claude, and I told about this?"

"Because you were ordered off the case to work the investigation begun by the British," the senior officer said

"But now this man is running loose in the city, don't you think I would be a possible target for retribution?"

"I'm aware of that possibility, and there are other officers besides you and Detective Lemieux who can search for this man."

"So, I'm supposed to walk the streets like nothing ever happened?"

"In my experience, which is years more than yours' detective," Captain Duval continued, "leads me to believe you're not going to be a target for this man or is his associates."

"And why is that Captain?" she asked. Why shouldn't I be concerned, I shot a man who had a gun, she told herself.

"Because his friends would have retaliated by now if they wanted to," Duval said. "Is that all you wanted to ask me?"

"No, it's not sir. I'm sorry Captain. I was coming to ask if you had contacted the cruise line for their crew manifest so Detective Lemieux and I could search them for the Asian woman."

"They are sending it by courier today, we should have them just after lunch," Captain Duval said. "Now, if you don't mind, I need to go to the men's room."

"Oh..., of course, thank you Captain," she said blushing at the thought she'd kept her supervisor from relieving himself.

Tearing back into her office, Detective Benoit was beside herself with angst and frustration as she retold the story from the patrol officers outside Captain Duval's office.

"Well now, seems your victim is now a fugitive," Claude said hearing Geneviève recount the patrol officers' story.

"Yes, and then Captain Duval said I shouldn't worry about being a possible target for retaliation," she said, pacing back and forth in the small office.

"He has a point. If this Louis Clement, had been a key player in something greater, his compatriots would have made it their cause to make an example out of you."

"It still irritates me that we weren't notified; I mean, the prisoner was arrested because of our efforts," Geneviève said, as she continued venting her frustrations to Claude.

"Well, as he said, there are others who can go looking for him, we've other things to do," Claude said pointing at the stack of manifests.

"It seems strange though, as the officers said, that someone knew about the transfer at such a late time," she said sitting back at her desk.

"Well, look at it this way. We're investigating the drug trafficking by cruise ship members, and one member was in our prisoners' company," Claude said. "So, it's quite possible that you might just meet him again."

"Oh, if I could be so lucky, I'd make the next encounter our last."

Chapter Twenty

Grasping his bag, and exiting the customs terminal, Nazim Aziz made his way to the taxi stand. The change in climate from the dry heat of the Algerian capital to the French seaport did little to temper his mood.

"67 Rue Etienne Miege, Chateau-Gombert district," he said entering the first taxi in line. Resting in the back seat, Nazim's mind raced, my first order of business will be contacting Gregory and finding out if he knows anything about our hijacked container.

Getting the call from Klaus while he was in Algiers instilled a level of distrust for the mysterious Irishman, which only comes from being deceived. Glancing out the window, Nazim didn't see the tourists walking or the cars and buses making their way through the city. All he saw were images of the container that held a half-million euros worth of hashish vanishing from his sight.

"We're here," the driver announced pulling Nazim from his thoughts. "The fare is 29.50 please."

Pulling thirty euros from his billfold, he handed the money over to the driver before stepping out of the taxi, "Merci."

Going up to the house, he was met by his companion Lauren, who gave him a brief hug and kiss, before entering the house.

"Gregory left a message for you yesterday, he had to go to Toulon to pay a debt," she said watching Nazim place his bags in the bedroom.

"Did he say how long he would be gone?"

"No, he did not."

"Please prepare the bath, I'd like to clean up before we eat," he said to Lauren. Why didn't Gregory call me directly? Is he hiding something from me as Omar suggested, he thought entering the large bedroom he shared with her.

"Of, course. Would you like a glass of wine as well?"

"No, not at the moment," he said.

Staring at himself in the mirror, Nazim could see the strain of the situation edged on his face. Gregory and Louis had set up transferring the drugs between the support boats and the oil derrick. So, there's a problem between the boat crews and the freighters now? And if not the freighters, is it the crews on the support boats and their dealings with Klaus?

Lauren looked at Nazim and said, "Your bath is getting cool."

"Oh, um... yes, I'm just... I'm trying to handle something which makes little sense."

"Then you need to sit in the warm water and relax," Lauren said pulling his shirt out of his trousers and unbuttoning it, baring his hairless but muscular chest.

"Yes, you're right," Nazim said pulling the shirt off while Lauren undid his belt and clasp on his trousers.

***

The detective's office door swung open as a member from the mailroom delivered a special delivery parcel. "Here's a package for you Detective Benoit," the office clerk said dropping off a large envelope bursting at the seams.

"Merci," Geneviève said taking the package and handing it over to her partner.

"And what do we have here'?" Claude asked taking a letter opener to the edge and sliced open the end.

"It should be the cruise line rosters," she said.

"And you are so correct mon Cheri; all five companies' worth, courtesy of the Marine Magistrates office."

"We should've asked the people at 'Papillion Transport' for their crew rosters while we had McDermott and his partner, um..., what's his name, the young one?" Geneviève asked, "Oh hell, I can't remember it now."

"Don't you mean 'Fletcher'?" Claude said correcting his young partner.

"Yes, that's him; anyway, we should try to have Captain Duval get those as well."

"I agree, since our investigation involves them," Claude said. "So which cruise line had the most 'questionable' port calls?"

"It was Nordic if I recall," Geneviève said.

"Ah, here we are," Claude said pulling out a thick stack of bound listings. "Five vessels, each one averaging, oh I'd say about, one-thousand crew members each."

"That's five thousand names we have to read over," she said dejected.

"Oh, you're sharp this afternoon Mon Cheri; yes, five-thousand names."

"And we're only looking for one member," Geneviève said sounding defeated before they even started their search for Grace Mendoza.

"Correct, and the other thing to keep in mind, much of the cabin staff come from Asian countries," Claude said. "We're talking, Korean, Filipino, Malaysian, Chinese, Thai, just to name a few."

"And our only lead is an Asian woman, and she's only five feet tall."

Claude chuckled at the description of the suspect. "Right now, yes, she's our only lead to the cruise ships, but we've also the French man, Francois Laurent to search for as well."

"But he wouldn't be listed as part of the crew?"

"No, I would not think he would be on the cruise ships, but remember, he was seen on a freighter in Toulon."

"So, you're saying we can drop European surnames in our search on the cruise ships, but not the freighters?" Geneviève asked, hoping to decrease her effort in the search.

"Mostly, yes, but we're still looking at everyone as a potential member of a drug trafficking ring," Claude said burying his nose back into the documents.

"And thanks to Scotland Yard's investigation, they think we can narrow the search to just 'Papillion Transport' freighters."

"Yes, it seems that way, but I wouldn't be surprised to find other freighters involved in the drug trafficking either as we dig deeper."

"Let me know when I can quit digging then," Geneviève said pulling a stack of the shipping manifests across to begin her own search.

***

Remaining in the holding area of the courthouse, Phillip Gaston looked optimistic. After pleading not guilty, he was assigned a public defender, or advocate, to present his case to the judge.

"Phillip Gaston?" the court officer asked.

"Oui, I'm Phillip Gaston."

"You're next, please come forward."

Passing his way through the doorway leading into the courtroom, Phillip waited for his case to be presented to the judge.

"Phillip Gaston," the judge said beginning the hearing process. "You pleaded 'not guilty' earlier in court to charges of 'obstructing a police investigation' and 'possession of an illegal firearm' is that correct?"

"Yes, your honor," Phillip said, his advocate standing beside him in silence.

"I've reviewed the case file, and it appears when placed under arrest, you were not in possession of a firearm, were you?"

"No, your honor, I was not."

"In that case, the firearm charge is dismissed," the judge said. "And in the absence of the arresting officers to substantiate the obstruction charge, I'm dismissing it as well due to lack of evidence showing involvement in any earlier crimes."

"Thank you, your honor," the advocate said finally on Phillips behalf.

"Officer Dubois, please see that Monsieur Gaston's release is processed."

"Yes, your honor," Claire said looking over at Phillip.

Exiting the courtroom, Phillip was led to the processing office for his release. Seeing him there was Officer Dubois, with the judge's order in hand ready for her fellow clerk to begin the discharge process.

Moving into the evidence locker, Claire Dubois pulled a box containing Phillips personnel belongs and slid it towards him.

Turning towards her fellow officer, Claire noticed the woman was busy inputting the information on Phillip into the computer. Getting out an envelope, she handed it over to him, "its instructions, money, and a bus ticket, from Gregory," she whispered.

Phillip stood there, looking confused at the envelope at first, and upon hearing Gregory's name mentioned, then one of surprise.

"Merci," Phillip said taking the envelope and stuffing it into his pocket.

"You must sign for your belongings," Claire said, returning to her role as a police clerk.

"Of course," Phillip said signing the inventory sheet confirming he was receiving all the items that the police took possession of when he was arrested.

"You're free to go," the other clerk said walking to the counter and handing a copy of the release form to Phillip.

"Good luck," Claire said turning away and returning to the courtroom.

Stepping out of the courthouse, Phillip made his way to the nearby park located down the boulevard. Relaxing at an empty bench, he pulled out the envelope and opened it. He took the money and bus ticket and placed them in his billfold. Unfolding the instructions, he began to read the letter.

Phillip, you were released due to a technicality found out by a friend of mine. Because the police still consider you a possible link to Louis, I need you to meet me in Toulon. The bus ticket will allow you to travel without question on any day you wish to leave. I encourage you to pack lightly and leave as soon as possible though. When you arrive in Toulon, I'll have you work with an associate of mine, but I'll also need your help keeping an eye on my niece, Sophia. Do not attempt to go to the warehouse or to see Louis, he is not in the city. Remember, the police still have a file on you, so travel cautiously my friend, signed Gregory.

Glancing around, Phillip suddenly felt alone in the city. For as many years he could remember, this had been his home, but now he was being asked to leave for his own good. Standing, he made his way to his apartment, resigned to the fact he needed to pack and begin his life anew.

***

Having ended her day pouring over the crew rosters, Geneviève made her way to the local market before heading to her apartment. Strolling through the aisles she chose the various staples she needed; assorted vegetables, fruits, cereal, bread, and milk. Proceeding to the checkout counter, she stood behind a man engaged in conversation with the clerk.

"Looks like you're preparing for surgery?" the clerk asked.

"Oh, no, my friend was hurt at work so he asked if I could change his bandages for him that's all," Julien LeBlanc said. He was unaware the woman who stood next to him was the one responsible for shooting his friend, Louis Clement, three weeks earlier.

Geneviève looked at the counter where the man had placed his items; bandages, gauze, tape, and antiseptic ointment. Everything one would need to keep a wound clean and sterile, she observed.

"Looks like you're treating something more than just a simple a cut," Geneviève said.

"It was an industrial accident; he's been to the hospital, but with the raising costs of visiting, he figured he'd asked me to take care of some basic things," Julien said.

"That'll be 35.40," the clerk said bagging the items.

Getting out forty euros, Julien passed them to the clerk who quickly counted out his change.

"Good luck," the clerk said watching Julien leave the market.

"Hope he knows what he's doing," Geneviève said.

"Oh, I'm sure he does, he's mentioned he used to be a medic some years back," the clerk said.

"So, he comes in often?"

"Yes, I see him at least three, maybe four times a week."

Geneviève thought of the possibility of this man being linked to the escaped prisoner, Louis Clement. But do I tell Claude, or wait until I have something more concrete?

***

Stomping up the stairs, two steps at a time, to his third-floor studio, the former Legionnaire handled the bags cradled in his arms. Stepping into the small apartment, Julien placed the medicinal items on the table. "Louis, you missed it my friend."

"What is that?" Louis asked limping into the front room.

"I had the most wonderful experience at the market. A woman, dark hair, with a strong athletic figure in a pair of slacks that look like they were painted on her by Michelangelo himself. Not even the telltale sign of panty lines," Julien said describing Geneviève to his friend.

"I'm surprised you noticed her hair color," Louis said sitting at the kitchen table.

"And her eyes, a smoky darkness they were, like those of a Brazilian dancer I once had."

"Can we get to my leg please?"

"I'm sorry. I just haven't seen this woman lately," Julien said. "And come to think of it, she reminds me a lot of Sophia," he added cutting away the dressing from Louis' wound.

"Don't let Gregory hear you speak about his niece, or he'll use you for 'shin kendo' training," Louis said referring to the ancient samurai practice.

Examining the area where the surgeon removed the bullet, he lightly touched the surrounding flesh. "It seems your leg's healing nicely, the

157

stitches can probably come out tomorrow," Julien said. Placing some antiseptic ointment on some gauze, he placed it over the wound and wrapped it.

"Now, let's look at your arm, shall we," Julien said cutting away the bandage from where the doctors repaired his elbow. "Um..., you seem to have a little inflammation around the stitches," observing the pinkish area around the wound.

"So, I've got an infection?"

"Possibly, how does this feel?" Julien asked pressing on the stitches.

"It's tender, but not painful," Louis said with a slight grimace.

"Well, we'll give it one more day and see if it goes down. If not, I might have to lance the areas," Julien said in a more serious tone.

"You're the 'doctor' I guess," Louis said.

"If that's the case, I'll have to see if the woman from the market would like to be my 'nurse' for the procedure."

"Will you get your head out of the bedroom and just fix the bandage," Louis said.

Laughing as he wrapped the bandage over the wound, Julien just shook his head. "What do you think kept me from killing everyone in our squad back in Indonesia ten years before?"

"I've always been too afraid to ask," Louis said.

***

In a small, sparsely furnished apartment; seventy kilometers from Marseille in the city of Toulon, Gregory sat at the table. Across the room, Sophia was preparing a simple dinner in her new apartment.

"Your friend Giuseppe, he seems like a very nice man," she said plating the linguine and shrimp.

"He's an honorable man, and he's promised me he'll take care of you until you're settled," Gregory said. "Um..., this is very good," taking a bite of the meal.

"My friend Celine taught me how to cook it."

"I never realized you could cook like this," Gregory said taking a drink of wine. "Your mother certainly never fixed a dish like this," alluding to his sister in law.

"Giuseppe said he could put me to work at the restaurant if I wish," Sophia said sitting at the table to eat.

"And do you?"

158

"I know I need to earn money; mama can't keep giving part of the money you pay her for the information she provides you."

A look of disbelieve crossed Gregory's face. "How do you know about that?"

"Mom and I talked after your African partner sent me to the hospital to pass information to Louis," Sophia said, unwilling to acknowledge Nazim Aziz having any French parentage.

"I see. I guess you're no longer the child I would bounce on my knee are you," Gregory said, a hint of sadness in his voice.

"No, but I still need you and mama from time to time, just like every child does," Sophia said.

"Well, in the next day or two, you'll be meeting a young man who works for me," Gregory said. "His name is Phillip Gaston."

"And why do I need to know about this person?"

"Because both of you will need someone you can turn to, and I'll be asking Phillip to keep an eye on you for your safety," Gregory said.

"As you just said, I'm no longer that little girl, I can watch after myself."

"I promised your mother to see you safe; that and I'm concerned that recent events with Nazim may cause him or one of his associates to do something drastic."

"So, you expect him to come for me and use me as leverage to have you involved in one of his criminal activities?" Sophia asked.

"Maybe, or I could just be paranoid; but either way, I will do what I can to keep you safe."

***

Strolling up to her apartment, Geneviève pulled out her keys and unlocked the door. Going in the hall, she slid her hand across the wall, flipping on the lights. Making her way to the kitchen, she placed the bag of groceries on the table before entering her bedroom. Tossing her jacket on the bed, she pulled her pistol from the holster and placed it on the nightstand. Back in the kitchen, she turned on the radio sitting on the kitchen table, putting away the things bought at the market.

Heating up leftover coffee in the microwave, she tried to piece together the events of the last several weeks. So, should I dismiss the possibility of the gentleman from the market being just a 'Good Samaritan' or is he someone else? Claude found out that Louis Clement was a former Legionnaire, so it's possible he knew a friend who could

159

help. He escaped, and it seems with help, but how? asking herself a myriad of questions with no real answers.

Chapter Twenty-One

Getting in the office later than his normal time, Detective Lemieux noticed Geneviève was already busy poring over the crew rosters. "You're in earlier than usual," he said, placing his coffee on the desk and tossing his coat over the chair.

"I couldn't sleep, so I figured I'd get a head start on these lists," Geneviève said holding up a handful of sheets.

"And have you encountered anything?"

"Yes, that there are too many damn Asian women working on these cruise ships."

"Keep in mind, for many of them, this is their escape to a better life," Lemieux said.

"You're probably right, it just seems like every other name is someone from an Asian country," Geneviève said.

"So, what else do we have on our docket?" the detective asked.

"I've an appointment in less than an hour with the security director at the airport to review their tapes."

"That's right; Chief Inspector McDermott's idea of seeing his 'mysterious Arab' from Aberdeen in our airport."

"I know it seems like a reach, but a possible lead is a lead nonetheless," Geneviève said.

"Well, it might just turn out to be nothing, so don't get your hopes up," Lemieux said. "You can't expect having the same success as we did with the hospital staff."

***

Stepping into the airport terminal, Detective Geneviève Benoit likened the scene to one of Western movies. One where the lone cowboy rides through the town while the townsfolk line the street allowing for a grand entrance. It was the same here, businessmen, families, and students all moving about with some place to go. Roaming through the terminal, she came across the security offices and entered.

"Can I help you?" the clerk asked.

"Yes, I'm Detective Benoit, and I'm here to see your director, Monsieur Dupont," she said, showing her police credentials to the clerk.

"Just a moment, I'll see if he's in."

In moments, a well-dressed gentleman emerged from the back office and walked up to Geneviève, "My name is Hector Dupont, Director of Airport Security," extending his hand.

"Detective Geneviève Benoit," she replied shaking hands.

Gesturing towards the back of the office, Hector said, "Please let's go into my office where we can discuss your request."

Showing Geneviève to the office, Hector offered her a chair at a small table in the room. "I understand you wish to review our security tapes?" he asked.

"Yes, an inspector from Scotland Yard believes he identified a suspect in his investigation while he was waiting for a flight home," Geneviève said. She then spent the next few minutes providing the description and location Chief Inspector McDermott had given her.

"In that case, we'll need to go to our control center," Hector said, showing her to the door.

Going down a back hallway, they soon found themselves standing in the back of the security control center. Along one wall was a bank of HD video monitors, each one displaying an image of the airport grounds, switching views every five-seconds.

"Oh my…," Geneviève muttered to herself.

"Yes, it seems overwhelming, but my people are well versed in picking up nuances on each screen and reacting to it," Hector said hearing her comment.

"It's quite a lot to take in."

"It is, so let's move to this station and see if we can pull up this gentleman for your visiting inspector," Hector said.

Sitting next to the director, Geneviève felt a sense of confidence from the man, not to mention the subtle scent of his Dolce-Cabana cologne.

"So, here we've the cameras from that departure terminal," Hector said, pointing to the computer monitor.

"There are sixteen different views," Geneviève said leaning in to see the playing card-size images on the screen, taking in the masculine scent of Hector. "Can you make it like a slide show, so it cycles each image?" she asked.

"Yes, just a moment," Hector said tapping away on the keyboard.

Soon, Geneviève and Hector were looking at each single image, moving from camera view for the moment in time that Conor had mentioned to her.

"There, that's Conor," Geneviève said pointing to the image of the Scotsman, his auburn hair and faded field coat giving him away.

"Ok, so we can narrow our search based on the time stamp and the corresponding camera feeds," Hector said manipulating the display.

Searching through the images, Hector pointed out one, "There, is that your inspector?" noting the weather field coat.

"Yes, that's him but he's looking the other way."

"So, let's look at what he sees from the other angle," Hector said.

Switching camera views, the image of Conor was now in the background behind the image of an Arab gentleman.

"Do we have a view of this man's face?" Geneviève asked, hoping she'd just identified Conor's mysterious individual.

"Let us see," Hector said pulling up the image opposite of the one they were looking at.

Slowly the image appeared on the screen, and Geneviève peered closely at it. Pulling out a copy of the photo from Aberdeen, she held it up to the monitor.

"It seems like you've found your man," Hector said a hint of disappointment in his voice.

"Can we re-trace his steps based on the camera views?"

"It'll take a few minutes, but yes, I believe we can," Hector said. Signaling one of the staff over, he instructed the technician to piece together the images of Nazim Aziz from their current image until he entered the terminal.

"It may take a few minutes to piece the images together; shall we go and get some coffee?" Hector asked.

"Yes, I'd like some," Geneviève said.

After leaving the control center, Detective Benoit and Monsieur Dupont were soon sitting in one of the airport cafés. "So, after working five years at De Gaulle in Paris, I decided I needed a break from the pace," Hector said with a chuckle taking a sip of his coffee.

"So, that's how you came to be in Marseille; it's not for the sunshine and the warm climate?" Geneviève asked with a gleeful tone.

"No, but I must say it has its benefits," Hector said gazing at the auburn-haired officer. "And you, why did you choose to live and work in Marseille?"

"Well, I've always loved being near the ocean," Geneviève said. "I grew up in Cherbourg before attending the police academy. So, when there was a position opening in this department it made my choice easy. Not to mention, I hate cold weather."

"Monsieur Dupont, please call your party at extension 101," the airport announcement could be heard.

"It seems continuing our conversation will have to wait," Hector said standing up from the table.

"Is it trouble?" Geneviève asked instinctively reaching for her pistol.

"Oh, no, that's just a means of letting me know the staff wants to see me," noticing her arm moving away from behind her.

Making their way back to the security offices, Hector and Geneviève were presented with a series of printed images of Nazim Aziz. From him entering the terminal, walking up to the Air Algeria counter, and checking in. Each image provided a clear path of the French-Algerian took through the terminal. The last image ended where he was walking past Conor by what appeared to be a mere 2-meters distance.

"So, so close," Geneviève said.

"It does appear if your inspector from Great Britain had known he was that close, you could have made the arrest right then," Hector said.

"Yes, it does," she said. "Now, to make my way to the Air Algeria counter to get this man's name."

"Oh, you don't have to go, I can provide that information for you."

"You can?"

"It'll only take a few moments," Hector said, sitting at the computer, and pulling up the flight status report, providing names and times when passengers checked in.

Reading over the print-out Geneviève said, "Not too many passengers are listed?"

"Let's just say that Algiers is not a popular place for many tourists," Hector said. "It takes government approval for most visitors to enter the country."

"Glancing at the image time stamp, and the roster, it seems the 'mysterious Arab' is actually a Frenchman. Based on this record, his name is Louis Remesy, of Marseille," Geneviève said writing down the name.

"So, it seems."

"What type of relationship do we have with the Algerians?" Geneviève asked.

"I'm not sure I'm following you Detective Benoit?"

"Can we contact the Algerian airport security, I mean, to see if they can see who this Louis Remesy met when he landed in Algeria."

"I'm sure we can contact them, but I'm not guaranteeing their surveillance systems are anywhere close to ours," Hector said.

"I think it be worth a try, and I'll discuss this with my captain to see if we can use the normal channels to request the information as well."

"Then it seems I've a few calls to make," Hector said.

"I can't thank you enough Director Dupont," Geneviève said, taking her copy of the images and report. "I need to take these to my office and send it off to Inspector McDermott."

"You could always agree to accept a dinner invitation," Hector said showing her to the door.

"I'll keep that in mind," Geneviève said, handing over her business card. "Call me."

After leaving the airport, Geneviève drove back to the police station, her thoughts swirling between finding a clue for Scotland Yard, and her sudden attraction to Hector Dupont. Entering the police station, Detective Benoit was making a beeline for her office when Captain Duval stopped her in the hallway outside his office.

"Detective Benoit, a moment if you don't mind," he said motioning her to the open doorway.

"Certainly sir," Geneviève said walking behind him into his office.

"Please have a seat," Captain Duval said, pointing to the empty chair next to her partner, Detective Lemieux. "It was just brought to my attention another one of your suspects, Phillip Gaston, has been released on a technicality."

"What technicality?" Geneviève asked.

"The report that was filed, and one which you both attested to, stated you arrested him for possessing an illegal firearm," the captain said.

Glancing at her partner, she said, "I don't recall placing that on the report, do you Claude?"

"No, but we did sign it and we're both responsible for the error," Claude said. There goes my chance at being promoted after this investigation, he thought.

"We do know he implicated himself by being associated with Louis Clement," Geneviève said. "So, once we find him again, we'll make sure the reports are filed correctly."

"Yes, your escaped prisoner from the hospital who has yet to been found," the captain said, a hint of regret in his voice.

"Have the other detectives considered checking other hospitals; maybe he went to another for treatment of his wounds?" Claude asked.

"I'm not aware if they'd considered that, but I'll pass it along," Captain Duval said. "So, what had you smiling so broadly before I ruined it, Detective Benoit?"

Staring at Claude and her captain, "Well sir, I believe I identified the Arab from Chief Inspector McDermott's investigation in Aberdeen," Geneviève said.

"Oh, and how did you do that?" Claude asked.

"Well, Hector and I ..."

"Hector? Who's Hector?" Captain Duval asked getting the jump on Claude before he could ask his partner the same question.

"Oh, I'm sorry. I mean Director Dupont; he's the head of airport security," Geneviève said blushing slightly.

"And what did he provide you with?" Claude asked.

"He and his staff were able to trace the steps of the suspect based on the information Conor, I mean Chief Inspector McDermott gave us."

"And so, we've got a name to go along with a face now," Captain Duval said. The senior officer wanting to show movement on the case to Chief Superintendent Collingsworth of Scotland Yard as well as his Superintendent Chevallier in Paris.

"Yes sir, so with your permission, I'd like to get this information to Chief Inspector McDermott as quickly as possible," Geneviève said.

"Yes, do so; also, I'll keep these tucked away for the time being." Captain Duval said holding a folder in his hands.

"And those are…?" Claude asked.

"Oh these. They're your letter of reprimand for improper record keeping and filing false reports," the captain said. "You didn't think this was just a simple talk and a 'slap-on-the-wrist,' did you?"

Stepping out of the captain's office, Claude and Geneviève made their way silently back to their office before speaking to each other.

"So, while you were out trying to get a date, I came across something interesting," Claude said poking fun at his partner.

"I was not trying to 'get a date' as you say," Geneviève said sitting at her desk. "But nonetheless, what did you find?"

"I was researching 'Papillion Transport' and came across a reference for the owners," he said. "It seems Adrien Richelieu III, LLC is actually two people, not one."

"Two men, how can that be?"

"The registered name is that of a corporation, but the documents filed for the corporation listed the owners individually," Claude said pulling out his notepad.

"Are they still alive?" Geneviève asked, forgetting about the information on Nazim Aziz for the moment.

"Based on the records on file, the owners are identified as Emilio Carbone of Brest and Arnaud Guerini of Lyon," Lemieux said. "I'm wondering if this Emilio has any ties back to Pasqual Carbone," alluding to the former Corsican mafia don.

"So, it appears we need to begin planning a couple of trips to visit these men?" Geneviève asked.

"Yes, and that will allow you to go see your 'Hector' again," Claude said, once again chiding his partner.

"Are you jealous?" Geneviève asked knowing her partner had yet to find someone to replace his deceased wife.

"I'm no such thing. I'm too old to be jealous of you and your personnel habits," Lemieux said. *It would have been nice if Claudette would have stayed instead of returning to Calais*, he thought. *Then I'd have someone to share my wine with instead of drinking them alone at night*, wishing for the company of the divorced journalist.

"So, what do you make of the captain's discussion regarding this supposed technicality on our report?" she asked.

"I'm pulling up my copy right now," Claude said, typing away at his keyboard.

"Well, while you 'hunt and peck', I'll call Conor and let him know about his 'Arab suspect' actually being a Frenchman." Shuffling the piles of paper across her desk, Geneviève came across the number to the Scotland Yard inspector. Dialing the number, she waited for the call to be answered.

"Police-Scotland, Aberdeen District Headquarters, Sergeant McKee speaking," the constable said answering the call.

"Good day sergeant, this is Detective Benoit of the French DCJP in Marseille, is Chief Inspector McDermott available?"

"I'm sorry ma'am, but the inspector's out of the office, can I have him call you back?" the sergeant asked.

"Yes, please have him call me at my desk, he has the number," Geneviève said.

"Very well, I'll see that he gets the message."

"Thank you," Geneviève said ending the call.

While this was taking place, Claude pulled up and printed his version of Phillip Gaston's arrest report for his partner to review. "There, it clearly states that we arrested him for his association with a known felon," he said pointing to their narration on the report.

"Yes, I can see that, so why was the report used at the courthouse different from this?"

"It seems there might be an issue with who's handling our reports," Claude said.

"A possible associate of that young man, handling the like of our police reports, I think not," Geneviève said. "I mean, he was too young and naive to have something or someone that sophisticated in place."

"If that's the case, then our escaped prisoner, or maybe even his associates, has someone working for them at the courthouse," Claude said hypothesizing aloud.

"You might be onto something, but we've no time for that," she said picking up the cruise ship rosters. "We've got our hands full with these." Resting back in her chair, Geneviève picked up the roster for the Nordic Constellation, looking at the names she had circled earlier in the morning. "I've identified eight possible candidates for our Asian accomplice from this ship," she said.

"Why only eight?" Claude asked.

"The night we first saw our suspect, don't you remember, she was still in her uniform, right?"

"Yes, I recall that too, so, what's your point?" Claude asked tiring of the game before it began.

"Well, a 'junior' member of the crew would be quick to shed their uniform, were as 'senior' members would be proud to wear it, wouldn't they?" Geneviève asked.

"Ok, so you're saying our suspected drug trafficker is someone of the crew who has greater privilege and freedom," Claude said.

"Correct, so I identified these eight based on their shipboard ranks, each one being listed as a 'chief' or a 'senior' steward."

"And they're all of Asian ethnicity?" Claude asked.

"Yes, I excluded those who didn't fit the profile," Geneviève said with a smug grin on her face.

"All right, and if that's the case, when do you propose we go about interviewing them?"

"The ship is due back on the 15th, after making its voyage from Milan."

"I recommend you brief Captain Duval on your theory," Lemieux replied. "That way he can pave the way with the cruise line for us to interview these ladies," getting up from his desk. "I'm going to get another cup of coffee."

Having already prepared her notes before talking with her partner, Geneviève called Captain Duval's office.

"Captain Duval's office, Officer Bernier speaking," the female officer said.

"This is Detective Benoit, is the captain available?"

"I'm sorry detective, Captain Duval was called into the commodore's office. Can I take a message?" the officer asked.

"Please have him call me when he has a moment," Geneviève said.

"Certainly, ma'am, I'll leave him a note."

"Merci," she said hanging up the phone.

Noticing the frown on his partner's face, Claude asked, "Something wrong?"

"Officer Bernier said the captain was called into the commodore's office," Geneviève said. "Do you think that has anything to do with the errors on our report?"

"No, I don't, if that was the case, he would have had us sign the letters," Claude said. Julien and I have known each other a long time, he would have given me a fair warning if it had anything to do with us, I hope, recalling his friendship with the captain.

"So, are we just supposed to sit and wait?" Geneviève asked, fearing the worst.

Circling up from his desk, Claude said, "No, we'll not wait or dwell on the possibility of bad news, you'll buy me that lunch you owe me."

***

Sitting across from the senior officer, Captain Duval waited patiently while his superior read the dispatch he held in his hand. "It appears that the inspectors from Scotland Yard have made an arrest into the drug trafficking," the commodore said.

"Is that based on our cooperation?" Duval asked.

"It doesn't say, but it does shed more light on the fact there's a problem beginning here in Marseille."

"And their arrests stem from something with one of the freighters of 'Papillion Transport' then?" Captain Duval asked.

"Partially, a patrol boat spied the *M/V Bonaparte* near the support vessel which was the focus of their arrest," the commodore said, placing the report back in the folder.

"But the report doesn't address anything more than that?" Duval asked.

"No, it doesn't. But, I want your detectives focusing their investigation solely on that company, the freighters and anyone they can associate with them," the commodore said handing the folder to Captain Duval.

"Yes sir, is there anything else?"

"Yes, you can inform Detective Lemieux I've forwarded his promotion package to Paris for consideration. It's up to the review board to determine his fitness for the vacant captain's position now."

"Certainly sir," glancing up at the clock. "He's done for the day, but I'll let him know first thing in the morning," Captain Duval said, smiling inwardly at the news his friend would soon receive much-needed recognition.

Chapter Twenty-Two

Walking off the bus, Detective Benoit glimpsed her partner Detective Lemieux spilling some of his coffee as his foot struck the top step leading into the District office. "Damn that's hot," the officer exclaimed shaking his hand.

Striding up the steps two at a time while clapping her hands, she proclaimed, "Bravo, Monsieur."

"Oh, you thought it was funny, did you?" Lemieux asked, embarrassed at the attention his partner's clapping had brought on him by the officers and citizens outside the police station.

"At least you didn't spill much of your coffee," Geneviève said.

"And if I did, I know a certain young lady who'd be buying my next one," the senior detective said, walking towards the building entrance.

Pausing at the clerk's counter, Detective Lemieux was handed several messages that had been received over the evening by the central operator.

"Here, this one's for you," he said, holding out one slip to Geneviève.

"Oh..., it's from Hector," she said.

"A dinner invitation I suppose?" Claude asked.

"I'm not sure, but I'll find out once we get to the office."

Opening the door to their office she allowed her partner to walk in before she did, "age before good looks," she said chiding the senior detective.

"Don't start your day on the wrong foot now," Claude said, setting his coffee on the desk while tossing his jacket over the chair.

Sitting at her own desk, Geneviève picked up the phone and dialed the office number for Marseille airport's head of security.

"Marseille Providence Airport, Monsieur Dupont speaking," answering the caller.

"Bonjour, Monsieur Dupont, it's Detective Benoit returning your call from last night."

"Ah, good morning, Geneviève, how are you?" Hector asked.

"I'm well, I was just returning your call from last night," she said, toying with her ponytail.

"Yes, I have some more information from the Algerian airport officials," Hector said, pulling out his notepad from the desk drawer.

"I hope it's good news?" Geneviève asked.

Detective Lemieux waved another message slip in Geneviève's face, this one from Chief Inspector McDermott in Aberdeen. Taking the slip, she shook her head in acknowledgement.

"It seems I underestimated my colleagues in Algiers," Hector said. "They could offer me with several images from their security camera of your suspect, Louis Remesy entering customs, and one from the terminal meeting an older gentleman."

"I'd appreciate getting a copy of the images," Geneviève said.

"I already have one of my clerks preparing them for you."

"Why thank you, I'll be by shortly to pick them up then," she said, feeling a warm glow cross her face.

"Until then," Hector said, hanging up the phone.

"Au revoir Hector," she replied hanging up.

"Well, what did your 'friend' have to say?" Claude asked, finishing his coffee.

"The Algerians' security has a series of photos showing our suspect, Louis Remesy entering the country and meeting an older gentleman," Geneviève said.

"Ok, so we found out the suspect has a family member he was visiting," Claude said.

"Possibly Claude; but what if it's someone of more importance? Maybe he's the supplier to this man 'Remesy,' since Scotland Yard considers him a party to drug trafficking, you never know."

"And to whom do you wish to ask that question?" Claude asked slurping the hot coffee.

"I'm not ready to hand this off to the Algerians if that's what you're asking." Geneviève said. "It might do us well if I made a trip to Algiers to determine if I can find out who this elderly gentleman is first hand."

"Oh, and what makes this your case to lead?" Claude asked. "I'm the senior detective, I could just as easily make the trip to investigate as you could."

"Yes, you could; but I'm a woman, and they might not be as intimidated by me asking the questions, as they would if you did. Plus, I can move about town more easily without being recognized."

"How do you propose to do that?" Claude asked.

"It's easy, I'll just need to pack a hijab, and um, I'll dress conservatively so I don't show any skin. Or I could wear a burqa, making sure I don't show or draw attention to my figure; I'm sure I'll be safe."

"The captain will never go for it," Claude said, hoping his partner didn't notice his concerned tone.

"Well; we'll never know until I ask him," Geneviève said. "But first, let's hear what the good inspector of Scotland Yard has to say," picking up the phone once again.

Dialing the number to her counterpart in Aberdeen, Geneviève twirled a pencil between her fingers while the phone rang on the other end.

"Aberdeen District Headquarters, Inspector Fletcher speaking," Andrew said answering the call.

"Inspector, this is Detective Benoit of the French DCJP in Marseille."

"Good morning detective, what a pleasant surprise to hear from you," Andrew said.

"Is Chief Inspector McDermott in at the moment?" she asked. "I'm returning his call from last night, but I've got information to share with him about his suspect from the airport in return."

"Yes, he is, just a moment," Andrew said passing the phone to his partner.

"Chief Inspector McDermott."

"Conor, this is Geneviève returning your call."

"Aye lass, how're you this morning?"

"I'm doing well, thank you for asking. I've got good news on your suspect from the airport," Geneviève said. "But you first since you called me," alluding to the purpose behind the call.

"Aye, we've confirmed one of the boats did meet up with a freighter out of Marseille," McDermott said. "And the service boat had drugs on board."

"And you're sure it originated from here?"

"Like we mentioned before, the freighter was the only one we can tie to the activity," McDermott replied. "You said you had some information. Well dinnae keep me in suspense lass, what've you got to say."

"Your 'Arab' suspect is really a French citizen as you thought. And his name is Louis Remesy, and he's living here in Marseille."

"That was fast work, how did you come across his name so quick?" Conor asked.

"Based on the description you provided, airport security was able to scan the video images until we had him standing next to you," the detective said. "From there, they retraced his steps to the Air Algeria ticket counter." Geneviève added.

"Do you know where he is today?" Conor asked, hoping to place another puzzle piece together in his investigation.

"No, it suggests he is still in Algeria, based on our current information," Geneviève said. Dammit, I should've asked Hector to contact me if the suspect re-entered the country. "As soon as we're notified, I'll pass the information to you though."

"Aye hen, that'll be a great help. Andrew and I need to get ourselves spruced up for court, so keep in touch," Chief Inspector McDermott said ending the call.

"I'll do that, au revoir," she replied hanging up the phone.

"So, they're happy to have a lead in their investigation?" Claude asked.

"Yes, he sounded like they were," Geneviève said.

Just then the phone rang. Picking it up, Claude answered, "Detective Lemieux?" Listening to the caller on the other end, "Oui…, I'll be there in a moment," he said putting the receiver back.

"There's a problem?" Genevieve asked.

"I'm being called up to the commodore's office," he said.

"Just you, they didn't ask for me to join you?" Geneviève asked,

"No, just me," Claude said, walking out of the office towards the elevators that would take him to the fifth-floor office to meet with the senior officer.

Looking at her partner walk out of the office, Detective Benoit decided to make her way to the airport to retrieve the documents obtained by the security director, Hector Dupont.

Parking the unmarked police car in the empty stall, Geneviève made her way into the airport terminal where security was located. Going in the office, she heard Hector discussing an issue with one of the uniformed security members at the back of the office space.

"Good morning, detective," waving her toward him.

"Good morning, Director Dupont."

"Keep me informed of the condition," he said to his security detail, turning to Geneviève. "Please shall we discuss things in my office?"

Stepping into the office, Geneviève once again sat at the small table while Hector took a seat opposite of her.

"So, your Algerian counterpart surprised you?" she asked.

"Yes, it shows Director Salah was full of surprises when I asked him about your suspect," Hector said. "He said the older gentleman your suspect met is a well-respected and very well-connected member in the city."

"And does he have the name of the older gentleman 'Remesy' met with as well?" Geneviève asked.

"Yes, the gentleman's name is Omar Khalid, based on what the director was able to find out." Hector said. "But when Director Salah asked for more information, he was told that he was being given everything on file."

"That sounds very suspicious, essentially as if designed to deceive anyone trying to gain information into this Monsieur Khalid." Geneviève said.

"It would suggest so," Hector said.

"Based on the wealth of information you've provided," she said, "I'm compelled to accept that offer to join you for dinner."

"I'd like nothing more than to have you as my guest," Hector said. "How about Friday night, um, say seven o'clock? We can meet at Alexander Mazza, near the velodrome?"

"I'll make sure I place it on my calendar," Geneviève said, blushing. "Now, back to business, you said you had the images from the Algerians."

"Yes," he said reaching back to his desk for a folder. "Here are the ones from their video feeds," passing the folder to the detective.

Studying at the images, Geneviève could see Louis Remesy at the customs kiosk, and the older gentleman, Omar Khalid. "The older one doesn't appear to look like a relative, does he?" she asked holding out the picture.

Accepting the image from the detective, Hector looked at the photo. "No, I can't perceive any similarities between the two."

"Well, I've got detective work to do, so I'll leave you to your exercises," Geneviève said standing next to the table.

"Oh, we're not conducting an exercise, we've been alerted by INTERPOL about a suspected pedophile trying to leave the country. I was reminding my security chief to keep the suspect alive," Director Dupont said, showing Detective Benoit to the door.

"Good luck, I'm not sure I'd be capable of exercising restraint with that type of suspect," Geneviève said a chill coming over her body. *Filthy rat, preying on innocent children, I'd cut his sack off and stuff it in his mouth given the chance.*

***

Sitting outside the commodore's office, Detective Lemieux considered why he was being called in to meet the senior officer in the district. *I know it wasn't the reports, Julien would've said something,* knowing his friend and captain. *I know I was up for promotion again,* recalling he had just provided his sixth submission of accomplishments. *It might have to do with something the British have found in their arrests. As lead investigator, he'd be the first to be made aware of something of significance.*

"Senior Detective Lemieux, the commodore will see you now," the police clerk said motioning for him to enter the office.

Stepping in to the office, Claude was surprised to discover not only his captain, Julien Duval present but also the other three captains assigned to the office. "You wish to see me sir," Claude said.

"Yes, I did, Captain (Detective) Lemieux," the senior officer said, addressing Claude by his new rank.

"Excuse me, sir?"

"Congratulations Claude, you've been promoted," Captain Duval said happy to confirm what his friend had just been told.

Learning the news, Claude broke down, tears welling up in his eyes. "I'm sorry sir," he said, wiping them away.

"It's all right, we've all been there," the commodore said extending his hand to Claude.

"I didn't expect this to happen so soon," Claude said. "The results from the board are not made known until the first week of August."

"It shows that your name has been on the top of Paris' list for some time," the commodore said. "And it's been obvious to us you're most deserving of this," handing over the badge and credentials for his new rank.

"Thank you, thank you, all," Claude said looking about the room at his peers, accepting the items.

"Now, let's go back to work, shall we?" the commodore said, "Oh, and I expect we'll meet you this evening at La Carravalle, Captain Lemieux?"

"Certainly sir," Claude replied, knowing he'd be expected to take part in the traditional 'wetting down' festivities that go with being promoted.

Making it back to the office, he found his partner, Geneviève, comparing the photos she received from Hector. "Where've you been?" she asked, looking up from the images.

Tossing the shiny new badge on her desk, Claude said, "collecting this."

Picking up the badge, she smiled, "Congratulations, you've waited a long time for this promotion."

"It seems like a long time, I just wish Nadine was here to share it with," once again wiping tears from his eyes.

"She'd be very proud," Geneviève said, embracing her partner, and kissing him gently on the cheek. Walking back to her side of the desk, "So, it looks as if our 'Monsieur Remesy' met with a prominent figure in Algiers."

"Oh really, how prominent?" Claude asked, rubbing his thumb across the golden shield.

"It seems when the Algerian security director tried to get information, he was given the impression having just his name was enough," Geneviève said.

"It could mean nothing," Claude said picking up his empty coffee cup and tossing it in the wastebasket. "Let's go get some coffee, I'll buy."

"It's a deal," Geneviève said, putting her coat on following Claude out of the office.

***

Switching the channel on the television for the tenth time, Louis Clement turned the unit off in disgust having nothing to watch. Remaining in the apartment while his friend Julien purchased more supplies to clean his infected elbow, he was reminded how a caged animal feels like.

Hearing a key entering the lock, he raised the pistol until he noticed the familiar face of Julien passing the door's edge, carrying the bags from the market.

"Any other time I'd felt confident coming through the door knowing your 'good' arm is still weak," Julien said. "Except I likewise know you're just as adept with a pistol using both hands."

"And you're fortunate my eyesight is as good as it is, lest I mistake you for some ruffian," Louis said, placing the pistol back on the end table.

"You'll be pleased to know I ran into Gregory," Julien said, handing the note to Louis.

"Oh, and all you got was just a note, nothing more?"

"It was done in passing, and he didn't look in the mood to talk," Julien said, putting away the purchased items from the market. "So, what does Gregory have to say?"

Unfolding the paper so he could read it, Louis read aloud, "The last shipment has been compromised. Henri contacted me and it suggests the Irishman has used us as part of a deception against Nazim Aziz. Because of this, I've decided it's time to sever our tie with Nazim and his drug trade. As soon as you are able, gather some men and remove all of our files from the La Cabucelle offices. I'll contact you soon so we can set up a new base of operations for ourselves. Signed, Gregory."

"What part of town are we going to move to?" asked Julien.

"There's the Saint-Andre' section, it's near the docks," Louis said standing up from the sofa. "But that means we'd be dealing with members of the Unione Corse," alluding to one of Marseille's criminal families.

"So, that's it, we're just supposed to pack up and move?"

"No, you're more than welcome to stay here, but what will you do, continue working for Nazim?" Louis asked. "He has little regard for you or any of the other men, unless it benefits him and him alone." Opening the refrigerator, he pulled out a bottle of beer, uncapped it, and took a drink. "Have you noticed that he only had his cousin Hakim working with us? If it weren't for you, me, Phillip, or the others, he'd still be back in the slums of Algiers licking that pompous camel's ass, Omar Khalid."

"And what of Franco, what is to happen to him?" Julien asked, not seeing, or hearing of his friend for the last four weeks.

"He got involved in something he shouldn't have, making a decision that could very well have cost him his life," Louis said. "And he knew it," taking another drink.

"I don't understand, what did he do?" Julien asked.

"He took upon himself to peddle drugs on his own, to people working the cruise ships," Louis said.

"I never knew about that. How did you find out?" Julien asked, opening a bottle of mineral water.

"About a year ago, he came to Gregory and me, saying he could handle some small transactions with a ship's steward," Louis explained. "And he convinced Gregory, but it got out of hand because he got caught up with a woman from a cruise ship and they got greedy," finishing his beer. "Turns out he had a connection with one of the Maghrebis gangs from Lyon supplying him."

"So, he's on his own from this point forward?" Julien asked.

"Yes, and if he's smart, he'll get himself to a place that's not easily found," Louis said. Because if I find him, he'll never have the use of his arms again, the pain in his elbow reminding him of the cost of loyalty betrayed.

***

Relaxing in the café frequented by the police staff, Geneviève and Claude waited for their order to be brought to the table. "So, how many times did your record get reviewed?" she asked.

"Oh, at least seven times if I recall," Claude said. "Each time, the waiting became worse. The thought of all this time, working the streets was never going to be enough," waving his arm at the traffic as it passed by the café.

"But it sounds this time, it paid off," Geneviève said just as their drinks and pastries arrived.

"Yes, this time, but it also came several years too late," he said, thinking of his wife Nadine and the suffering she endured battling cancer. Her strength came from holding out hope for her husband's promotion until it became too much.

"I know she'd be very proud that you didn't give up," Geneviève said, offering a napkin to her partner.

Drying the tears from his eyes, Claude said, "You're right; plus, I now have the opportunity to see you get promoted into my seat."

"And I'd be honored to have you mentor me to that end," she said raising her coffee cup in salute.

"Salute," Claude said in return.

Glancing at her watch, Geneviève stood up. "Should we get back to finding the 'bad guys' hiding in the fair city?"

"Yes, we owe it to our citizens," Claude said with a chuckle feeling rejuvenated by Geneviève's youthful spirit.

***

Returning to Marseille, Gregory Arsenault's first action was getting the note to Julien without making a scene. He knew Louis would understand his decision, and unless he had underestimated their friendship of twelve years, Louis would follow his direction.

After meeting his friend, Gregory knew his next action was getting word to his freighter captain's regarding his decision to sever ties with Nazim. Entering the maritime registrar's office, Gregory made his way to the counter identified as 'communique's'.

"Can I help you?" the clerk asked.

"Yes, I'd like to send a single telex to four separate vessels, is that possible?" he asked.

"Yes, we can have it transmitted. Will it be four separate telex's or just one notification?" the clerk asked, pulling out a blank message form.

"Just one message," he said wondering if the clerk heard him the first time.

"Please place the name of the vessels here," the clerk said pointing to the space at the top of the form. "And print out your message here," identifying the space at the bottom. "You can sit at the table and fill it out and then return it when you're done."

"Thank you," Gregory said, walking over to an empty seat.

Picking up the form, he first listed out the vessel names at the top; *M/V's Bonaparte, Cousteau II, De Gaulle and Joan of Arc*. And then moving to the bottom section, added the message to the captains on each vessel. "Choosing to sever ties with partner; stop. You may hold in port two additional days upon receipt of this message; stop. Need all captains and first officers to meet in Valencia the day after receiving this communique; stop. Arrangements have been made at Westin Hotel for all parties; stop. Answers will be provided upon meeting; stop. Papillion sends." Stepping back to the counter, Gregory handed the form back to the clerk.

"That'll be two hundred and fifty euros, please," the clerk said preparing the telex machine to send the message.

Getting out his billfold, Gregory handed over three hundred euros to the clerk, who in turn gave him the change.

180

Within minutes, the clerk had typed out the message for Gregory and sent it out to the vessels. "They should have it in the next hour baring any technical difficulties," the clerk said.

"Merci," Gregory said turning away from the counter and knowing his next stop was to arrange for his flight to Spain.

Chapter Twenty-Three

Picking up her notes, Detective Benoit made her way out of her apartment and hurried to catch the bus heading downtown. Standing amongst the other riders, she felt a hand touch her side near her pistol. Twisting back, she noticed a young student swaying to the music playing in his earphones.

After the brief bus ride, she exited and made her way into the police station, walking directly to meet Captain Duval. Entering the outer office, she watched the clerk stepping out of the captain's office. "Is the captain busy?" she asked.

"Oh, ah..., just a moment detective," the clerk said, sticking her head back into the office.

"Show her in," Captain Duval said loud enough for Geneviève to hear.

"Merci, officer," Geneviève said, walking past the clerk before closing the door behind her.

"What do I owe for this early morning visit, Detective Benoit?" the captain asked looking up from the papers on his desk.

"I've been given new information on the suspect that Chief Inspector McDermott had," she said, handing over the folder with the security images.

"What am I looking at here?" opening the folder.

"The first image was provided by Chief Inspector McDermott during their surveillance in Aberdeen. The next three images are of his suspect, Louis Remesy here in Marseille, and the last three are of Remesy being met in Algiers by Omar Khalid," Geneviève said.

"And this has some significance I take it?" Captain Duval asked.

"Yes sir, it does," Detective Benoit said. "Besides the fact that Remesy is wanted by Scotland Yard as part of their investigation," pausing to turn over her note. "Information provided by Director Salah of the Algerian airport security reports Monsieur Khalid is a well-connected individual within the district. But all other pertinent information is being withheld."

"So, he's a private person who doesn't appreciate being spied upon," Captain Duval said.

"Sir, I believe it goes deeper than that. If Remesy is suspected in drug trafficking by Scotland Yard, wouldn't it be safe to assume anyone in contact with him could also be part of the smuggling operation?" Geneviève asked.

"Be careful young lady, you know what they say about 'assuming' things," Captain Duval said.

"Yes, of course I do, it makes an 'ass out of you and me'," chuckling at the metaphor.

"And, if we follow the possibility that Scotland Yard's suspect met with this Omar Khalid, what do you propose should be the next step?" Duval asked.

"With your permission, I wish to travel to Algiers to meet with the Algerian officers and see if we can gather other information," Geneviève said, hoping to convince her supervisor.

"What other information do you hope to gather other than the meeting between the two?" Captain Duval asked.

"Based on the photos, I'm curious to learn if our Louis Remesy is actually of Algerian decent," she said. "It would explain the possibility of his relationship with this gentleman Khalid."

"And Captain Lemieux, he supports your theory?" Captain Duval alluded to her newly promoted partner.

"Yes, we've spoken about this yesterday," Geneviève said.

"Very well Benoit. I'll contact the Algerian authorities, you prepare for your trip," he said. "Oh, you shouldn't expect Claude in anytime soon. He had a rough evening," emphasizing the activities from her partner's activities from the past evening.

"I understand," Geneviève said, walking out of the office. Pushing passed the groups of officers milling about the staircase, she ascended the steps two at a time until reaching the second floor. Turning to her right she reached her office.

Sitting slumped in his chair, the newly promoted 'Captain' (Detective) Claude Lemieux was feeling the after effects of his congratulatory festivities from the preceding night.

Entering the office, Geneviève took one look at her partner, "Oh…"

"Not one more word," Claude said, shutting her up.

"I was just going to say, ah... good morning, that's all," she said, sitting at her desk.

"The hell you were; I noticed it on your face, you had something devious on the tip of that tongue of yours," Claude said, leaning forward to drink his coffee.

"You're right, I did, I um..., I was, oh..., you know what I mean," Geneviève said.

"Keep in mind, the older you are, the harder it is to overcome activities you didn't think twice doing when you were younger," swallowing two aspirins.

"I'll keep that in mind, if I ever find myself drinking like you do," Geneviève said gently, reminding him of his wine consumption.

"Point taken, Mon Cheri; so, what did Captain Duval think about your little plan to visit Algiers and snoop around the city?"

"Did he call you about it?" she asked.

"Yes, of course he did," Claude said. "Because while you're jet setting, I'll be here planning to follow-up on the two supposed owners of 'Papillion Transport' later this month."

"Oh, we have more information?"

"No, but Captain Duval was instructed by the commodore our main priority was finding the owners and anyone else involved with 'Papillion Transport,'" Claude said. "Which, I might add, includes the freighter crews, and conduct a thorough investigation."

"We'll need a few extra detectives to make that happen," Geneviève said.

"Captain Duval is already adjusting the work rosters to make that happen. He said it would be my 'first' supervisory task as Captain," the senior detective said, brushing his thinning hair to one side.

"And when are we beginning the interrogations?"

"As soon as Captain Duval arranges for the other detectives, and you return from your trip, we'll begin," Claude said. "Oh, by the way, you have a 4 pm flight to catch as well," looking at the clock. "Here's your ticket voucher and documents," handing over a manila envelope.

"If that's the case, I need to go pack," Geneviève said. Grabbing the envelope, she put the file and her pistol away in her desk, locking the drawer before leaving her partner sulking in his chair. Scurrying back to the bus stop, she headed back to her apartment to pack, mentally creating a checklist of what she would need.

***

Strolling through the terminal, Detective Benoit felt oddly out of place, wearing a hajib over her hair and wrapped around her neck.

184

Choosing to wear a blouse with long sleeves to cover her arms and loose-fitting slacks, she felt capable of passing for a common Algerian woman. The downside to this attire was traveling without the aid of her service pistol, directed to leave it behind by Captain Duval. Walking up to the counter, she handed over her passport and police credentials to the ticket agent.

"Merci, mademoiselle," the agent said, handing back the documents. "Here's your boarding pass, you leave from gate 13," motioning to the left side of the terminal.

"Thank you," Geneviève said, taking back the documents. Walking away from the counter, she placed the documents into her satchel, and bumped into a gentleman, "Oh, I'm so sorry," she said.

"That's perfectly all right," Gregory Arsenault said, unaware he'd just encountered the woman responsible for shooting his friend, Louis Clement.

Making her way to the security gate, Hector Dupont met her. "That's not much of a disguise."

"It's not meant to be a disguise, at least not for the flight," Geneviève said.

Escorting her through security, Hector made sure that there was no delay in her making the flight. "So, I see we'll be postponing our dinner date for this Friday?" Hector said.

"Hector, I'm sorry about this, but it's important that I follow-up on the leads you provided as promptly as possible," she said.

"Don't worry, I understand. I'll be waiting for your return," watching her walk thru the jet-way toward her flight.

Sitting for two hours with the benefit of the plane's air conditioning, Geneviève could relax, but, stepping out of the airliner, she soon felt the heat generated by the tarmac. Looking around, she spotted the azure blue waters of the Mediterranean Sea off in the distance as the sun began to set. Walking into the customs terminal, she made her way to an empty kiosk, surrendering her passport.

"And what is your purpose in Algeria?" the agent asked.

"Business," Geneviève said.

Peering at the woman, the agent looked at the computer screen and showed her profile identifying her as a member of the French police. Stamping her passport, he handed it back to her, "Welcome to Algeria."

"Merci," she said taking back her documents and securing them in her satchel before leaving. Walking past the exit doors, she soon discovered a well-dressed gentleman holding a placard with her name written on it. "I'm Detective Benoit," she said walking up to the man.

"Good day detective, I'm Inspector Karim Haddad," he said in passable English. "Your Captain Duval asked that we see to your arrival," leading her away from the gathering crowd in the terminal.

"I'm glad for the company," she said, following the officer to a car waiting at the curb.

"We've secured a room for you at 'Hotel Sofitel Algiers Hamma Garden'; it's where most Europeans stay," Karim said, driving away from the airport towards the center of the city.

"Thank you," Geneviève said, "I don't want to look disrespectful, but it'll be nice to remove the hajib."

"Admittedly, I was surprised when you walked off the plane wearing it, but I'm likewise pleased to recognize you make the attempt to fit in as well."

"I thought it might help in the event I meet someone who doesn't share the viewpoint of women wearing modern attire," she said sensing her scalp needed scratching.

After a few minutes of silence, Inspector Haddad continued with their conversation. "I've still planned for you to meet with Director Salah of airport security tomorrow morning," he said.

"Will it be possible to look for some new information from your records?" she asked, hoping to gather more on Omar Khalid.

"Yes, of course, I'll do my best to help you with anything you need," Karim said, pulling the police vehicle into the driveway of the hotel. "I'll be back at eight o'clock tomorrow morning."

"Merci," she said, stepping out of the car as the doorman held it open for her.

Chapter Twenty-Four

Rising early and doing her normal series of yoga stretches. Geneviève worked out her stiffened muscles after sleeping in a strange place. After a quick shower, she was soon getting dressed, which included wearing the hajib once again.

Finishing her breakfast, Geneviève looked over her notes on Louis Remesy which she merged from files supplied from Scotland Yard, including what she'd put together over the last week. Sipping her coffee, she looked up to notice a familiar figure walking out of the hotel elevator.

Hakim Talib, cousin to Nazim Aziz, the man she knew as Remesy, was leaving the hotel after spending the night with his girlfriend, who worked as the night bookkeeper.

Stuffing her notes back into the satchel, Geneviève raced out of the dining room hoping to catch the Algerian before she lost sight of him. Exiting the front lobby, she spied him getting into an older Mercedes-Benz just as Inspector Haddad pulled up the driveway.

"Follow that Mercedes," Geneviève exclaimed, jumping into the front seat next to the Algerian policeman.

"Why, what did he do?" Karim asked, accelerating the police car out of the hotel's driveway.

"The passenger is a suspect who aided in the escape of my shooting suspect," she said catching her breath.

"Are you sure?" the officer asked.

"Yes, I'm positive, I conducted the interrogation of him in Marseille just two weeks ago," she said.

Pulling out his radio, Karim called ahead to one of his fellow officers to help pull the vehicle over.

"Don't your cars have a siren or lights?" Geneviève asked, realizing that they were pursuing the Mercedes without the usual fanfare associated with other police cars.

"This is from the car pool, used by our Administration staff; it's not meant for pursuing other vehicles," Karim said, turning the corner he thought he saw Hakim take.

Soon, the sound of sirens could be heard as two more vehicles joined in the chase. Searching ahead, Karim noticed one vehicle had blocked the roadway in front of the Mercedes path.

Hakim noticed this as well, not knowing he was the focal point of the police activity. Fortunately, the police car was situated a block beyond the gate leading to Omar Khalid's compound where Hakim drove and parked behind.

Halting at the gate as it shut, Karim Haddad exited the car, and pounded on the steel facade. Soon a young man appeared at a smaller gate meant for foot traffic, seeing Geneviève and Karim standing at the gate he spoke, "what is it you want?"

"I'm Inspector Haddad, I wish to speak to the driver of the car that just entered."

In a moment, Ismail, Omar Khalid's servant walked out of the compound, "I'm the driver, what is the problem officer?" he asked.

"That's not the man I saw," Geneviève said looking up to Karim, her back facing Ismail.

"You're sure?" Karim asked glancing at her.

"Yes; like I said, I recognized the man exiting the elevator, and it wasn't him," she said.

"I'm sorry, there looks to be a mistake," Karim said, turning away from the compound escorting Geneviève by the arm.

"Aren't you going to question him about a possible passenger?"

"No, I've got a bigger problem on my hands to attend to," Karim said, holding the door open for her. Slipping behind the wheel, he started the car and drove away from the compound and Ismail.

"What are you talking about?" Geneviève asked.

"The officer in the other car purposely parked a block further way than he should have," Karim said.

"And how do you know he was doing it on purpose?"

"Didn't you notice, he never came to our aid or assistance after we stopped," Karim said. "Unfortunately, there are many members of the force who are paid to look the other way in some circumstances."

"And you believe this officer might have been one?" Geneviève asked.

"Yes, so after our meeting with Director Salah, we'll look at who lives in that compound."

***

Browsing through the images from the security cameras, Detective Benoit was shown the same photos that were provided to Hector Dupont.

"I'm sorry Detective, but that's all the images we have available that shows your passenger entering Algiers," Director Salah said.

"I understand. Well then, I wish to thank you for your cooperation on this matter," Geneviève said, standing and shaking hands with the security director.

"If there's anything else we can do to help, please feel free to contact me."

"I will, once again, thank you," she said, stepping out of the office.

"So, where does that leave you?" Karim asked, walking outside the terminal to the police car.

"We still need to determine who lives at the compound from earlier this morning," Geneviève said, sitting in the police car.

"And we shall find out momentarily," Karim said, maneuvering the police car into the morning traffic. Dodging past the jumble of taxis, motor-scooters, and delivery vehicles, Inspector Haddad soon had them back at police headquarters.

Pulling the records from the file cabinet, the police clerk handed the file over to Inspector Haddad. Signing the custody log, Karim handed back the book while taking the file from the clerk. "You'll safeguard this information, and my name, won't you Karim?" the clerk asked.

"Of course, you have my word."

Walking to the table where Geneviève sat, Karim opened the folder. "Omar Khalid, has had a very eventful past, Detective Benoit," he said.

"What do you mean?" Geneviève asked.

"I would ask you to look for yourself, but unless you are fluent in reading foreign languages, it might be quite difficult. The reports are all in Arabic, I'm afraid," Karim said, pointing out the written dialogue.

"So, what is it you found interesting?" she asked. "I assume it's not that he was a saint as a child."

"No, just the opposite," the officer said. "Based on this report, he was one of the youngest insurgents to lead men during the uprising with the French authorities. It says he was also responsible for the death of at least three French Army officers," Karim read. "After the hostilities ended, he became known as a ruthless gang leader, killing two senior gang leaders to establish his territory."

"So, he's made enemies of both the French and Algerians," Geneviève said. "This might be a means of exploiting him."

Turning the page, the officer continued. "It also says he had a brother, but he died at the hands of a Legionnaire," Karim said. "About two years after Algeria claimed independence from France, all the entries ended."

"Which means someone in the 'new' government must have covered up Omar Khalid's dealings afterwards, giving him a new lease on life," Geneviève said.

"Learning this information about Khalid, what do you plan to do next?" Karim asked.

"Ask him about his brother," she said. "It might just be he's the uncle of Louis Remesy and that they're related."

"And this would mean what to your investigation?"

"Based on his past, Omar Khalid could well be the source of the drugs that 'Remesy' is trafficking through Marseille," Geneviève said, developing her plan to confront Omar Khalid.

Glancing up at the clock on the wall, Karim said, "your meeting should wait; it's nearly time for evening prayer."

***

The soft glow of the setting sun filled the rooms of Omar Khalid's residence. Sitting in a small room off the veranda, Hakim Talib was relating the events from earlier to his uncle Omar Khalid. "She's the same policewoman from Marseille, the one from the hospital," he said.

"Are you sure?" Omar asked, considering the ramifications if he was right.

"I'm certain, I'd never mistake her. She sat no closer than you are right now when she interrogated me," Hakim said, wiping the sweat that had formed on his brow.

"First, we must inform your cousin," Omar said. "Then we'll prepare for her return."

"Do you really think she'll be back?"

"Yes, she's here looking into Nazim's visit last week from what my sources in Marseille can tell me."

"And how would she know about his visit? Even I wasn't aware he was coming to Algiers," Hakim asked.

"That's not important for the moment; you need to remain in the compound and keep out of sight for the time being," Omar said, "I'll have Ismail take care of her."

"I trust your judgement Omar, but you can't kill a French police officer," Hakim said.

"I'll do no such thing, trust me; but when one travels in a foreign country, things happen that can't be explained," the Algerian crime boss said, rising from the chair, and walking out the door. Glancing at the group of men standing near the garage, Omar motioned for Ismael to join him. "See that the police woman is discouraged from asking any further questions," he said.

"Of course, your excellency," the crime boss' servant said.

***

Sitting in her hotel room, Geneviève recounted the conversation she had with Inspector Haddad about Omar Khalid and his past. Killing three officers is murder under French law and there's no limitation of charges being held on that, I just need to get my hand on Omar Khalid. And, the Algerian from the hospital in Marseille, he's as good as caught too, if Karim can help me apprehend him, she thought to herself.

A knock at her door interrupted her thoughts. Walking to the door, she said "Yes, who is it?"

"It's hotel management mademoiselle, we've a situation that needs to be addressed," came the response.

Without the aid of a spy-hole in the door, Geneviève was at a loss in her attempt to determine if it was a member of the hotel staff. "Just a moment," she said looking around the room for a usable weapon. Having her back to the door, she was surprised as Ismail and two others of Omar's men crashed into the room.

Pulling herself off the floor, Geneviève found herself outnumbered. Opposing the three men, the detective took a defensive stance, glancing at each of them, her heart racing.

In an instance, the younger of the two followers lunged for her arm, which resulted in a sharp punch to the throat by Geneviève. Falling to the floor, the young man grabbed his throat, fighting to breath, his larynx bruised from the impact of the blow.

"Who's brave enough to make the next attempt?" Geneviève asked glancing at Ismail and the other assailant.

Pointing to his partner, Ismail shouted, "Go for her legs," as he lunged for her arms.

With years of disciplined training, Geneviève avoided the attempt by the second assailant going for her legs, kicking him squarely in the

191

jaw. Regaining her balance, she swung around catching Ismail with a back-handed swing as he tried grabbing her arm. The blow caught the Algerian against the temple, knocking him unconscious, causing him to fall against the dresser, lifeless, blood oozing from his forehead.

"You need to consider your next action with great care," she said looking at the second assailant staggering to his feet, while the younger one lay on the floor, still holding his throat.

Staring at his fellow felon laying on the floor, the second assailant grabbed the arm of the younger one trying to escape just as Inspector Haddad and another police officer appeared at the doorway.

"You're not leaving," he said slapping the assailant across the face hard enough to make the man stagger backwards in Genevieve's direction.

In an unrehearsed action, Geneviève landed a solid punch to the jaw, knocking the assailant to the floor.

"Looks like he tripped trying to escape," Haddad said looking at the youngest of the three still cowering on the floor, his hands raised in defeat.

"So, it would seem," Geneviève said, her racing heart settling down.

"Are you all right detective?" the inspector asked, looking at the lifeless figure of Ismail.

"Oh..., yes, I'm fine," she said sweeping a few loose hairs from in front of her eyes. "I grew up near the docks in Cherbourg, lots of sailors trying to take advantage of me taught me how to say 'no' as it were."

"I can see it works well for you," Haddad said. "Make sure you secure these two away from each other," instructing the other officer.

"Yes sir," the officer said, placing the handcuffs on the younger suspect.

Glancing down at Ismail, Inspector Haddad said, "It appears you might have been right about your suspect. This is the same man from this morning at Khalid's compound."

"I'll need to contact my captain about this, but I also want to meet this Omar Khalid as well," she said, flexing her left hand.

"Let's make arrangements with the hotel manager for a new room, and then we'll pay a visit to Monsieur Khalid," the officer said. "And I'll see that two of my men are kept here for security as well."

Picking up her things, Geneviève followed Inspector Haddad to the manager's office while the officers and medical attendants cared for Ismail, who laid unconscious on the floor.

***

Moving to another room, Geneviève spent a restless night of sleep, even with Haddad's officers providing security, she knew Khalid had made her a target. Just as she faded off the alarm rang on her phone signifying the start of a new day.

Having returned to the police station, Geneviève freshened up, making herself presentable for their meeting with Khalid, wearing the hajib and long sleeve blouse from the previous day.

Pulling up to the gate, Karim glanced to his left and right, insuring that his officers were in position at either end of the street, just in case they were needed.

Sliding out of the passenger seat, the detective stepped confidently forward to the metal gate. Walking to the intercom on the fence, Geneviève pushed the 'talk' button. "I wish to speak with Monsieur Khalid, now."

In moments, a young Algerian boy opened the gate. "This way mademoiselle, his excellency will meet you."

Peering at Karim, she stepped forward in to the compound, taking in all the possible danger areas, following the boy towards the veranda at the back of the house.

Karim kept his pace a step or two behind the French police detective, just in case he needed to defend an assault from behind by Khalid's men.

Walking up the steps, Geneviève spied two women swimming in the infinity pool under the watchful gaze of an older gentleman she took to be Omar Khalid.

"Good day mademoiselle, I am Omar Khalid. I understand you wish to see me?" he asked, rising to his feet, approaching Geneviève.

"Bonjour, Monsieur Khalid, I'm Detective Geneviève Benoit of the French DCJP in Marseille," holding up her police credentials. "I would like to ask you a few questions concerning this gentleman," holding out the photo of Louis Remesy from the airport.

"Hmmm, I know this young man," Omar said, taking a seat at the table.

"And how do you know him?" she asked.

"He's a business acquaintance of mine, from Marseille."

"And what types of business are you engaged in Monsieur Khalid?" Geneviève asked, noticing the two near-nude figures of twin sisters, Aisha and Ketifa exiting the pool.

"I don't believe my business is any concern for the French authorities," glancing up at her. "And I don't think it's important that you be made aware of what business I'm engaged in either," Omar said sipping his mineral water turning his gaze toward Officer Haddad.

"This gentleman you met; he's under investigation for possible drug trafficking activities, both in France and in Great Britain," Geneviève said, standing before the Algerian crime boss.

"Then why are you here in Algeria detective?" Khalid asked. "I'm not aware of any transactions that this gentleman made outside of our business arrangement. So, detective, I suggest you discuss your concerns with him," Omar said glancing at Inspector Haddad standing at the edge of the veranda.

"Do you know where he is today?" the policewoman asked.

Reclining in his chair, a smug smile noticeable on his face, the elder Algerian answered. "No, we concluded our business the other day," Khalid said. "He did mention having another meeting elsewhere but he didn't offer any specifics," he replied lying in the attempt to shield his young apprentice.

"In that case, I thank you for your time then. Shukran," Detective Benoit said, stepping away from the table. Walking away from the veranda, the French officer noticed two men making their way into a small shed. Pausing to watch them, she didn't realize she had stopped directly in front of Karim, who walked into her.

"I'm sorry, I didn't notice you stop," Karim said. "Is there something wrong?"

"That man; the taller of the two, he looks familiar," Geneviève said nodding her head towards the men.

"It'll have to wait, my captain has started the process for our warrant to search the compound," he said. "It should be ready by the time we get back to the police station."

Geneviève didn't hear Karim finish his statement as she concentrated on determining where she met the strange man before today.

Taking the last few steps toward the shed, Franco Laurent ducked his head while entering the small building where he was being held. Every morning and evening he was afforded the opportunity to move around the compound, walking fifty meters to the far end and back. Returning to the shed, he glimpsed Detective Benoit near the gate, but didn't realize it was her because of the hajib she wore. Soon, the two of them would meet again.

Chapter Twenty-Five

Pulling his car into the compound past the police officers who were leaving, one of Omar Khalid's followers, a lawyer, made his way towards the veranda. "Your excellency, I've some terrible news," the lawyer said.

Glancing up, Omar could see the disturbed expression on his face. "What has you so concerned Mister Alvaro?"

"The three men you sent to the Frenchwoman's hotel," glancing over his shoulder, "they're in custody I'm afraid."

"I was told she was not armed, and she was alone, how in Allah's name did they fail to apprehend her?" Omar asked in frustration.

"I'm not sure; but Ismail and his young cousin were taken to the police infirmary because of injuries," Mister Alvaro said. "And the third man is being held at the Central police station."

Motioning to Aisha, "Have Hakim come to me in the study," Omar said, standing from the table, and making his way inside the house.

Tapping at the closed door where Hakim lay sleeping, the servant girl spoke. "His excellency wishes to see you in the study."

Hearing the noise, Hakim heard the woman speak, "Ok, I'll be there in a moment," he said raising from the bed and dressing. Shuffling into the study, Hakim saw Omar pulling out a cell phone from his desk drawer. "You wish to see me?" Hakim asked.

"Yes, it seems this woman with the French police, a Detective Benoit from Marseille, is making a case relating your cousin to me," Omar said. "And she's information about his dealings in Great Britain."

"I recall Nazim talking to his partner about that trip. He came back to Marseille rather quickly from Scotland not too long ago," Hakim said. "Nazim mentioned that things didn't go well because of several policemen being near the meeting place with his contact."

"I know this already Hakim," the criminal leader said. "What concerns me, is she's being helped by an officer I might not have any influence over here in Algiers," alluding to Karim Haddad.

"So, what am I supposed to do?"

Opening up the cell phone, Omar selected the number for Nazim. "First thing is for me to contact your cousin, and then I'll look at what I can do to have you moved before the police return to search the compound," looking out the window.

***

In the darken bedroom of a non-descript house, a figure stirred awake. The ringing of his cell phone woke Nazim Aziz from his sleep. Reaching over the slumbering form of Lauren, he answered the call on the fourth ring. "Hello?"

"Nazim? This is Omar, we need to talk."

Sitting up and rubbing his hand across his eyes, Nazim grabbed his watch to look at the time, eighteen minutes after ten in the morning. "Give me ten minutes, and I'll call you back," ending the call. Making his way to the bathroom, he relieved himself, then splashed some cool water on his face, chasing the cobwebs from his mind from last night's wine with Lauren. Pulling on some clothes, he grabbed the phone and walked into the kitchen to fix a cup of coffee. Holding the phone, he re-dialed the number for Omar.

"Are you ready to talk?" Omar asked answering the call.

"My apologies Omar, but I was weak last night and drank too much," Nazim said drinking his coffee.

"We'll discuss that later; we've a much greater problem that has come up. There's a police woman here in Algiers looking for you," the elder Algerian said.

"A local officer?" he asked.

"No, this one's with the DCJP and she's from Marseille. She mentioned her name was Detective Benoit," Omar said. "She alluded that you're involved in drug trafficking in Britain," he said watching Hakim stare at Aisha bringing out food and drinks for them.

"How is that possible?" Nazim asked.

"It seems your precautions were not enough," Omar said. "She had a photo of you, but it turns out that it was from airport security here in Algiers."

"So, there's someone there that passed information to the French about my travels," Nazim said. "I'll just have to make other arrangements for my next trip to North Africa then."

"It's not just that, she likewise recognized your cousin Hakim, from when he was visiting his lady friend at the hotel," Omar said.

"So, what you're saying is this police woman not only tracked me to Algiers, but she's also tracked down him," Nazim said, his frustration growing.

"Yes, from what Hakim said, she's the same one who interrogated him at the hospital," Omar said seeing Hakim shake his head in agreement.

Nazim paced the front room, his mind awash with possibilities of how and who might be responsible for compromising his travels. "I need to contact Gregory and have his police informant can get me information on this detective," he said. "I'll call you when I find something out."

"And I'll see that Hakim and your fugitive are placed in a safe location until the police leave," Omar said ending the call. "Come we have much to do and little time to accomplish it," he said motioning to Hakim.

***

Making his coffee, Nazim 's mind raced at the possibilities of being found out by the French police. I've used my fake passport when traveling, and I've always addressed myself as 'Louis Remesy', so how did this police woman find out about me? Scrolling through his phone, he came across Gregory's number and pushed it to start the call, which was answered on the first ring.

"Hello Nazim," Gregory said.

"Gregory, I need you to contact your informant; there's information on a woman I need quickly," Nazim said an even controlled tone to his voice. "I've been told there's a policewoman investigating my travels. I need know how much information she knows and how it was obtained," he added.

"I'll look at what I can do and I'll call you back," Gregory said ending the call abruptly.

Staring at the phone, Nazim looked puzzled at the demeanor of his partner.

Wandering into the kitchen, Lauren asked, "Is everything ok?"

"Yes, for the moment; is it possible for you to fix me some breakfast?" Nazim asked.

"After last night, that would be a fair trade," the woman said making her way into the kitchen.

***

After waiting two hours for the local judge to sign the warrant authorizing a search of Khalid's residence, the two officers returned.

198

Coming back to the compound, Karim stood at the entrance, his court document in hand. Depressing the intercom button, "My name is Inspector Haddad; I wish to see Monsieur Khalid please." After a minute in the sun, Karim could already sense the beads of sweat cascading down the center of his back.

Opening the gate, Mister Alvaro, Omar Khalid's lawyer stood in front of the police officer. "I'm Monsieur Khalid's legal representative. How can I help you officer?"

"I'm here to execute this search warrant," Karim said pushing the document against the lawyers' chest. "If you'll please step aside, I'll make this as quick as possible," striding past Mister Alvaro and straight for the main house, followed by Detective Benoit.

After forty-five minutes, Karim and Geneviève walked outside and stood in the shade of the entrance. "Nothing, just the house staff," he said.

"He was tipped off," Geneviève said, walking toward the small shed she spied earlier in the day. Freeing the door, she was assaulted by the stench of a person who sweated profusely within the four walls, the stained cot the only clue to the occupant. Whoever was being kept here wasn't staying willingly.

"Is there something I need to know?" Karim asked, sticking his head in the doorway of the small shed.

"Earlier, I thought I recognized someone I'd last saw in Marseille, a drug dealer. I think he might have a connection to the others," Geneviève said. Pointing to the sweat stained cot she said, "And I don't think the person sleeping on this was doing so by choice."

Pointing to the far wall, "Not likely, look behind it," Karim said.

Pulling the cot aside, they both looked at what Karim had noticed, a loop of steel held in concrete. Peering closer, Geneviève could follow the wear marks from a chain or cable on the metal protruding from the ground. "Someone was here against their will," she said, walking past the Algerian policeman and back into the sunshine and fresh air.

"The two young women looked too well kept being subjected to living in the shed," Karim said alluding to Aisha and her twin, Ketifa from their earlier visit.

"So, we're looking for someone who has found himself at odds with Omar Khalid?" Geneviève asked.

***

Hearing Nazim once again demand his help in solving one of his problems only strengthened Gregory Arsenault's resolve to leave him and his drug trafficking endeavor. Resting in his study, he dialed the number for his sister-in-law, Claire.

"Police Municipale, Officer Dubois speaking."

"Officer Dubois, I'm hoping to gather information concerning a court case for a friend, his name is Louis Remesy," Gregory said.

"Oui, and what is it you wish to find out Monsieur?" Claire asked.

"I need the officers' names in the case, and when they began their investigation," Gregory said, not wanting to confuse Claire with a cryptic message. "Everything they have on him."

"I'll see what is available," she said.

"Oh..., and one other item," Gregory said. "I've been told your daughter is safe, and she's being looked after by an associate."

"Merci, I appreciate the fact you kept your word," Claire said, tears rolling down her cheek.

"Please call this number if you have questions," Gregory said ending the call.

"Yes sir, I will," Claire said to the dial tone buzzing in her ear.

***

As Benoit and Haddad were searching the compound of Omar Khalid, a van followed by two sedans drove up to an abandoned building near the railroad yard in Algiers. Dragging the fugitive from the back of the van, Omar's second most trusted servant, Malik, tugged at the chain binding Franco Laurent's hands together.

Setting a chair near a steel pillar in the middle of the warehouse, he wrapped the chain around the column and locked it. Sitting on the chair, the French fugitive spied Hakim standing near the small office talking with several men of Omar Khalid's band of thieves, drug dealers, and extortionists.

"Hakim, if this keeps up, it won't end well for you," Franco shouting across the open warehouse floor.

Hearing his name come from the Frenchman, Hakim walked over to the captive. "You made a poor choice Franco, and soon, you'll discover how Nazim dispenses his discipline for those too weak or who fail to follow his example."

"Is that so?" Franco asked. "Is that why your cousin exiled you from the work in Marseille, to this..., this shit hole," nodding to the warehouse and its surroundings.

Swinging hard, Hakim caught Franco's jaw with the back of his hand, splitting the lower lip of the Frenchman. A shower of blood sprayed across the ground as Franco's head jerked at the impact.

Bringing his head up, the Frenchman flexed his jaw back and forth. Spitting blood from the open wound, Franco said, "You're nothing but a coward, letting your cousin protect you instead of handling things on your own."

"And you're nothing but an insect," Hakim said raising his fist to strike again.

"Enough!" exclaimed Omar who had heard the exchange between the two former friends as he entered the warehouse.

"My apologies," Hakim said, looking at the elder Algerian walking towards him.

"You will have a chance to discipline the infidel in time Hakim," Omar said. "And as for you Monsieur Laurent," moving closer to the captive. "I'd begin praying to your god of choice, because your time will soon end on this earth," whispering in his ear so only he could hear it.

***

Meeting in the air-conditioned office, Inspector Haddad and Detective Benoit looked over the reports they'd prepared for their respective supervisors. The reprieve from the afternoon heat was needed as it was reported to be near 35 degrees Celsius by 2 pm.

"Inspector, I've been asked to give you this message," a clerk said, handing over a folded slip of paper to the police officer, before walking away.

"What does it say?" Geneviève asked.

"It's an address," Karim said, looking at the map on the office wall. Moving his finger across the laminated image of the city, he found what he was looking for. "We need to move, now," he said, grabbing his ball cap.

Walking in behind Karim as he raced out of the office, Geneviève asked, "Where are we going?"

"The clerk provided an address to a warehouse known to be used by Omar Khalid," Karim said, sliding behind the wheel of the police car.

In less than ten minutes, Inspector Haddad and Detective Benoit found themselves outside an abandoned building near the railway station. Stepping out of the car, Karim motioned for the four other officers that had joined him to split up and move around either side of the building.

"We'll use the front door," he said to Geneviève. Racing up to the single-entry door, Karim grabbed the handle and turned and found that it was locked.

"You don't happen to have a spare one on you?" she asked pointing to the pistol.

"Sorry, but I don't have it in my authority to offer you a weapon; plus, your position on this raid is as an observer," Karim said.

"Then please, allow me to open the door for you," Geneviève said raising her foot into the air before crashing it down on the door handle, rendering it useless. Swinging the door open, the officers found a half-dozen men, including Hakim Talib milling about a half-constructed office.

"Police, stand where you are," Karim shouted, pointing his pistol at the six men, as two of his fellow officers gained entrance to the warehouse from a rear door. Each man stood where he was, hands raised in fear of being shot by the officers. Ambling towards the group, Karim spoke, "Everyone, move against the wall, placing your hands as high as you can reach."

As Karim and his fellow officers placed handcuffs on Omar's men, placing them under arrest, Geneviève made her way to where a swollen and bruised Franco Laurent was sitting. Looking down at the fugitive she saw he was chained to the steel column, a trickle of dried blood set against the corner of his mouth. "Monsieur Laurent, you've come a long way from Marseille in a few short weeks. You'll be happy to know your friend, he escaped custody last week," Geneviève said.

"My friend? You mean Louis, he escaped?" Franco asked in bewilderment.

"Yes. So, when you're returned to Marseille, I'll expect your full cooperation with his apprehension."

"Really? In exchange for what?" Franco asked.

"For saving your life of course," Geneviève said.

Franco looked up at the woman knowing she was perhaps right. He knew he wouldn't have left Omar's compound alive, and if he did, he'd been crippled for life at best.

"Officer Benoit, the van is here to transport the captive," Karim said.

"Who had the keys?" she asked.

"The proud looking one, third from the left," Franco said, pointing out Malik to the officers.

Karim walked up to the young man and asked for the keys that secured Franco. A sneer from Malik cost him a chance to avoid being the target for Karim's police baton as it struck the young man in the abdomen. Pulling Malik to his feet from where he crumbled in pain, Karim reached into the front pocket and retrieved the keys, tossing them to Geneviève.

Undoing the chains from his wrists, Geneviève stepped aside as one of Karim's officers replaced them with a set of handcuffs.

***

Again, Inspector Haddad and Detective Benoit found themselves toiling over paperwork in the air-conditioned office, this time accounting for the arrests of Khalid's men and Francois 'Franco' Laurent.

"Inspector Haddad," the senior officer said stepping into the office. "The paperwork to extradite Monsieur Laurent is being processed, but the courts don't expect to have it signed by the judge until tomorrow afternoon at the earliest."

"I understand sir," Karim said. "Looks like you'll need to stay an extra day," turning to Geneviève.

"Well, in that case, I'll need to contact Captain Duval and appraise him of the case," she said. "Is there a private office I can use to make the call?"

"You can use our supervisor's; by the way, what do you say we go and have dinner before it gets too late," Karim asked, pointing to the clock reading seven pm.

"I'd like that, it's not as if the paperwork will find a way to walk out of the station," she said. "And the odds are Captain Duval has left for the evening, anyway."

Unknown to the officers, instructions from Khalid had already made its way to a follower in custody, arrangements were now set in motion to see Franco Laurent never left Algiers. In a basement holding cell of the police station, an older Algerian was handed a crude weapon made from a toothbrush as he drifted toward the Frenchman.

In a well-choreographed act, all the Algerian prisoners turned their backs as the elder Algerian struck Franco in the neck. The impact was just below the ear piercing his carotid artery, sending a shower of blood against the backs of those in the holding cell.

Shock and horror etched itself across Franco's face, his life spewing out of him with each beat of his heart. Struggling to stem the flow of blood, he turned to face his assailant, realizing that he'd seen the man before doing Omar's bidding. It was the same older Algerian that confronted him at the docks in Tunis while he was trying to escape Nazim. The last thing Franco saw before dying in the middle of the jail cell, were the brilliant white teeth of the elder Algerian assailant.

***

Word of the Frenchman's death spread quickly from the basement staff to the police officer's ward room, which included Karim and Geneviève as they returned from having dinner.

"How did this happen? He was in custody, right here in this building," Geneviève asking the question that would haunt her for days, if not weeks.

"It seems Omar Khalid's reach is greater than we gave him credit for," Karim said, looking across the desk at the detective.

"And what am I supposed to say to my Captain?" the female detective asked, the shock of the event still fresh in her mind.

"I'm sure he'll understand you had no control over what happened."

"That might work for you Karim, but I told my captain I would have something significant to show for this trip," Geneviève said. Omar Khalid is a more powerful man here than I thought I could handle, and he's hiding something about this 'Louis Remesy' as well. What am I going to say to Captain Duval when I return? And what do I tell Conor about his suspect 'Remesy' and the drug trafficking? wondering if she'd failed in her duty.

***

Avoiding his compound because of the police, Omar Khalid sat in the penthouse suite of the Hotel El-Aurassi, draining the last of his mineral water from the glass. Taking his cell phone, he dialed the number for Nazim, wishing to break the news about his cousin personally. On the third ring, his call was answered.

"Hello, Omar?" Nazim asked, "It's nearly ten pm, why are you calling?"

"Yes, I know what time it is Nazim, but I've got more dreadful news to tell you."

For the next ten minutes, Omar related to Nazim what had transpired. From moving himself, Hakim, and the fugitive to the warehouse and their arrests. And his order for the 'accidental' death of Francois Laurent at the hands of a hardened criminal.

"And what of Hakim? How long do you expect the police to hold him?" Nazim asked, knowing his younger cousin knew much of his drug activity and its location in Marseille.

"It's hard to say, with the involvement of the policewoman from Marseille, it will be harder to influence some of the weaker officers to help," Omar said.

"Please do what you can, if nothing else, keep him from being harmed while in jail," Nazim said. "I'll look at what I can do from here."

"You have my word, I'll do everything in my power to insure he's left unharmed," Omar said. I can't allow my nephew, to be treated like a goat while in jail. I'll need to be very careful when I contact the superintendent of the district when discussing this matter, contemplating how he'd approach the police.

***

The ringing of his cell phone caught Gregory Arsenault by surprised as he sat alone in his study overlooking the city. Setting down his cognac, he picked up the phone from the end table. "Hello?"

"Monsieur, this is Officer Dubois with the information you requested," Claire said.

"Thank you for getting back to me so quickly officer," he said looking at his watch noting how late in the evening it was. "What information do you have for me?" Gregory asked.

"It seems Detective Benoit and Captain Lemieux are investigating 'Monsieur Remesy' for drug trafficking," Claire said in a cold, uncaring tone. "Their investigation has been ongoing for three weeks, and it also includes passing information to inspectors from Scotland Yard."

"I understand," Gregory said. Not just the local police, but Claire just confirmed that Scotland Yard is investigating Nazim, but how are they making the connection? Can I make a move fast enough to avoid being a suspect as well, assessing the risks to his organization?

"There's more," she said. "It seems that Detective Benoit also found a fugitive by the name of Francois Laurent during her recent visit in Algiers."

"Thank you, I'll not keep you from anything further," Gregory said. Placing the phone back on the table, he took the last little bit of cognac from the snifter and swallowed it. The burning sensation soon replaced the sweet taste of the liquor as it moved through his body.

Chapter Twenty-Six

Pulling the police car to the front of the departure terminal, Inspector Haddad looked at Detective Benoit, who sat in quiet solitude since being picked up from the hotel. "I'm sorry things didn't work out as you'd hoped."

Geneviève took a deep breath before answering. "So am I; but, at least I've got a solid lead on Louis Remesy to follow up on when I return. And we've uncovered his connection with Omar Khalid," she said, stepping out of the car.

Stepping to the back of the police car, the Algerian officer spoke. "I'll do my best to keep you informed on the extradition proceedings for Talib," Karim said, pulling out her bag.

"Thank you, Karim," she said taking her bag from him. Shuffling into the terminal, Geneviève's shoulders sagged, her head hung low. How could I be so naïve as to think I could accomplish this arrest on my own? And what will Claude think of my failure, not to mention allowing our drug trafficking suspect Laurent to be killed. Stepping up to the counter, Detective Benoit checked in for her flight, and with little fanfare, made her way to the departure gate and the flight back to Marseille.

***

Two men stood next to each other outside the customs section of the Marseille airport. Detective (Captain) Lemieux and the director of airport security, Hector Dupont waited for the same young woman, but for separate reasons.

Using her status as a police officer, Detective Benoit made sure she was among the first passengers to exit the jet from the flight. Stepping quickly through the customs process re-entering her homeland, she soon walked through the exit doors into the waiting space.

Watching his partner walk through the sliding doors, Claude walked up to Geneviève and put his arm around her shoulder, placing a kiss to her forehead.

"Welcome home, mon Cheri," he said, showing his relief knowing she was back with him.

Glancing up at her partner, a tear rolling down her cheek, "Thank you, Claude."

Noticing Hector standing off to the side, she smiled, wiping the moisture from her face as he walked up and said, "Welcome home. I'm glad to see you return unharmed Detective Benoit," kissing her cheek.

"Thank you, Hector," she said. "If that dinner invitation is still available, I'd like to keep it," forcing a smile to her face.

"Yes, of course it is," Hector said. "I'll call you tomorrow," kissing her briefly again as he walked away leaving the two detectives alone.

Making their way to claim her luggage, the two officers moved through the crowd in silence. Reaching baggage claim, one of the ground crew walked up and passed the single piece of luggage to the officer. "Merci," Geneviève said.

"So, tell me everything," Claude said grabbing the baggage, assuming the role of the senior police officer again, guiding her towards the terminal exit and the car park.

"Where do I begin?" Geneviève asked. "Claude, I was so sure I could handle meeting this Algerian. And then the next thing I know, I see one of our suspects leaving the hotel. I'm attacked in my room, and…."

"Wait, what did you just say?" Claude asked turning to face his partner.

"The day after I arrived. I saw the suspect from the hospital, oh…, what's his name, um…, Hakim Talib, that's it," she said. "And later that same evening, three men tried to attack me in my room at the hotel."

"But you didn't have your weapon with you, how did you go about defending yourself?"

"Just as you said before, I'm always armed," waving her hands in his face, alluding to her hand-to-hand combat skills.

"And after all that, the Algerians are still willing to cooperate with the release of…, you said his name was Hakim Talib, right?" the detective asked reaching his car. "The Algerians will simply hand him over to us for his role with our escaped suspect, Louis Clement?" Claude asked.

"Yes, Inspector Haddad; did I mention his first name's Karim, he's a good officer; he promised that he'd keep me informed," Geneviève said, getting into the police car.

"And what of the other suspect, Laurent?" Claude asked, having been briefed by Captain Duval as to the events surrounding his capture by the Algerians.

"Karim found out from one of the medical staff that our suspect, Francois Laurent, died when he was stabbed with a home-made shive, slicing open his carotid artery; he basically bled out," Geneviève said. "Dammit, Claude!" slamming her hand on the dashboard, "he was our one strong lead to the drug trafficking on the cruise ships."

"No, he wasn't," Claude said, moving the police car into traffic. "We still have the ship's steward, the Asian woman, remember? When we find her, then we'll track down other dealers; I'm sure that this man Laurent wasn't the only one she was in contact with dealing drugs."

"So, we continue to investigate, but in reverse?"

"Yes, but first thing is to get you home, we'll start looking again tomorrow," Claude said, driving into the city and towards Geneviève's apartment.

***

Pacing around his office near the docks, Nazim Aziz contemplated the actions he needed to take, trying to determine who was responsible for the loss of the drug shipment. The arrival of his partner, Gregory Arsenault interrupted his thoughts.

"Where have you been?" Nazim asked.

"I left a message with Lauren. I told her I was in Toulon repaying a debt," Gregory said defensively, but lying with ease. "The information on Franco came with a price needing to be dealt with in person."

"Yes, well you'll be happy to know it was wasted money," Nazim said. "Franco's dead."

"What do you mean he's dead?" Gregory asked. "How did it happen? Wasn't he in your 'associate's' care in Algiers? Did one of your associate's henchmen kill him for sport?"

"What are you talking about?" Aziz asked. "No; it seems the police here in Marseille found out something and were trying to extradite him," Nazim said lying to his business partner.

"And yet somehow he died?" the Legionnaire asked. "What do I tell his family? Surely his ex-wife needs to be told something for the sake of his son," Gregory said.

209

"I'll leave that to you and Louis to handle," Nazim said. "And speaking of Louis, how is he doing anyway?" he asked trying to change the tone of the discussion.

"He's being looked after, his wounds are still healing, but he's safe," not wanting to disclose his friends' location.

"I'm glad to hear that; and now that you're back, what can you tell me about our latest shipment?" Nazim asked holding in his anger for the lost revenue.

"It was delivered to the support vessel by the freighter Bonaparte, why do you ask?" Gregory replied.

"Because, Klaus Schmidt contacted me just the other day. He said the normal vessel didn't have the shipment. He was told by the captain of the *Standard-Apollo* the freighter gave it to another one earlier that morning," Nazim said staring at his partner. "This method was your arrangement; you vetted those captains as being capable of handling things discreetly."

Staring back at Nazim, Gregory came clean on the call he received. "I was contacted by Sean Gilmore, the counselor for the Irishman, your 'Monsieur Higgins' a few days before the ship entered the channel," he said. "He told me they weren't happy with the current vessels handling the drugs and wanted to make a change. So, I agreed to their request to making this onetime change," mentioning the discussion.

"So, without calling me," Nazim's anger coming to a head. "Without discussing what we originally planned and had in place, you made a change to the arrangement costing me five hundred thousand euros in hashish," pounding his fist on the desk.

"What do you mean your half-million in euros? Don't you mean ours," Gregory replied, standing in front of the desk.

"What story did the Irish concoct to convince you to make this change?" Nazim asked, his temper rising at the thought his partner had somehow benefitted from the theft.

"They said that they'd concerns over the vessels mishandling the drugs," the Frenchman said. "Which I took as things happening after the freighter offloaded the drugs onto the support vessels, but before delivery to the derrick," Gregory said. "For an additional hundred-thousand euro, they offered the service of their captain to make a onetime transaction. I assumed their captain would deliver it to the derrick."

"It took my contact nearly six weeks to provide twenty-five thousand kilos of hashish for this transaction, and now it's gone," Nazim said. "There won't be another shipment ready from the lab in Africa for at least another four weeks. What do I tell the groups waiting for their share?"

"I'm not sure what you'll need to tell them. I've a meeting with the members of 'Papillion Transport' next week, I'll see if I can get more information regarding the first vessel," Gregory said. And this will be the last time you and I undertake any transaction as partners deciding that this would end their affiliation. "Until then, I recommend that you discuss this past event with your 'other' business partner, the one in Algiers."

"And who do you think that is?" Nazim asked suspicious at Gregory's last comment.

"Your friend, Omar Khalid; that's who you went to see the other day isn't it?" Gregory said, acknowledging that he knew of the Algerian crime boss and Nazim's mentor. "Don't look so surprised Nazim. You're not the only person who has the means of getting information on suspicious activities, like private phone calls, or sudden departures from the city."

"Be careful with what you say from this point forward Gregory, it might not end as well as you think," Nazim warned.

Glancing at the ships riding at anchor in the harbor, Gregory spoke. "I expect that you'll see that any outstanding payments for past transactions are made to 'Papillion Transport' by the end of the week."

"And if I see that my financiers' withhold the payments to account for the loss of the last shipment, then what?" Nazim said.

"I would caution you to not take that action Nazim. I'm not sure you want to find out how the members of 'Papillion' terminate their business transactions," Gregory said, walking out of the office.

***

Squatting in the holding cell at the Algerian police department, Hakim Talib and Omar Khalid's henchman Malik sat beside each other, discussing their plan to escape. "You're sure this will work?" Hakim asked, unsure of the ploy described by Omar's henchman.

"We've done this before, trust me, your wounds will heal quickly," Malik said. Glancing about the cell at the other six prisoners, he nodded to the others before grasping Hakim's head and hitting it against the concrete wall.

Dazed from the impact, Hakim swung mindlessly at his foe, shouts from the other prisoners growing louder. Being kicked and punched by each cellmate, he finally collapsed onto the floor, clutching his side with one arm, shielding his head with the other.

Soon, he felt the cold spray of water as the police officers manning the holding cell tried to subdue the assault without using their guns. As the six other prisoners' coward in the corner as instructed by Malik, Hakim could feel himself being dragged from the cell by his feet. Lifted from the floor and placed on a gurney, he was soon wheeled away from the cell toward the infirmary to have his wounds treated.

As the gurney was pushed into a waiting elevator, the two-medical staff members dumped him into a linen cart. "Do not make a sound, you'll be free soon," the voice said, dirty sheets being pulled on top of him. Still dazed from the assault, he couldn't sense if the elevator had move, but he heard the doors re-open as the cart was wheeled out.

In a matter of minutes, Hakim found himself inside a van being driven away from the police station, a familiar voice instructing him to sit up.

"It seems that Khalid has little regard for your well-being," Inspector Haddad said looking at the prisoner's bruised and beating face.

"Where're you taking me?" Hakim asked as handcuffs were secured on his wrists.

"A safe place for the night, then, we'll be going to meet a friend of ours in Marseille," the inspector said.

"What do you think will happen when it is found out what you've done? My associate will hunt you down like a lame camel and dispatch you and your associates," Hakim spat at the policemen.

"For the moment, I'm not concerned about your associate," the officer said. "I am concerned about how I'll explain your injuries to my superiors if you don't shut up," Karim said placing a black hood over Hakim's head.

***

Stepping into the lobby of police headquarters after spending a restless night of sleep in her own bed, Geneviève headed towards her office before the desk clerk stopped her. "Detective Benoit, these messages are for you," handing over the slips of paper.

"Merci," Geneviève said looking at each. Let's see, there's one from Conor, there's one for Claude from a detective in Lyon, one from Hector, oh..., and one from Karim.

Going in the office that she shared with Detective (Captain) Lemieux, she sat at her desk, looking closely at each message, with the one from Karim catching her eye. 'Call immediately, important news to pass.' Picking up the phone, she dialed the number to the Algerian officer.

"Hello, Inspector Haddad speaking."

"Karim, this is Detective Benoit in Marseille."

"Ah, good morning detective, I'm glad you called," the Algerian officer said. "But I'm sorry to say, I've got some unpleasant news to pass along. But, it could also be considered 'good' as well."

"Good news, bad news, you're not making any sense Karim, what are you trying to say?" Geneviève asked.

"It seems your suspect, Hakim Talib, tried escaping last night from his cell, we believe with help from Omar Khalid," the inspector said in a sullen tone.

"I'd ask how it happened, but being there when Francois Laurent was killed, I don't think I need to ask," she said slumping into her chair, dejected.

"But I'm happy to say, we're able to thwart the undertaking, and in doing so, we're now expediting his extradition to Marseille," Karim said. "We'll be arriving on the two pm flight."

"We? You mean you're handling this yourself?" Geneviève asked. "I need to inform my Captain of this so we can arrange transport."

"Of course, I'll be looking forward to seeing you at the airport," Inspector Haddad said hanging up the phone. "Soon, you'll be in the hands of the French police Talib. And I can go about cleaning up my department," he said knowing the weak officers were the easiest to bribe.

***

Hustling to Captain Duval's office to relay the information she had gotten, Geneviève nearly ran over Officer Dubois turning the corner in the hallway, causing the officer to drop several folders.

Peering up at the detective, Claire said, "I'm sorry Detective Benoit, I didn't see you coming."

"My apologies officer, I'm in a hurry and wasn't paying attention."

Crouching over and helping pick up the folders, Geneviève noticed one marked 'Gaston, P.' with evidence tape sealing the edge. "Officer, why is this file sealed?" she asked.

"Judge's orders detective," Claire responded, small beads of sweat forming on her brow.

"I see," Geneviève said, handing the folder to the officer as they each stood up.

"Thank you," Claire said, making her way back to the records room to deposit the folders. I wonder if she suspects something. She looked surprised at the seal on the file recalling the manner that she persuaded the judge to seal the court documents.

Walking the last few meters to Captain Duval's office, Geneviève entered to catch her partner, Captain Lemieux waiting to see their senior officer. "Well, newly promoted and you're finding excuses to avoid working in our office already," she said, poking fun at Claude.

"Mind your manners Detective Benoit or I'll see you go back to patrolling the less favorable areas of our fair city," Claude said. Voicing his displeasure with his partner for the benefit of the young clerk, while winking at Geneviève.

"My apologies 'Captain' Lemieux," Geneviève responded as the door to Captain Duval's office opened.

Looking at the detectives standing before him, their captain spoke. "It's a wonder you catch any crooks with the time spent seeing me. What is it this time?"

"Captain Lemieux was here first," she said, referring to her partner.

"After getting our orders from the superintendent, I reassigned Masson and Berger to look closer into the owners of 'Papillion Transport'. And we've gotten a lead on the two individuals registered as the owners of 'Papillion Transport' from our offices in Lyon and Brest," Claude said referring to his notes. "It seems the two 'owners' are Emilio Carbone of Brest and Arnaud Guerini, of Lyon. They have possible ties based on their time as members of the Foreign Legion," he continued closing his notebook.

"Interesting to say the least," Captain Duval said. "I'm not happy to hear of one with the surname of Carbone," alluding to the link to a mafia family.

"I had the same concern too Captain," Claude replied.

"Captain Lemieux, begin making arrangements to liaison with our other offices, but keep the information on a need to know basis for the time being. And see that you make arrangements for Detective Benoit to share in the workload as well."

"Of course," Claude said. "Your turn Mon Cheri," relinquishing the floor to Geneviève.

"Thank you, Captain," she said. "Captain Duval, I've just learned that our prisoner is being extradited from Algiers later today," she said.

"Is it the dead one or the live one?" Captain Duval asked.

Wincing at the reminder of Franco Laurent's death, Geneviève said, "It would be the live one, Hakim Talib. He was our suspect we interrogated at the hospital. He was seen visiting the escaped suspect Louis Clement." Glancing at the phone message, she continued. "He'll be arriving at two o'clock, escorted by Inspector Haddad of the Algerian State Police."

"The remains of the suspect Laurent were returned the other day," Detective Lemieux replied ahead of Geneviève. "They're being held at French Armed Forces Hospital until his family can be notified."

"Very well," the captain said, "Claude, contact the detention center supervisor to arrange for transport; Detective Benoit, you may contact Monsieur Dupont and inform him of the prisoners' arrival later today. That'll be all," dismissing the two officers.

"Oui, Captain," they said leaving the office.

After struggling through the daily traffic heading towards the western end of the city and the airport, the two detectives were soon parking their sedan in the short-term area across from the terminal which housed the security offices.

Entering the terminal, Detective Benoit and Captain Lemieux made their way to Hector Dupont's office. Contacting the clerk inside the security office, they were soon shown to the director's office.

"I'm glad to see you both again,' Hector said, standing to greet his guests.

"You have everything in order?" Geneviève asked.

"Of course, my senior officer is preparing the tarmac for the flights arrival at this very moment," Hector said.

"Will there be an escort ready for our transport?" Claude spoke this time.

"Yes, your supervisor from the detention center contacted me to confirm our procedures and his drivers know what's expected."

Glancing at the clock, Hector motioned towards the door. "Shall we go; the flight will be on approach by now," gesturing to the outer office. Stepping out of the terminal, the two officers followed the director making his way to the marked vehicle used for patrolling the airport grounds.

In a few minutes, they were under the shade of an empty jetway, avoiding the harsh summer sun, while the Air Algiers flight taxied to the designated rendezvous space. With the aircraft coming to a stop, ground crews rolled a mobile stairway to the front door, allowing the airport's security detail to enter the aircraft.

"It's time to take possession of your prisoner," Hector said, driving out toward the aircraft.

Approaching the jet, Geneviève saw the familiar figure of Inspector Haddad, pulling a hooded man dressed in a green and black striped jumpsuit by the arm, making their way down the stairs. Soon the police van from the detention center arrived.

"Welcome to Marseille," Geneviève said, approaching Karim and his prisoner.

"I caution you to keep the hood on, our flight might have been leaked to the wrong people," Karim said, handing Hakim Talib over to the police officers.

"Claude, I'd like you to meet Inspector Karim Haddad of the Algiers Police," Geneviève said, introducing her associate from Algiers to her partner.

"Thank you for looking after my partner," Claude said, shaking hands with Karim.

"And this is Director Hector Dupont, head of airport security."

"Pleasure to meet you Inspector," Hector said shaking hands. "If you don't mind, we need to let the plane park now," pointing to the waiting ground crew at the terminal.

"Of course," Claude said, walking back to the waiting car.

As the vehicles cleared the tarmac, the pilot added power to the idling engines allowing the jet to make its way to the terminal.

"So, Karim when do you need to return?" Geneviève asked, taking a seat next to the prisoner in the van.

"My superiors said that I'm allowed stay the night, just so long as your department processes the documentation on the transfer," he answered.

Pulling off the black hood covering Hakim, she noticed a swollen and blacken eye. "Did he stumble?" she asked.

"Unfortunately, yes. It turns out wearing shackles caused him to stumble getting out of the van when we arrived at the airport," Karim said with a smile on his face. The French officer sitting next to Hakim chuckled at the response given by the Algerian officer.

***

Picking up his bags, Nazim Aziz looked around the front room of his house. Nothing looked out of place, except for his lady friend Lauren, who stood wiping tears from her face.

"You'll let me know you're safe when you can," she asked.

"Yes, it might be a day or two, but I'll get word to you that I'm safe," kissing her on the cheek. "Remember, if anyone, including Gregory, asks about me, I'm on a business trip to La Havre," Nazim said.

Stepping out of the house, Nazim got into the waiting cab, "the train station please." Resting in the back, he contemplated the steps needed to take leave the country. First, I need to make my way to Lyon, from there, catch a flight to Milan. Omar said he'd contact his friend Alberto, so I had someone to meet in Italy. Soon, I'll be in Tangiers, mentally mapping his route to freedom.

Twenty minutes later, Nazim found himself in a rail car with other travelers, making his way towards Lyon. Upon deciding to join Omar, he contacted a friend who helped plan his travel out of the country. Arriving in Lyon, he made his way to the airport. Here, using his new passport and alias, Nazim made his way through customs without incident and sat waiting for the flight to Milan.

***

His eyes closed, Omar Khalid found himself sitting alone in the penthouse suite of the Hotel El-Aurassi, lost in thought, learning of Hakim's apprehension from his lawyer. Opening his eyes, he looked out the window at the azure blue waters of the Mediterranean, the cell phone ringing interrupting his gaze. Reading the number, Omar answered the call. "Hello?"

"Good day my friend," Alberto Scuderi said, hearing the Algerian answer.

"Ah..., good morning Alberto," Omar said.

"I apologize for the call, but I thought important to tell you that I've been in contact with your apprentice Nazim; he's safe and resting comfortably with several of my associates in Milan."

"Thank you for helping Alberto," Omar said.

"Tell me, what type of trouble has this young man brought upon you my friend?" the Italian asked.

"It seems his eagerness to prove himself to me and others has clouded his judgment. He failed to remember what our goal is in the activity we're involved in," Omar said finishing his glass of water.

"The younger ones usually do have to learn a harder lesson than what we did in our youth," Alberto said, looking over the harbor in Naples from his villa.

"It's worse this time. His cousin was apprehended by the police and extradited to Marseille," Omar said, looking out the window but not seeing the sea in the distance.

"Is there something I can do to help you with the situation?" Alberto asked, having been in a similar condition himself.

"I don't wish to burden you my friend," Omar said as Aisha entered the penthouse carrying a tray of fruits. "But if you could, I would appreciate any information about the location where the police are holding Nazim's cousin. And likewise, I need you to find out about a woman for me. I'd be indebted to you for helping."

"Of course, what is the woman's name?" the Italian asked, skewering a piece of prosciutto and cheese with a toothpick.

"Benoit, Detective Geneviève Benoit of the DCJP," Omar said. "I'm willing to pay a quarter-million euro to insure I have her join me here in North Africa."

Learning the sum of the bounty his Arab friend was willing to pay for the policewoman made Alberto Scuderi choke somewhat on the meat and cheese. Drinking some wine, he cleared his throat, "that seems like a princely sum for the touch of a woman, Omar?"

"She'll never have such luxury Alberto. But, she's becoming a nuisance, the more she's involved, the more she learns," Omar said, taking the peeled orange offered by Aisha.

"Is there anything else?"

"Yes, please let Nazim know I look forward to seeing him again," Omar said.

"I will, it shouldn't be but a day or two before he can leave the country without suspicion," Alberto said. The French-Algerians' passage made easier with payment to the customs agent for not recording Nazim's entry into Italy the other day.

"Thank you, we'll talk again soon," Omar said hanging up on the Italian.

Staring at the handset, Alberto Scuderi contemplated his next move to help his friend in Algiers. Seizing a French policewoman is not a hard task, having done it before with officers of the Italian police. But to do so in France, that's another matter altogether, thinking through the various scenarios. If we could draw her out of France, maybe to Sicily, then we could pull it off, having done so with Italian officers in Naples.

Dialing a new number on the phone, Alberto Scuderi formulated a plan to abduct the French detective, on the second ring, the call was answered.

"Pizzeria La Italia, how can I help you?" Sophia Dubois asked.

"Monsieur Ricci if you please," Alberto said.

"Oui, one moment please."

"This is Giuseppe; can I help you?"

"Yes, you may Giuseppe, this Alberto Scuderi, and I'm in need of your help."

EPILOGUE

Sitting in the afternoon sun, Gregory looked at each face of the men gathered around him. Each vessel captain and first officer, shareholders in 'Papillion Transport' operations, had been called to the Westin hotel in Valencia Spain.

"Gregory, does this meeting have to do with the last shipment?" Henri Levet, captain of the *Bonaparte* asked.

"Yes, in part it does," Gregory said. "But be assured my friend, it has nothing to do with anyone sitting here at the table." Looking at each man, he continued, "In simple terms, I've grown tired of Nazim's blatant disregard for what we've built as part of 'Papillion Transport' and the relationships through-out the Med."

"So, we're going to sever our tie with the Arab," this time it was Marcel Dumont, captain of the *Joan of Arc* showing his disdain for Nazim at every chance.

"Yes, we've got several accounts still in place; between the Italians, Greeks, and Turks, we'll still be in business well after Nazim is apprehended because he can't control his ego," Gregory said. "The biggest problem we'll encounter will be from a gentleman in Algiers."

"Why do we care about an Arab in Algeria?" Olivier Girard, first officer on the *M/V De Gaulle*, captained by Sebastian Dubois, said draining his Heineken.

Looking at the young Frenchman, Gregory chose his words carefully. "Because the people we continue to do business with will undoubtedly have business dealings through him. Not to mention, my greatest concern is your safety and well-being while you work for me."

Yves Clement, captain of the *Cousteau II*, sat quietly while listening to the conversation that surrounded him. As the senior captain, he was the first member of 'Papillion Transport' to be recruited by his brother Louis and Gregory when they took control of the vessels. Over the years, he had numerous conversations with Gregory and Louis, routinely making lucrative decisions that benefitted everyone at the table.

"The important thing to remember gentlemen," Yves said, "your first responsibility is to ship and crew, without them, you are nothing."

"But what do we do when one of the crew, like that Spanish bastard Guillermo Ochoa, takes matters into their own hands?" Anton Huet, first officer on the *Joan of Arc* asked.

"Simple," Gregory said. "You dispense the necessary discipline while at sea, your captain has that authority. It wouldn't be the first time your captains' have had to do it," knowing each of the vessel masters had killed someone in the past. "Enough of the negative," Gregory said standing, his drink in hand. "A toast; to 'Papillion' and the future. Asante!"

Raising in unison, each man held up his drink. "To 'Papillion' and the future."

***

Observing the Mercedes pull into the villa's driveway, Inspector Haddad and the Moroccan police officer photographed the activity. Soon, they saw the occupant of the large German car exit from the back seat, it was an Arab who the inspector had seen before from a previous photograph.

"What do you think they are discussing?" the Moroccan officer asked.

"Something illegal, if my last meeting with the elder one is any indication," Karim Haddad said. "Something very illegal."

"And you said the French DGSE is involved as well?"

"Yes, our information will be relayed to them," Karim said. "Let's head back to the city, I need to get these images sent off."

As the police officers left their vantage point, the men meeting at the villa exchanged pleasantries.

Looking about, Nazim strolled up the path from the car until he met his mentor, where he and Omar exchanged embraces. "Thank you for helping me get out of Marseille," Nazim said stepping back from Omar.

"I'm sorry I failed you and your cousin," Omar said leading the younger man into the villa.

"You mentioned that so far, he's being treated well," Nazim said.

Motioning Nazim to the chairs situated on the patio, Omar said, "Yes, the information I've been given is that he's being held in isolation, but he is well." The familiar sight of Aisha and Ketifa soon came into view as the twins brought forth a pitcher of water, glasses, and a platter of fruit for the men to enjoy.

"So, tell me, what help can your Moroccan friend provide to move our drugs?" Nazim asked taking the proffered glass of ice water from Ketifa.

"Youssef has the means and contact for the use of a vessel, possibly two to move our product to France, but no further," Omar responded taking his glass from Ketifa.

"So, we're back to the way things were five years ago," Nazim said. "Before I met Gregory and his connections."

"Yes, for the time being," Omar said. "I've also taken the liberty of discussing this issue with my friend Alberto, there may be another avenue at our disposal, but he's not given me an answer recently."

"And what of this policewoman, what are we going to do about her?"

"I've also discussed this with Alberto, he and his men have much more experience in dealing with the authorities than we do," Omar said. "I trust him to develop a plan and provide us with his intentions before acting.

"If anything happens to Hakim, I want her to pay a price that will be long and painful," Nazim said. "Something akin to the ancient ways would seem appropriate," envisioning the woman staked spread-eagle in the desert under the relentless heat of the sun.

***

The camera clicked as each image of the French policewoman was recorded. Having spent the last two weeks in the city, the Italian mafia member observed the routine of the target. From her early morning walk to the bus stop, the small market where she bought her goods to the few evenings meeting with a tall dark-haired gentleman at a local café, he built his plan for abducting the woman.

Today, he was watching the detective make her way around a local park, stopping periodically to exercise at pre-determined locations with built-in equipment meant for accomplishing certain movements.

Swinging her leg back and forth, Geneviève spotted the same car she saw earlier in the week near the market she frequented. Shifting her weight to her other leg, she began swinging in the opposite direction, but kept her head turned to face the suspicious vehicle.

Completing the exercise circuit, she took off in a slow jog in a direction that would take her past the car. With each stride, she picked up her pace, arms keeping cadence with each step, until she was nearly sprinting. Making the turn at the far end of the park, she could see the outline of a person in the car holding something to their face.

Seeing the woman turn towards him, the Italian brought the camera up and snapped off several images. In doing so, he failed to notice the approach of the police officers from behind until it was too late.

Opening the door to the rental car, Claude Lemieux grabbed the camera from the startled mafia member. "The city officials frown on visitors conducting themselves like voyeurs at city parks," he said.

"I don't understand what you mean," he said looking up at the French police captain who glared down at him.

"Well, let's look at the images and see if I can explain it a little better for you," Claude said turning the camera on and selecting the images. "Read this gentleman his rights," he said to the accompanying officers.

All the images were of his partner Geneviève Benoit, several of them with her in a compromising position while stretching, her running shorts riding high on her thighs, and two views of her in her apartment from across the alley.

Looking over his shoulder, Geneviève saw the images, "these are from all over the city," she said pointing out the various locations of each photo. "Do you wish to explain yourself?"

"I'm a man, you're an attractive woman, there's nothing wrong with what I was doing," the mafia member said, leaning against the car hood as he was hand-cuffed.

Pulling his partner aside and out of ear-shot of the prisoner, Claude said, "You've made an enemy, mon Cheri. This is not some man with a fetish for women exercising," holding up the camera.

"It seems that Omar Khalid has the means to reach across the sea then doesn't it," Geneviève said alluding to her meeting with the Algerian gang-leader and suspect of aiding with drug-trafficking.

"This is more serious than three locals trying to rough you up in your hotel room though," Claude said. "This shows that they're willing to apprehend you."

Looking about the park, she'd always felt safe in the city she called home, now with Claude pointing out the possibility of being abducted by a foreign criminal, she began to feel vulnerable.

Discover other titles by Anthony J. Harrison:

Obscure Intentions – A Geneviève Benoit Novel

The Irishman's Deception – A Conor McDermott Novel

Betrayed by a Scot – A Conor McDermott Novel

Provide your comments or feedback at;

mailto:fairwayscribe@gmail.com

Thank you for reading my book. If you enjoyed it, won't you please take a moment to leave me a review at your favorite retailer?
Thanks!
Anthony

Acknowledgements

First and foremost, I'd like to thank my wife, Mary, for letting me scratch this itch called writing and for supporting me with her comments and encouragement, even after I locked myself away for hours at a time. Also, a big thank you to my daughter's Rebekah and Jennifer for letting 'Dad' to his thing without the need to keep asking "why'd you write that?"

Next, to my good friend and co-worker, Doretta Burgess, for providing the first level of sanity checks, grammar checks and being that punctuation pundit on all the many pages of my random thoughts and ramblings. Also, to the members of the Ventura Fiction Writers Group; Dru, Wendy, and Ron for helping me understand the difference between 'showing' and 'telling' in my writing and Robin for encouraging me to 'just keep writing'.

About the Author

Anthony is a first generation American and native Californian, the son of Scottish immigrants, and who's fraternal grandparents hailed from Ireland. A product of a mixed education (part parochial and part public schools), he developed a thirst for reading early in his childhood and took to writing fiction as an escape from his work as an Instructional Systems Designer. When not working on improving his writing, Anthony can be found on the local golf course, honing his game invented by his ancestors.